# Voluntary Silence

## By Kevin L. Bouyer

# Chapter 1

It was at this moment that Kayla realized her decision to embark on this nighttime road trip would be a regrettable one. She strained to keep her eyes focused on the double yellow lines in the middle of the road, which only revealed themselves in small increments as she drove through the dense fog. She had no idea about the posted speed limit, but she could almost guarantee she was nowhere close to exceeding it.

"Are you able to see?" her college roommate, Jordyn, asked, sitting in the passenger seat.

Kayla continued to squint. "Barely. I don't remember hearing anything about a fog advisory when we left campus. This came out of nowhere."

"Hopefully, it will clear up a little down the road," Jordyn said.

Kayla glanced at her phone. "Do you have any service?"

"Yes, at least for now."

Kayla let out a heavy sigh. "So, how much further do we need to go to get back on the highway?"

Jordyn looked at the GPS map on her phone. "It's another five point two miles, to be exact."

"And remind me again why you didn't want to listen to the GPS? I don't think this shortcut of yours is doing us any favors. This just seems like it's straight out of a horror movie with two college girls driving on a foggy road at night. Nothing good ever comes out of that scenario in movies," Kayla said.

"First of all, we're not in a horror movie. And second, I've taken this road before, and it really does save some driving time going home. I have no idea why the GPS doesn't take us this way."

Kayla gripped the steering wheel with more conviction after seeing a pair of headlights pressing through the fog in the left lane and driving by in the opposite direction. "I'm not too comfortable with these other cars driving by. If I can't see them until the last second, that means they can't see us until the last second, either. Not to mention any deer that could come running across the road. It's hard enough avoiding them on a clear night. But with this fog . . ."

"Don't even jinx us," Jordyn interrupted. "Let's just keep going while thinking positive thoughts."

After driving for a few more miles, the dense fog eased, allowing Kayla to get a better visual of her surroundings, although the lack of streetlights still made this a difficult task. She also had no help from her eight-year-old Honda Civic struggling to light the road sufficiently, suffering from cloudy headlight syndrome. However, the lighting was strong enough to reveal the silhouettes of a row of monstrous pine trees flanking both sides of the road.

"You see what positive thinking can do for you? No more fog," Jordyn said.

"Thank goodness."

Jordyn reached down to her midsection. "I've been holding this for a while and can really use a bathroom break."

"You can't wait until I drop you off at home?"

"Definitely not. We have another forty minutes of driving, and I can't wait that long."

Kayla twisted her head and pointed to an empty Gatorade bottle on the back seat.

"Are you crazy? Do you think I'm a guy that can whip it out and pee in a bottle?"

"My only other suggestion is for you to squat on the side of the road," Kayla said.

"That's not happening. I can probably hold it a little while longer. Hopefully, there's something up ahead."

Kayla continued driving as the fog eventually dissipated completely. She looked on the right-hand side of the road, toward a sign reading, "*Welcome to Arcadia*." She tapped Jordyn on the knee and pointed to the sign. "Hopefully, this town has a public bathroom you can use."

*****

A few minutes later, a faint glow of light appeared in the distance.

Jordyn leaned forward in her seat. "Is that a mirage, or am I seeing signs of civilization up ahead?"

Kayla squinted, noticing a faded neon sign coming into view. "Last Chance Gas," she said. "Are you kidding me? That's the name?"

As they approached, a small cream-colored building revealed itself with red trim lines surrounding the outer edges of the structure. Two old-fashioned gas pumps were standing in front of the building, appearing to have been built decades ago. A two-car garage with square glass panels on each door was located on the right, indicating an auto shop existed on the premises. To the left of the front area stood a glass door with a sizable window next to it, providing a clear view inside of the building. The lights were on, and an open sign hung across the front door.

Kayla slowed and turned to Jordyn. "Do you honestly want to stop here for a bathroom break?"

"Unless you have some adult diapers in the glove compartment, then I don't think I have a choice."

Kayla pulled onto the dirt-covered lot and parked off to the side of the building. She scanned the area, trying to get a sense of her surroundings. A slightly bent lamppost next to the building cast a dull yellow light, struggling to illuminate the front area of the gas station. With the help of her headlights, she spotted two vehicles parked on the opposite side of the lot. The first vehicle, a battered pickup truck speckled with several areas of rust and a missing headlight, had no doubt seen much better days. The second vehicle was a dark-colored sedan, which appeared to be in much better condition.

Kayla peered through the oversized windows and spotted a man standing by a counter, wearing gray overalls and a baseball cap. She observed the rest of the inside area within her field of vision, searching for any other signs of life, but all was quiet.

She glared at Jordyn with one eyebrow raised. "And this doesn't make you nervous at all?"

"Hey, when you gotta go, you gotta go."

Kayla thought for a second. "Okay, how about we both go in? This will make it two against one if he tries something."

"Don't worry; it'll be okay."

"I'm not feeling comfortable about this. But if you insist on going in by yourself, can you open the glove compartment and take out the pepper spray I have resting in the corner. My dad always thought it was a good idea for me to have some form of protection at school." Kayla grabbed her duffle bag sitting in the back and pulled out a pocket knife. "I also have this."

"Wow, I didn't know you were so serious about protecting yourself, but I get it. Better safe than sorry." Jordyn proceeded to unbuckle her seat belt and reach for her knapsack sitting on the back seat. "Thanks for the offer, but what I have in here will give me all the protection I need."

"What's in there besides your clothes? Do you have a gun?"

"I plead the fifth. Trust me; I'll be fine."

Kayla watched Jordyn exit the car with her knapsack slung over her shoulder and approach the entrance to the gas station. She double-checked, making sure the car doors were locked, and watched Jordyn move toward the counter. She could see Jordyn talking with the man who pointed to an area behind him. Jordyn eventually walked down a hallway and disappeared out of sight.

Kayla looked at her phone and noted the time, while also realizing she no longer had any cell service. She thought of a self-imposed time limit, giving Jordyn no more than five minutes to do her business and return to the car.

Not wanting to be lulled into a false sense of security, Kayla perused the area outside once more to make sure nobody was lurking in the shadows. She then turned her attention back to the man inside who hadn't made a move since Jordyn had entered and seemed occupied with his phone. He eventually left the counter and disappeared out of sight.

Kayla's heart rate increased while she waited for him to return. Moments later, she noted the time she'd given Jordyn to come back was almost up. She reached for her knife and contemplated what to do.

The man eventually returned to the counter, appearing calm and relaxed, but still no visible sign of Jordyn. Kayla closed her eyes, said a silent prayer, and exited the car with the knife in her back pocket.

She surveyed the area once more as a light breeze kicked up, rustling the leaves above in the trees. She approached the door and entered.

The gentleman immediately looked up. "Oh . . . didn't expect more company. Are you friends with the other young lady that came in here a few minutes ago?"

"Yes," Kayla said.

The gentleman leaned forward. "I figured since I don't get many visitors at night, and I find it highly unlikely there would be two separate customers in this short amount of time. So, how can I help you?"

"I was wondering what was taking my friend so long in the bathroom."

The gentleman shrugged. "I guess it all depends on what level bathroom break this was. Know what I mean?"

Kayla offered a hint of a nervous smile and remained standing by the front door.

"You can come in. I won't bite you. And if it makes you feel any better, I can run in the back and knock on the door to make sure your friend is all right."

"That's okay. I'll give her a little more time."

Kayla took a deep breath to help calm her stress levels and reluctantly stepped farther inside. There were two short aisles with an assortment of potato chips and candy, along with a small, refrigerated section with cold beverages. As old as this place looked, Kayla couldn't help but imagine that all of the snacks on the shelves were way past their expiration dates. She surveyed her surroundings to confirm all the exit points, including any additional doors, besides the entrance or any windows. Her father always made it a point to make sure she was aware of her surroundings, especially in unfamiliar places, and map out a plan to exit as quickly as possible, if needed. Unfortunately, the only visible exit point was the front door, though she imagined there had to be a back door somewhere.

Another minute had passed, and Kayla hadn't even heard so much as a toilet flush. Droplets of sweat developed on her forehead as time slowed to a crawl. She peeked over at the gentleman again who continued to sit with his head down, buried in his phone. Kayla quickly shifted her eyes away from him after he unexpectedly flashed a look in her direction.

*Enough is enough. There's no way she should be taking so long to use the bathroom.* "Excuse me, sir. Do you mind if I go back to the bathroom and make sure she's okay?" Kayla sounded confident on the outside but had a mountain of fear building on the inside.

The man pointed toward the hallway. "Be my guest."

Kayla tugged on the back of her shirt to confirm the knife was concealed and out of view in her back pocket. She wasn't too keen on the idea of having to come near this gentleman, but for her to get to the bathroom, she needed to bypass the counter where he sat.

While nearing the counter, she displayed a cordial smile and commenced with a quick visual inspection of this man. He appeared well groomed, although she couldn't determine the state of his hair with the baseball cap covering his head. He sported a five o'clock shadow, layered over a square jawline, and by all accounts was a handsome middle-aged man. While he nodded to encourage her to continue walking past him, she picked up on a concerning sight. With his hand wrapped around his phone, his knuckles appeared red and somewhat raw as if he'd been hitting something. Acting on impulse, she stopped and tried to quickly avert her eyes away from his knuckles.

He looked at his hands and said, "Oh, this is embarrassing, I see you looking at my horrible-looking knuckles. I can explain. I'm also a mechanic here at the shop, and after working on cars during the day, my knuckles normally end up looking like this. Probably a good idea for me to start wearing gloves."

The explanation seemed plausible to Kayla as she continued her march past the counter and made sure he remained still with no sudden movements. She had her hand near her back pocket, making the knife easily accessible if needed.

She focused on the hallway, approaching a door on the right, which from the looks of it, appeared to be a utility closet. A few more feet to the left stood a door, slightly ajar with only darkness peering from the crack. Kayla noted an exit sign hovering over a door at the far end of the hallway, confirming her assumption of a back door exit.

She continued her cautious stroll until she arrived in front of a door with a restroom sign plastered on it. She knocked gently, waiting for a response.

She knocked again. "Jordyn, are you okay?"

Nothing but silence followed.

Kayla's face grew flush with fear as the muted response immediately placed her in a frightening scenario. Her fight-or-flight instincts became further challenged by the gentleman at the counter who unexpectedly appeared in the hallway.

Without hesitation, Kayla reached into her back pocket, pulled out the knife, and flicked the switch to display the blade. "Stay right there," she warned with a quiver in her voice.

The man placed his hands in the air and said, "Hold on, young lady. I'm not here to cause you any harm. You can put the knife down."

Kayla continued standing with her left arm extended and shaking ever so slightly. "I'm not doing anything until you tell me what happened to my friend!"

"I honestly don't know what happened. She asked to use the bathroom, I pointed to where it was, and that's the last time I saw her."

"So, why the heck isn't she responding now? What did you do to her?"

"I did absolutely nothing to her. I'm telling you, I'm as clueless as you about what's going on."

She sighed heavily in disgust and continued to point the knife at the gentleman.

"Listen, young lady, I understand you may feel nervous and scared at the situation, and I'm only trying to help. But that can only happen if you stop threatening me with your knife. Besides, what sense would it make for me, being the owner of this gas station, to attack you as my customer?"

With all the high-intensity stress consuming Kayla's body, her common sense was somewhat impaired, and she hadn't thought of a good reason why the owner of a store would attack a customer. The chances of this happening were close to zero unless a customer threatened the owner, which ironically was exactly what she was in the process of doing.

Kayla swallowed hard as she struggled to interpret this man's threat level. He'd appeared calm and sincere with his words and actions up to this point. The hardest part was gauging whether or not his motives were truly genuine. Even though he owned the gas station, he was still a stranger. And in her mind, a stranger was always guilty until proven innocent.

She made a jabbing motion with the knife. "Step back!"

The man complied and took a couple of steps back.

"Keep moving," she said.

He continued to backpedal with his hands in the air until Kayla was comfortable with the gap between him and the bathroom door. She kept her left hand extended with the knife and reached for the doorknob with her right hand.

She let out a sizable exhale before twisting the knob ever so slowly and pulling the door open. She eyed the gentleman before opening the door wider and peeking beyond the cracked bathroom door.

"It's empty. Where did she go?"

Kayla slammed the door shut and focused her attention on the gentleman. Her adrenaline spiked, accompanied by an intensified level of fear. Any benefit of the doubt she awarded this man for being the owner of the gas station was immediately thrown out the window. In her mind, Jordyn had disappeared under his watch, and he was the last person to have seen her. This made him prime suspect number one.

She imagined what her father would tell her to do in this scenario. He didn't advocate for violence but was a firm believer in self-defense. Although this man hadn't physically threatened her, she realized the situation could easily escalate, and she had to be ready to defend herself.

"You're welcome to check inside the garage," he said, pointing to a door on Kayla's left side.

She refused to follow his finger and divert her attention away from him. The art of distraction came in many forms, and taking your eyes off the ball was the oldest trick in the book. She remained laser-focused on the gentleman, checking his body language for any subtle hints of aggression.

"Why would she go into the garage? And is there somebody else here besides you?"

"I have another mechanic who works with me, but he left about an hour ago." He shook his head. "I'm telling you, I didn't go near your friend."

"Don't lie to me. I saw you leave the counter."

"Yes, and that was to check in the hallway because I thought I heard a door slam."

Kayla raised the knife over her head. "Step back!"

The man took a couple of steps back while Kayla moved forward. "Keep moving," she said.

He continued to move with his hands in the air. She motioned for him to step in the opposite direction of the counter since she had no clue if he potentially had a weapon hiding behind it. She moved beyond the hallway, making sure to maintain a safe distance.

"Get down on your knees!" she shouted.

He obliged and kept his hands in the air.

Kayla continued backing away, down the aisle, until she made it to the front door. She took a quick peek outside to confirm no unexpected guests were roaming and sprinted into the parking lot. She immediately stopped for a second and whipped out her phone to take a picture of the two vehicles sitting in the lot with the license plates in full view. She approached the dark-colored sedan, kneeled, and proceeded to jab the knife into the left front tire. She rounded the car and did the same to the right front tire. She stood and was distracted for a second by a glitzy red disco ball hanging from the rearview mirror of the car. She then focused her attention on the truck, prepared to do the same and disable the vehicle. But after a glance, she noticed the right front tire had already been relieved of air.

She twisted her head back toward the station and noticed the man was no longer in view. She snapped a photo of the station before running to her car and yanking open the door. She started the car and was about to shift it into gear but immediately stopped when her phone chimed and a text message appeared from Jordyn, indicating her service had been restored.

*I hope you get this message on time because the service here is horrible. I know you're wondering where I am, but I'm ok.*

*Can't explain what's going on right now.
Please do me a favor and promise u won't
mention this to anyone. Should be back on
campus in a couple of days. U can continue
going home without me.*

Kayla struggled to keep her emotions in check after reading the mysterious text. On one hand, the crushing weight of stress that held her in a chokehold did subside knowing Jordyn was alive and well. But on the other hand, a sense of anger swelled, based on the poor timing of her receiving the message. If it had not been for the service disruptions, she most likely would have received the text earlier and avoided the need to step foot into the gas station. She started to reply but immediately stopped. *What if this isn't really Jordyn texting and someone got a hold of her phone?* Kayla realized she had to keep all possibilities open and hesitated on what to do next. She bit her bottom lip and decided to proceed with replying to see what type of response she would receive.

*Glad to know you're ok. I'm so
confused. What are u talking about? I can't
leave u at this pitiful-looking gas station.*

She waited a minute for a reply, which never came. Her focus was immediately diverted away from the text conversation after seeing the gas station owner appear near the store window, looking in her direction with a cell phone by his ear. She quickly shifted in gear and sped out of the parking lot to distance herself from any further interactions with him.

# Voluntary Silence

The adrenaline-fueled rush consuming Kayla for the past hour had dissipated and the reality of what transpired began to sink in. It was only a short time ago that she and Jordyn had left campus for a quick weekend getaway to go home and escape the rigors of another school semester. And now, in what felt like a blink of an eye, she'd managed to drive through the thickest fog she'd ever seen in her life, threatened the owner of the Last Chance gas station with a knife, and lost her college roommate to a cryptic text with what appeared to be a voluntary disappearance that she was now burdened with keeping a secret.

# Chapter 2

Kayla peeked in her rearview mirror, waiting to see if any headlights appeared in the distance. Despite the fact there was no physical confrontation with the gas station owner, she felt like a criminal who had ransacked and robbed his store. She feared he might have called 9-1-1 to report Jordyn missing, along with her aggressive behavior while wielding the knife.

She took a deep breath in an attempt to calm down from the stratospheric levels of stress currently consuming her. She shook her head while a slew of thoughts careened back and forth. *Why would Jordyn want to voluntarily disappear for a couple of days? Why did she want me to leave her at that hellhole of a gas station? Is she really going to be okay?*

"Get a grip," she mumbled.

She had roughly thirty more minutes to calm herself enough to be able to speak with her parents without sounding like a complete basket case. She was rather efficient at hiding her emotions and concocting a lie when interacting with friends, but this was a different story with her father. Attempting to cover her tracks in the midst of lying was a damn near impossible feat with her father. She knew she had to suck it up and muster whatever was necessary to temporarily push this harrowing event deep into the recesses of her mind if she was going to have any chance of deceiving her father.

Her focus was interrupted by headlights appearing in her rearview mirror. The cone-shaped beams were initially a good distance away yet were becoming larger with each passing second, indicating the vehicle behind her was approaching at a rapid pace.

Two thoughts immediately crossed her mind. *Is this the gas station owner coming after me, or did he call the police to report what happened?*

She continued driving at her current speed and reached into the back, grabbing her duffle bag. She placed it up front to cover up the pocket knife and pepper spray resting on the passenger seat.

The vehicle came within a car length of her bumper and slowed to match her pace. She squinted in an attempt to look beyond the glaring lights in the rearview mirror and struggled to trace the vehicle's outline. She could tell there were no sirens affixed on the roof of the car, most likely ruling out the police scenario. But option number two wasn't much better if this was the gas station owner. She could only imagine his level of agitation was through the roof after what had transpired back at the station.

Her instinct told her to press harder on the accelerator to create some distance. However, she did the opposite and took her foot off the accelerator, letting the car coast at a slower speed. If this person were truly not following her, they would logically go around, as no other cars were coming in the other direction and there was plenty of room to pass on this two-way road.

"Come on; go around me," she mumbled under her breath as the vehicle trailing slowed to keep pace and did not initially offer to pass.

She slowed even more and put on her hazard lights to coax the mystery vehicle behind her to shift into the oncoming traffic lane and pass. The car finally did and proceeded to pass.

The vehicle pulled alongside hers, prompting Kayla to give a cursory glance. She noticed someone in the passenger seat wearing a hood, preventing her from seeing any facial features or hairstyles that could possibly provide a clue as to the person's gender. This individual continued to look straight ahead and did not reciprocate with a look back at Kayla.

As the car pulled ahead, she trained her eyes on the driver but could only catch the silhouette of a person wearing a baseball cap. And, like the passenger, this person didn't offer to look over.

Once the vehicle switched lanes in front of Kayla, she reached for her phone in the cup holder and proceeded to take a picture of the car, along with the license plate. Her curiosity was in full bloom, wondering if this was the same car in the gas station parking lot. But she figured that was impossible since she'd flattened the two front tires. She was tempted to look at her photos to compare the license plates but knew that could be a disastrous decision. Being distracted while driving on a narrow road in the dark country was probably not the best idea.

A part of her wanted to keep up and follow the vehicle before she realized this, too, was not a recommended option for anyone who had an ounce of common sense. She was proud of her decision-making ability up until this point and didn't want to ruin the evening with a regrettable miscalculation of judgment. Therefore, she refrained from following through with the chase and continued on home.

She pulled into her driveway thirty minutes later and tilted her head back against the headrest. The unexpected and nerve-racking events had made her little over an hour drive seem like a cross-country trek.

She immediately grabbed her phone and tried calling Jordyn, but it went straight to voice mail. She then compared the photo of the car at the gas station with the mysterious vehicle she'd encountered on her way home. The license plate numbers were completely different, which confirmed her suspicions that this couldn't have been the same car.

She put those thoughts aside for the moment and concentrated on the next hurdle. Even though she was extremely exhausted, she had to gather all of the mental strength she could summon to put on an Oscar-worthy performance in front of her parents.

She closed her eyes for a moment and let out an enormous exhale before exiting the car. While in a seated position, Kayla's tall stature was not initially evident due to her compact torso. But upon standing, her lengthy legs allowed her to stretch out to roughly half an inch shy of six feet. Her statuesque physique had its privileges, yet she felt extremely self-conscious about it and would always round down to five-foot-eleven whenever asked or tasked with writing her height on any documentation. With her wide eyes and rounded face, many people would place her as a junior in high school instead of college if they judged strictly on her facial features. Her height, however, did help in adding a few years to her perceived age.

She shuffled down the stone-paved walkway leading up to the thirty-year-old split-level home, the only one she'd ever known. The cream-colored house with vinyl siding and burgundy window shutters blended in with the rest of the contemporary homes surrounding the cul-de-sac. The recently installed landscape lighting provided the right amount of highlights to the home's exterior, while also allowing the pink and periwinkle flowers from the hydrangea bushes to shine, even at night. Her home always provided comfort, peace, and serenity whenever she needed to escape the sometimes cold and unforgiving outside world.

She approached the front door and stopped before closing her eyes to feed off of the positive energy. She needed it now more than ever to counteract the stress and anxiety ravaging her insides.

"Here we go," she whispered before opening the door.

She entered the foyer and immediately heard voices upstairs in the kitchen. Her tired legs struggled to propel her up the stairs with the duffle bag in tow.

Before she made it to the top, her father, Trevor, approached and grabbed the bag, giving her a warm embrace.

"Welcome home. I thought you were planning to arrive a little earlier than this," he said.

Kayla flashed a smile. "Me, too, but had to finish up a project before I left."

Her mother, Amara, walked over and reached up, giving her a massive hug. "You know how your father feels about you driving at night."

"Yes, I know."

Amara paused for a moment, looking puzzled. "No Jordyn tagging along? I'm surprised she didn't want to eat here for dinner tonight. That's the usual plan when you both come home for the weekend. I'm assuming you dropped her off at home?"

"She didn't come home with me this time."

Trevor narrowed his eyes. "You mean to tell me you drove home by yourself at night?"

"Yes. I know you're probably not happy, but you taught me well, and I can take care of myself. I had my phone fully charged, a full tank of gas, my pepper spray, the pocket knife you gave me, and a don't-mess-with-me attitude."

"Hold on; wait a second, Trevor. You gave her a pocket knife?" Amara asked.

He shrugged. "It's not like she's going to go around stabbing innocent people. She knows it's strictly used for self-defense purposes."

Trevor gave Kayla another hug. "I'm just happy you made it home safely, especially knowing you drove solo. I think this is the first time Jordyn stayed back at school while you came home. What does she have going on at school that's so important?"

*Here come the questions. Stay calm.* "Her sorority was having a campus event this weekend, and she had to stay behind to help set up," she said, impressed with her lie and the confidence in which she conveyed it.

"Since when did she join a sorority?" Trevor asked.

*About a minute ago.* "She joined this semester. Said she wanted to be more active in school outside of going to class."

"Good for her," Trevor said.

Doing her best to avoid any follow-up questions, Kayla walked deeper into the kitchen and opened a large black pot sitting on the stove, unleashing a flavorful aroma into the air. "What is this I smell? Could this be the seafood gumbo I've missed so much while at school?"

"Just a little something I whipped up for you," Trevor said.

They sat in the dining room to partake in the home-cooked meal. Kayla gorged herself with the gumbo, eating as if she hadn't been fed in days.

Amara laughed. "Slow down, Kayla. Nobody's going to take your food away from you. There's plenty more left."

Kayla dabbed the corner of her lip with a napkin. "You don't understand. Home-cooked meals taste extra special when you haven't had one in a while."

"I get it," Trevor said before pausing to eat a spoonful, with a portion of it spilling on his goatee. He wiped his chin and continued, "I'm surprised you decided to come home now when there are only a few more weeks left until spring break."

"I know, but sometimes you need the quick weekend trip back home to help recharge your battery."

"No complaints from me. Always happy to have you home. So, how's school? Keeping up with your studies?"

"Yes, I'm doing okay. It's been a little tough after switching my major last year, but I'm making it work."

"I told you it might be difficult switching your major. Now you need to play catch up to try to graduate on time. And Lord knows we don't have any extra money to pay for your tuition once your four years are up," Amara said.

"I know, Mom, but I'm confident I can catch up. I've even given up on the idea of trying out for the volleyball team so I can concentrate on my school work."

Voices were silenced for an instant as the sound of silverware clanging against the porcelain bowls could be heard.

"And what about Jordyn? How's she making out after taking a semester off?" Trevor asked.

"She's hanging in there."

"That's it? You don't sound too confident with your response," Trevor said.

"I'm giving you the response she gives me whenever I ask her how she's doing. You know she's a private person."

"I've always wondered why she took the semester off. Hopefully, everything is okay with her," Trevor said.

"There could be a million reasons why she took the semester off, so I wouldn't jump to any conclusions this was due to anything serious. Maybe she needed a mental break," Amara responded.

"I don't know, but I'll keep my eye on her and let you guys know if I ever find out what's going on," Kayla said.

*****

Kayla eventually finished her meal and dragged her tired body up to her bedroom. She closed the door and immediately collapsed on her bed from exhaustion, although it was more mental than physical. She was proud of the way she'd handled the dinner conversation and kept her anxiety under control.

She looked at her phone, hoping to see a text or maybe a voicemail from Jordyn. There were days when she longed for her phone to be silent so she could rest, but this was not one of those days.

She stared at the ceiling, doing her best to avoid conjuring up any unpleasant thoughts surrounding Jordyn's voluntary disappearance. Kayla had always been a glass-half-empty type of person, and when you combine that with her chronic worrying habits, her stress levels were always habitually high. But somehow, she was able to mask much of this negative energy with her bubbly personality and vibrant smile, which could bring hope and optimism to any difficult situation.

She sighed and eventually closed her eyes, knowing she needed that smile more than ever now.

# Chapter 3

The sun slowly descended in the sky as Kayla approached the familiar entrance to Flagstone University. Two brick columns on each side of the road supported a black metal banner, with the university name proudly stretched across the top about fifteen feet in the air. The red mulch and multi-colored flowers scattered along the ground provided the finishing touches to a welcoming entrance.

She heeded her father's wishes to leave early enough and arrive on campus before sunset. She would have normally enjoyed a weekend where time slowed to a crawl. But, the slowdown in time this weekend had only heightened her anxiety. Seconds seemed like minutes, and minutes seemed like hours while she hoped and prayed for some form of communication with Jordyn, which never happened.

As she drove on campus, there was renewed optimism that when she entered her dorm room, she would see Jordyn standing there, safe and sound.

She pulled into the parking lot and stared at the brick façade of Dario Hall. She was fortunate to be in one of the newer dorms on campus. The dorm was also conveniently located next to the dining hall, making it much less of a hassle to walk for a meal during those biting Rhode Island winter days.

She grabbed her duffle bag and proceeded inside, nodding her head at a few familiar faces upon approaching the hallway leading to her dorm room. The walk felt longer than normal, most likely due to her slower pace as she edged toward the room.

She stopped and stared at the "*K & J*" cardboard initials affixed to the door. Before entering, she listened intently to determine if any signs of life were stirring on the other side. She unlocked the door and bit her bottom lip as the room came into view. A touch of light from a small lamp illuminated the desk standing between their beds, giving her hope Jordyn might have found her way back. She walked farther inside, clearing the entranceway to get a better view.

She knocked on the bathroom door. "Are you in there, Jordyn?" she said, hoping to hear a response, but none followed.

Kayla didn't recall leaving the lamp light on when they'd left for their road trip home. *Maybe Jordyn came back to the room during the weekend.* She noted the time, realizing it was still early enough during the evening that Jordyn could come walking through the door at any moment.

She sat on her bed before closing her eyes and rubbing her forehead to help massage away a headache she felt coming on. She eventually opened her eyes and stared at Jordyn's empty bed.

An assortment of K-pop posters covered her side of the wall, along with candid photos of Jordyn's family in framed pictures on her desk.

She stood and walked over to Jordyn's desk. A calendar of daily positive affirmations stood by her desk lamp, but it was two days behind. Kayla flipped the sheets to the present date.

*"I am more than my circumstances dictate."*

She smiled at the message, thinking she needed to pay more attention to these affirmations. She proceeded to look around at the two closed notebooks sitting on Jordyn's desk containing various colored sticky notes jutting out from a few pages. Now, Kayla was never one to snoop around other people's property, knowing she wouldn't want anyone doing the same to her. But, she believed certain situations could warrant breaking this rule. And in her mind, that situation was now.

Her curiosity was beyond piqued as to what Jordyn might have been doing these past couple of days. She hated to think that if Jordyn were in trouble, she would sit around and potentially wait for something unthinkable to happen to her.

She looked over her shoulder toward the door before proceeding to flip through the notebooks on the desk. The pages contained various class notes and homework assignments—nothing of great importance. Kayla figured if Jordyn were trying to hide something, it wouldn't be sitting on her desk in plain sight, so she needed to dig a little deeper.

She looked back again at the door and decided to open her desk drawer. She made it a point to carefully peruse through the drawer contents, shifting a few items around and being careful to put them back in their place. Besides various pens, paper clips, a calculator, and loose sheets of paper, there wasn't anything of interest.

She sighed, realizing this search was most likely not going to result in finding a smoking gun. Jordyn's phone was the more likely place to contain any serious clues as to what was going on, and gaining access to her phone would be next to impossible.

Kayla stopped all efforts and plopped back on her bed as the headache intensified. At the moment, this was all out of her control, and her only wish right now was to see Jordyn walking through the door.

*****

Hours later, Kayla was asleep in her bed and eventually awakened by a noise. She squinted to see the door open with the silhouette of a figure standing by the entrance. She shook off the confusion that normally occurred when being semi-conscious and conjured up three scenarios. First, she might have been dreaming and this figure could be anyone her mind had conjured up. Second, someone had broken into her room and she had to be ready to defend herself from a violent attack. Third, this was really Jordyn finding her way back.

She continued to squint, pretending she was still asleep, watching the figure through her narrow slits as the person stood by the entrance for a few seconds before closing the door and coming farther inside. The figure stood in the middle of the room for a second and did not budge. Based on the cone-shaped outline of the head, it appeared this person was wearing a hood.

Kayla closed her eyes completely for a moment, unsure if the person was looking directly at her while standing in the center of the dorm room. This individual was moving oddly and wasn't behaving like the Jordyn she knew. Her fears were further heightened after she realized she never took out her pocket knife and pepper spray resting in her duffle bag and out of reach. She considered letting out a solid scream to hopefully scare the person away.

Just as the thought entered her mind, the person retreated to Jordyn's bed and casually sat. Since the bed was positioned close to the window, a small hint of light filtered in through the partially closed blinds from the campus streetlamps outside, allowing Kayla to get a better glimpse of the individual. Her fears did subside once the person removed their hood and Jordyn's patented ponytail revealed itself. The tension immediately eased in Kayla's body, and she continued to squint, watching Jordyn's behavior intently.

Jordyn sat with her head down and knapsack between her legs. She stayed still for a moment before standing and walking to the bathroom. She contemplated alerting Jordyn to the fact that she was awake when she returned from the bathroom, but she appeared exhausted and figured it was better to let her rest.

*****

Kayla blindly reached for her phone to shut off the alarm the next morning. She took a moment to gather her senses and rotated her head toward Jordyn's bed. The covers were pulled tightly up to the pillow, giving no indication the bed had been occupied during the night.

29

She quickly sat up in bed, confused as if she might have experienced a dream sequence during the night that Jordyn had returned. She stood still momentarily before her eyes roamed the room, looking for Jordyn's knapsack but couldn't find it. Her anxiety returned in full force, coming to the realization that Jordyn might still be missing and classes were resuming today.

She tapped her phone to make sure she hadn't missed a text or call during the night. The stress of keeping Jordyn's disappearance a secret was becoming too much to bear. A tidal wave of guilt immediately consumed her, as she felt disgusted with herself for not saying anything sooner.

Her ominous introspection was interrupted by the sound of a toilet flush and running sink water in the bathroom.

She let out a massive sigh, looked up above, and mumbled, "Thank you!"

The door opened and Jordyn stepped out. Kayla couldn't help but produce one of her award-winning smiles with the sudden urge to jump up and hug her. But Jordyn didn't respond with the same elation and only waved meekly before sitting on the bed.

There were few times Kayla ever struggled to initiate a conversation, yet this moment rendered her speechless. The only form of communication she could muster was a timid wave.

She closed her eyes for a moment, as if to reset the speech center of her brain, and said, "Welcome back."

A hint of a curl formed at the ends of Jordyn's lips, indicating a smile was fighting to come through.

"Did you get any sleep? Looks like your bed was untouched," Kayla said.

"I crashed and took a quick nap on top of my covers last night." She paused while shaking her head. "You need to excuse me if I don't seem too happy to see you. I feel like crap," Jordyn said.

"What's wrong?"

"Having some issues with my stomach."

Kayla tempered her eagerness to ask Jordyn about her mysterious destination over the weekend. She felt awkward asking and hoped Jordyn would volunteer to spill the beans.

"Did you eat something that's bothering your stomach?"

Jordyn leaned back against the wall and said, "Maybe."

Kayla tilted her head forward as if trying to coax Jordyn into revealing more details about what she ate or where she might have dined over the weekend.

"So, does this mean you're not going to your class?"

Jordyn nodded without saying a word as her furrowed eyebrows indicated she felt a bit of discomfort. Then, before Kayla could say another word, Jordyn pushed herself off the bed and ran to the bathroom, slamming the door shut. A gut-wrenching gag could be heard, followed by the sound of her emptying the contents of her stomach in the toilet.

# Chapter 4

Jordyn's eyes fluttered, waking up from her nap. She welcomed the two-hour snooze, providing her with some much-needed rest. As an added bonus, her nauseous episodes eased in intensity. She rubbed her eyes, attempting to clear her vision, and surveyed the room. All was quiet, indicating Kayla was out and about, attending her classes.

Jordyn produced a scowl, noticing a bitter and slightly metallic taste tickling the edges of her tongue. She promptly rotated her legs off the bed and gathered herself before standing. Her knees buckled for a moment before she could steady them.

She plodded her way to the bathroom and brushed her teeth to get rid of the unpleasant taste. Despite feeling rested, the mirror revealed a network of microscopic red veins invading the whites of her eyes, crisscrossing in all directions. Her hair didn't fare any better, as several strands of hair stuck out at various odd angles away from her scalp. She grabbed a brush sitting on the side of the sink and stroked her dark brown hair from front to back, matting down the untamed strands. She adjusted her elastic hair band to pull her ponytail tighter and produced an exaggerated smile.

"You still look like crap," she mumbled to her reflection.

She exited the bathroom and walked to the closet. She pushed aside a laundry bag and grabbed her knapsack, buried in the corner. She made note of the time, realizing there was roughly an hour left before Kayla's class would end.

She proceeded to extract the contents, pulling out a pair of black leggings, a sweatshirt, and a thin, long-sleeved white shirt.

She froze, hearing voices outside the door. She immediately prepared to launch the knapsack and laundry bag back into the closet, but the voices quickly faded away down the hallway.

She continued unpacking, grabbing her toiletry bag, along with two prescription bottles. She walked to her dresser, opened the drawer, and promptly stuffed the prescription bottles at the bottom, hidden under her folded clothes.

Upon closing the drawer, she noticed one of the blue ribbon awards she'd won for a group class project was on the floor, sticking halfway out from under the dresser. She hadn't seen that award in quite a while and didn't recall handling the ribbon in any way recently, which could have led to it falling from her hands and onto the floor. There was no way this ribbon would have ended up on the floor without someone opening the drawer and moving things around. Odds were pretty high if she could confidently remove herself from the suspect list, there was only one other possibility.

She slammed the drawer shut and fumed at the idea that the one person she trusted had violated her privacy.

# Chapter 5

Kayla's eyes momentarily closed before she abruptly opened them, feeling embarrassed someone might have caught her dozing in class. She surveyed the lecture hall and didn't find anyone looking in her direction. With only three hours of broken sleep the previous night, she longed for a power nap and had every intention to go back to her room and grant that wish once class ended.

Her attention span had bordered on nonexistent the minute her professor had uttered the first few words in his lecture. However, she couldn't afford to take this microbiology class lightly, as anything less than a B would drop her GPA below the 3.2 average she needed to maintain her largest scholarship. She never could have imagined struggling at this point to maintain her grades after being on the dean's list for the last two years at Flagstone. She hated to think how her parents would react, knowing how hard it had been for them to keep up with tuition payments.

She cringed at the possibility of having to work and keep up with her coursework at the same time. Her last job as a summer counselor had been a disaster while attempting to deal with a group of high-energy kids on a daily basis. It had quickly become apparent if she lost her scholarship, not only would she need to work during the summer, but a part-time job during the school year might also be necessary.

Her eyes closed briefly again before she was startled awake by the sound of students moving around, as class had ended. She grabbed her notepad and noticed her professor looking her way. *Oh crap, I know he caught me napping.*

"Up late last night?"

"Sorry, Professor Lawson. Didn't get much sleep," Kayla said while struggling to keep eye contact.

"Don't worry; I won't hold it against you. I don't know if it's the early morning class or maybe I need to change my lecture style, but you're not the first to be counting sheep during my session."

"I'm so sorry. It won't happen again. I just have a lot going on right now."

"As I said before, my door is always open if you need help with assignments or want to talk about anything else. I know this class isn't the easiest, and I can say that with confidence since I was a student here decades ago, trying to figure it all out like you. So, I completely get it."

Kayla displayed an embarrassed smile. "Thanks for understanding."

She quickly grabbed her backpack, not interested in carrying on the conversation any longer, and shuffled herself out of the lecture hall. She ignored her growling stomach as the need for sleep overruled any desire to eat at the moment.

Her attention shifted to Jordyn, wondering if she was feeling any better and what she could have been doing over the weekend that had made her sick. She also hoped Jordyn would be forthcoming in letting her know the reason for her mysterious disappearance, as Kayla's curiosity could no longer be contained.

She approached Dario Hall, feeling slightly more energized by the casual walk on campus and the warm spring breeze. The groundskeepers had applied a fresh coat of mulch around the various flowerbeds and trees on campus. An influx of students had invaded the open green grass, sitting and enjoying the warm sun rays. For a brief moment, Kayla considered grabbing a blanket and taking advantage of the picture-perfect spring day by napping on the grass. *Maybe another time.*

She neared her dorm room, wondering if Jordyn was still asleep. She opened the door to see an empty room. Her heart rate ticked up a notch, wondering if Jordyn had mysteriously disappeared again, but the crumpled sheets on her bed, the various hair care items, and an opened apple juice bottle on her dresser indicated she'd most likely stepped out for a moment. This also gave some comfort to Kayla, knowing she was well enough to venture outside of the room.

She walked toward her bed, noticing a blue ribbon sitting on top of the sheets. She thought that was odd since she didn't recall anything on her bed when she'd left for class. She grabbed the ribbon and placed it on her desk before planting herself on the bed. She kicked off her sneakers and was about to lie down when the door opened and Jordyn stepped in with a laundry bag slung over her shoulders.

Kayla immediately smiled and said, "I see you're doing better."

Jordyn rolled her eyes. "We need to talk."

Kayla waited with great anticipation, hoping Jordyn was ready to talk about her mysterious weekend escapade.

Jordyn pointed to the blue ribbon sitting on Kayla's desk. "Any idea where that came from?" she asked, looking annoyed.

Kayla shrugged. "I found it on my bed. I was going to ask you the same question."

"It's an award I won last year for a group project competition in one of my classes."

"But why was it on my bed?"

"I think the bigger question is; why was it on the floor by my dresser?"

*Busted.* Kayla was hit with a reality check that her careful shuffling through Jordyn's drawers hadn't been as careful as she'd thought.

"Okay, I have a good explanation. I'll admit I went through your drawers last night, and I want to first apologize for what I did."

Jordyn stood with her arms crossed. "Go on; I'm listening."

"I was worried about you over the weekend and was expecting to see you when I made it back to campus last night. When I didn't see you, I panicked and wanted to see if I could find something that would give me a clue as to what was going on with you—where you were."

"I told you in my text back at the gas station that I was fine and would be back on campus in a couple of days."

Kayla tried to remain calm but could feel a tinge of agitation setting in. "Was that text supposed to calm all my fears? Put yourself in my shoes. How the heck should I have reacted when you wanted to voluntarily be left at that dingy, isolated, perfect-setting-for-a-horror-movie gas station? You already know my nerves are bad, and your text didn't help one bit."

"Okay, I'll admit my text must have been confusing, but I have my reasons for doing what I did."

"Well, are you planning to let me in on what's going on? Maybe this is something I can help you with."

"I can't do that right now. You know I don't like to have my business out in front for everyone to see."

Kayla pointed to herself. "But I'm not everyone. I'm a concerned friend who wants to help in any way I can."

"I appreciate the show of empathy. I just can't tell you what's going on right now."

Kayla let out a sigh. "You're killing me, Jordyn!"

Jordyn focused her attention on the blue ribbon. "We still need to address the fact that you violated my privacy by going through my drawer."

"Yes, and I said I was sorry."

"That's not good enough for me. How would you like it if I went digging through your stuff and followed it up with a simple sorry? That doesn't give me confidence you won't do it again."

"You just need to trust me going forward."

"Easier said than done."

"Hey . . . I'm not the only one who violated trust in this relationship."

"How so? I didn't go through your stuff, sneaking around to see what I could find."

"No, but it's not like you to mysteriously disappear for an entire weekend and leave me completely in the dark as to what's going on. I think that's a violation of trust. I have no idea if you're in danger, or if I should be worried now about any type of threats coming my way since I'm your roommate."

Jordyn's face softened a bit. "No need for you to worry. Nothing's going to happen to you because of what I'm doing."

Kayla gave Jordyn a slow, appraising glance. "I hope you're right."

# Chapter 6

Trevor Devereaux pulled into the driveway and shut off the engine. He raised his left arm toward his nose and sniffed. As usual, the scent of various seafood dishes was embedded in the fibers of his clothes. For any seafood lovers, this would be a welcomed scent to have stuck to your clothes, but after smelling like this all day at the restaurant, it no longer invoked feelings of hunger like it used to when he'd first started there as a cook. He'd since worked his way up to head chef, resulting in him managing a large contingent of junior cooks. He truly had a passion for cooking and enjoyed sharing his knowledge with those junior-level chefs following in his footsteps.

Based on Trevor's physical appearance, most people were surprised by his profession. Not that a head chef had any specific characteristics they needed to conform to, yet based on his experience, most people speculated he was either a construction worker or might have even played professional rugby at one time or another.

He sported a clean, hair-free scalp with a trimmed goatee, possessed a sturdy body frame, and had an assortment of tattoos running down his right arm, along with his initials inscribed on the side of his neck. He experienced his share of sidewalk discrimination with people choosing to walk across the street to avoid him on occasion. Contrary to what many people would believe, he found this behavior amusing, especially those times when he considered crossing the street to avoid someone coming his way, but they beat him to the punch.

He grabbed his apron sitting on the passenger seat and exited his 2020 Chevy Tahoe. He was surprised to see Amara's car parked in front of his in the driveway. She was a pharmacy technician, which occasionally led to extended work hours. It was his initial understanding she would have been working late tonight.

He proceeded down the walkway and admired the recently installed landscape lighting, adding to the home's curb appeal during the evening. His house was no longer the only one around the cul-de-sac with no lights. Keeping up with the Joneses was always his motto.

He entered the house and walked into the kitchen where Amara was sitting, entertained by a show broadcasting from a small TV sitting on the counter.

"Welcome home. I was wondering when you were going to get here. I was about to start eating alone," she said.

He gave her a peck on the lips. "I'm surprised to see you home this early."

"Me, too. One of my coworkers asked if we could switch shifts today, so instead of working late tonight, I'll be doing it tomorrow."

Trevor took in a deep inhale, attempting to decipher the scent coming from the stove. "Is that my gumbo I smell?"

"Yes. Since we didn't get a chance to go grocery shopping yesterday, these were the only leftovers we had in the fridge."

"Oh, well. Leftovers are good for the financial diet. Speaking of finances, I think Kayla's tuition payment is coming up next week."

Amara looked at the calendar on the refrigerator. "Do we have enough money in the checking account to cover the payment?"

"I doubt it. I get paid on Friday, but my car payment is coming out at the same time. I can transfer money from our savings to help cover the tuition."

"Any thought about selling the Tahoe and buying a car with a lower monthly payment?"

"Not really. I only have two more years before it's paid off."

"That's also two more years of spending a fortune to fill up that oversized gas tank."

"I'll take paying a little extra for gas in exchange for a reliable vehicle. Other than the normal wear and tear on the Tahoe, I haven't had to spend much money on any big repairs. Knock on wood."

"We definitely can't afford any unexpected car repairs. We can barely stay afloat with our normal bills," Amara said, standing to grab a plate. "And I'm concerned about us keeping up with Kayla's tuition payments."

"We'll make it work. We always find a way."

"Speaking of finding a way, when were you planning to—"

Trevor stuck his hand out. "I know. Don't say it. I'll get around to it."

Amara sighed. "I haven't bothered you about this in a while, and I've been patient for way too long, but enough is enough. You act like it's no big deal. Unless you're planning to not ever say anything?"

"I know it's a big deal, but how the hell am I even supposed to start that conversation with Kayla? Believe me; this has stressed me out beyond belief and probably led to these gray hairs starting to pop up in my goatee."

Amara's lips curled in disgust. "You're not doing Kayla or me any favors about keeping silent on this. I've been doing all I can to keep my promise, but you're making it extremely difficult."

"Okay, I get it. I heard you loud and clear and will work on it. Can we please not talk about it now? I just want to eat, watch some TV, and go to bed."

# Chapter 7

Kayla spread out her blanket, joining the many other students who were congregating at Octagon Park. This was the epicenter of campus, which normally attracted a large number of students on the cushioned grassy surface.

She took a deep breath to soak in the air, closing her eyes and tilting her head up toward the sun. She needed this moment to release the stress that had inundated her world during the past week. She was mentally drained and had trouble focusing in class. With spring break only a few weeks away, she wanted to end the first half of the semester on a good note.

Her moment of serenity was interrupted by her chiming phone as a text message displayed on the screen.

> *Be there in a few. Professor Wilks wouldn't stop talking and class ended a little late.*

The message came from her friend, Avery, who was on her way to join Kayla for a quick chat in the afternoon sun. She felt guilty she hadn't been able to spend much time with her since the start of the semester. They'd been pretty much inseparable last year, but a major clash in their schedules this semester made it a challenge for them to meet up.

"Finally," Kayla said as Avery approached.

She had always admired how Avery walked with a sense of purpose, not letting her small stature get in the way of her abundant confidence. With her box braids dangling and bouncing against the sides of her face, round cheeks, and the whitest teeth you'd ever want to see, Kayla couldn't help but think Avery would one day end up in a toothpaste commercial.

Avery sat on the blanket and said, "Don't blame me. We can first start with Professor Wilks, who has a knack for always getting chatty at the end of class. And second, you can blame all my loyal fans who kept stopping me to talk on my way over here. You can't fault me for being popular." She said and smiled.

Kayla reciprocated with a smile of her own. "No egos allowed in this zone."

"So, how have you been, my friend? Seems like a while since we had a chance to talk," Avery said.

"I'm doing what I need to do to get through the day."

"Uh-oh. That's giving me some I'm-struggling-and-need-a-friend-to-talk-to vibes. Where's the sunshine and rainbows energy I normally feel when I'm around you?"

Kayla laughed. "It's still here, I guess."

"Okay, talk to me. What is it? Too much schoolwork? Feeling homesick? Boy trouble? Somebody bullying you?"

Kayla took a gulp from her water bottle. "None of the above."

"Well, whatever it is, you know I got your back."

"I know you do. I guess I need to get my mind right. Been in a little funk lately."

"I hear you. We all go through those moments, but I'm not going to allow you to feel bad about yourself in front of me. This is now the no-sulking-allowed zone. We got spring break coming up in a few weeks, we have some fine-looking boys on campus who would love to talk with you, and spring fever is here. What could be better than that?"

"Yeah, I know I should probably be in a better mood now, but I'm not."

"Speaking of boys, what's happening in that department? You still with Julian?" Avery asked.

"No, it didn't work out with him, so I'm back on the market and haven't found anyone yet."

"Are you kidding me? Definitely his loss. I'm sure you'll be locked up with someone else in no time."

Kayla let out a sigh. "We'll see. I honestly think most boys are intimidated by me because of my height. I don't know of many boys who would feel comfortable having to tilt their heads up to kiss their girlfriend."

"You do know we have a basketball team consisting of boys over six feet? Ever think about including them in your dating pool?"

Kayla laughed. "I'm not trying to be one of their groupies. I have a lot more respect for myself."

"Okay, that was only a suggestion. You know what's best for you." Avery stopped momentarily as a frisbee came floating by her head. "And what's going on for spring break? Doing anything fun?"

"I'm hoping I can make my way to the Cape for the annual spring break party, but my parents are already starting to complain about it, so I'll most likely be heading home."

"That sucks. Then you probably don't want to hear what I'm doing for the break."

"Probably not, but I'd feel funny if I didn't ask."

"I'm flying to San Diego to hang with my family and celebrate my grandma's eightieth birthday."

"Lucky you. Would you believe me if I told you I've never traveled anywhere outside of Rhode Island? At least not that I can remember."

"Are you kidding me? Don't you know that's travel neglect? Haven't you ever been to a family reunion or hung out with some relatives every once in a while?"

"Nope. Other than my parents, there isn't much family for me to talk about. I hear I have relatives in Virginia and Colorado, but I've never seen or spoken to them."

Avery put her hand on Kayla's shoulder. "What if I tell you I consider you family? Does that help?"

"Absolutely."

Avery looked at the time. "Sorry, my friend, I gotta run. My next class is starting shortly, and I need to walk to the other side of campus."

Kayla stood up. "I'll walk with you. I'm done with my classes for the day and don't mind getting more of this sun." She folded up the blanket before stuffing it in her backpack and proceeded to walk with Avery.

Although Kayla enjoyed Avery's company, she'd become even more self-conscious about her height whenever they both walked together. She had nearly nine inches on Avery and always felt like she was a parent walking with her child. She did her best to ignore the stares that came from people passing by, noticing the extreme height difference.

They eventually approached a stone-carved falcon, sitting on top of a pedestal, representing the school's mascot.

"Come on; how about a selfie?" Avery asked, grabbing Kayla's arm and dragging her to the pedestal.

Avery passed her phone to Kayla to take advantage of her longer arms for a better angle to take the selfie. Kayla bent her legs to even out the height difference as they both squeezed into the camera's view and displayed massive smiles in front of the mascot. Avery proceeded to text the photo to Kayla and said, "Next time you're feeling down, look at my irresistibly happy face and, hopefully, that will cheer you up."

Kayla laughed.

Avery pointed to the parking lot behind them. "I normally cut through here to save time going to class."

Kayla displayed a huge grin as the somber mood that had floated over her like a cloud a short time ago had disappeared. She could always count on Avery to bring some joy to her day, and she'd needed it desperately.

They proceeded through the parking lot, admiring the luxury cars that the financially privileged students owned. Kayla abruptly stopped and focused her attention on one car in particular.

Avery stopped along with her. "Whose car is that?"

Without saying a word, Kayla stared at a glitzy red disco ball hanging from the rearview mirror of the car. She quickly took out her phone and opened her photos, scrolling back a few days. She froze upon realizing the four-door sedan parked a few feet away from her was the same car that had sat in the gas station parking lot on the night Jordyn had mysteriously disappeared.

# Chapter 8

Kayla took a few steps back to distance herself from the car. She closed her eyes for a few seconds then opened them, staring back at the car.

"Are you okay? You're starting to scare me," Avery said.

Kayla let out a long exhale to try to absorb the blow from the tension that spread through her gut. She finally made eye contact with Avery. "I'm sorry. It's a long story, but I'll be okay. You should probably continue to your class. Don't want to make you late."

Avery put her hand on Kayla's shoulder. "If you need me to stay with you, let me know. I can skip class if necessary. Just want to make sure you're good."

She forced a smile and offered Avery a sincere gaze. "I'm good. I promise."

Avery took a step back. "Okay . . . if you say so." Avery departed, looking back at Kayla several times as she walked away.

Once Avery disappeared out of sight, Kayla twisted her head from left to right, canvasing the parking lot, looking for any unusual activity or people of interest. An image of the gas station owner flashed in her head as she wondered if he was on campus, following her. Then again, how would he know she was a student here at Flagstone? She also wasn't sure if the car she saw at the gas station was even his. At this point, all of these questions didn't matter. What did matter was the realization that a few days ago, this same car, sitting idle in a rural gas station parking lot, almost forty-five minutes away, was now staring her in the face on campus.

She shook her head, clearing her thoughts, now conscious of the fact she'd been standing in the same position for way too long. Anyone passing by might have thought she was in a state of hypnosis. But of greater concern, the possibility of her being stalked by the owner of this car became terrifyingly real.

She slowly turned in a complete circle, sweeping her eyes across the parking lot. She did gain comfort in knowing if someone were after her, they most likely wouldn't be brazen enough to grab her in broad daylight.

*Okay, Kayla, let's calm down and figure this out.*

She perused the area and noticed she was in close proximity to the campus library. Depending on what side of the building you were on, there was a clear view of the parking lot if you positioned yourself by the library's large glass panels.

Without any further hesitation, she scurried to the entrance. She darted into the building and focused her eyes on any males within her range of vision who might have had a resemblance to the gas station owner. Kayla's paranoia was in full bloom, as she couldn't escape the feeling that someone had their eyes on her from a distance.

She walked briskly around a set of tables where a few students sat with their laptops opened, diligently working and not paying her any mind. She focused her attention on the oversized windows and kept her eyes on the car, which remained parked and unoccupied. The tinted library windows, combined with the sun glare reflecting off of them, gave her the cover she needed for anyone attempting to look inside from the parking lot. She found an empty desk by the window with a clear view of the car.

A trickle of sweat slid down the right side of her temple and stopped at the edge of her jawline. She unlocked her phone and took one more look at the photo to make sure this wasn't a case of mistaken identity, but the Rhode Island license plate number in the gas station photo was an exact match to the one on the car outside.

She flinched when her phone chimed with a message. She hesitated, looking at it for a moment based on developing PTSD from the anxiety-inducing text message Jordyn had sent her a few days ago. She eventually positioned her eyes on the screen and let out a colossal exhale after seeing a text from Avery, checking in on her.

After responding to Avery, she sat with eagle eyes while waiting for the owner of the car to claim their vehicle from the parking lot.

Eventually, she saw a woman approach the car. She grabbed her phone and trained her camera on the woman before zooming in. She had her thumb hovering over the button to take a photo before she quickly realized the woman was getting in the car parked one spot over.

"Damn," she whispered.

She momentarily shifted her focus away from the car and checked her surroundings within the library. She didn't want to be lulled into a false sense of security, thinking the threat could only be coming from the outside. After a quick scan of the area, she darted her eyes back outside to the car. In her mind, she was convinced she would stay in the library all day long if she had to until someone showed up to claim the vehicle. However, there was one problem that suddenly became apparent, which could potentially derail her minute-by-minute focus on the car. Her bladder was full and started to groan in protest to be relieved. She did her best to ignore its plea, but the urge was becoming too hard to resist. She gritted her teeth, knowing that, with her luck, the moment she left the table would be the small window of time needed for the owner to hop in the car and leave undetected.

She stood and paused for a moment as a thought entered her mind. She walked to a nearby shelf and grabbed a couple of thick, hardcover books. Coming back to the table, she positioned the books toward the end of the table, near the window, and proceeded to prop up her phone against the books. She swiped to video mode and positioned the phone so the camera was in clear view of the car. She then hit the record button and quickly walked away from the table to make a beeline for the bathroom.

She understood she was taking a risk leaving her phone unattended, but it would be worth it if she could catch a glimpse of the owner of the vehicle. She also had comfort in knowing all of the students in her immediate area were completely focused on their laptops and oblivious to the fact she was even there.

She rushed into the bathroom and barged into a stall. She'd never paid attention to how long it normally took to empty her bladder, but this time around, it seemed like an eternity. She eventually finished, washed her hands, and exited the bathroom, darting back to the table. Her phone was exactly where she'd left it, along with the car. She stopped the video recording and replayed it to make sure she hadn't missed anything while she was gone, but there was nothing.

Another hour passed, and the owner of the car never showed up. As much as Kayla wanted to stay perched at the table, she had a couple of assignments due the following day and hadn't eaten since breakfast. She knew she had to abandon her mission, but this came with a heavy price. Her normal relaxing walks on campus would now turn into tension-filled journeys since the owner of the car had not yet been identified. This meant her head would constantly be on a swivel, hyper-focused on her surroundings, wondering if she was unknowingly being watched.

# Chapter 9

Amara honked her horn and protested against a car squeezing in front of her as she battled the late afternoon rush-hour traffic. She cursed under her breath, not only at the driver but also at herself for leaving work later than she should have. She contemplated forgoing the quick grocery store run she'd planned, but the refrigerator was bare and desperately needed to be replenished.

She eventually exited off of I-95, thankful she'd made it through the bumper-to-bumper traffic and could drive more than ten miles per hour. She switched to the 80's XM station and turned up the volume to Elton John's "I'm Still Standing." Music had always been her savior when it came to dealing with stressful moments and fighting through rush-hour traffic moved the needle up on her stress meter.

She pulled into the parking lot, praying there was a spot not too far from the entrance to Trader Joe's. After circling once and not finding an open spot, she drove farther away from the entrance until she found a parking space at the outer edges of the lot. She never had the patience to circle multiple times, waiting for that premium parking spot near the entrance of any store to become available.

She exited the car and tugged at her skirt to smooth out the material that had bunched up around her thighs while sitting in the car. Amara never considered herself a fashionista and preferred to stay on the conservative side when it came to dressing. Kayla had constantly teased her about spicing up her wardrobe to help show off her figure, which had held up extremely well against Father Time. She considered herself fortunate her twice-a-week gym routine kept her in optimum shape for someone approaching half a century. This was also evident by the constant attention she received from men, with the majority of them probably half her age. She couldn't lie, as the attention did provide a serious boost to her ego. But she was never one to flaunt what she had and was perfectly fine with staying incognito and blending in with the rest of the crowd.

She entered the store and immediately frowned at the crowd of shoppers bustling around the aisles. Her game plan had always been to get in and out as quickly as possible. But, with the mass of shoppers populating the aisles, she understood her game plan would be extremely challenging. She thought for a moment to turn around and try another day, but she decided to push on and get it over with. Sighing, she proceeded to fight through the throng of shoppers and swiftly grabbed what she needed.

She pushed her cart, artfully dodging the customers in various aisles and doing her best to remain patient when she was bottled up and couldn't move as quickly as she wanted. After working her way down a few aisles and adding several items to her cart, she noticed a gentleman out of the corner of her eye staring in her direction. She couldn't immediately tell if he was looking at her or somewhere beyond, but her sixth sense told her it was the former.

She grabbed a bottle of apple juice off a shelf and continued about her business. She rounded the corner into the next aisle and, a minute later, she spotted the same gentleman not too far from her. Now she could chalk this up as a coincidence, but since she was in the feminine hygiene aisle, she didn't know of too many men who were comfortable roaming this area without breaking into a cold sweat. Her heart rate increased, along with her discomfort about the situation. The man looked to be in his forties and was well dressed in beige khakis and a tucked-in, blue collared shirt. His hair was neatly trimmed and, by all accounts, he looked like a trustworthy individual. But Amara completely understood looks could be deceiving.

She continued and approached the section with products designed to treat yeast infections. She carefully perused the shelves, tugging at a few of the products while looking out the corner of her eye to see if he still had his sights set on her. Although she didn't need any of these products, she figured if he were physically attracted to her, this would deter him from pursuing her further.

She placed two boxes of Monistat into her cart to see if this would be the kryptonite needed to repel the gentleman. To her dismay, he continued to look her way on occasion and didn't seem to be deterred by her stunt. With this failed attempt at shaking herself free from the stranger, she decided to end her shopping experience early. She pushed her cart with extra zest and did her best to lose him among the host of other shoppers. She looked for the shortest checkout line, but they all contained a large contingent of customers. She stood in line, reluctant to turn her head for fear she would see him staring back at her.

She held onto the cart as her arms began to tremble. It had been a while since she'd experienced a panic attack, and she was well aware of the signs. She felt spots of moisture gathering around her chest and closed her eyes while taking in deep breaths. She opened them, and her periphery vision allowed her to see the gentleman in the checkout line, two lanes to her right. She could no longer keep her composure and broke the line, pushing her cart to an open space in an aisle and dropping it off before dodging through the crowd until she made it outside. Without looking behind her, she walked hastily to her car and called Trevor.

"I think someone's following me," she said, her voice trembling.

"Where are you?"

"At Trader Joe's. I was in the middle of shopping and saw a man following me."

"Are you still in the store?"

"No, I left my cart inside and walked out. I felt a panic attack coming on."

"Okay, relax. Do you see him following you now?"

"I'm afraid to turn around."

"But we need to know if he's anywhere near you."

Amara swallowed hard and twisted her head, looking behind her. "No, I don't see him," she said, approaching her car. "I'm about to get in the car now."

"Okay, good. Make your way back to the house, and I should be there in about an hour. If you see any vehicle following you, then don't lead them to our house. I would drive to the police station, and let's see if they're bold enough to continue following you."

"Okay, see you soon. Love you," Amara said.

She started the car and reversed out of the parking space before abruptly hitting the brake as a man seemed to come out of nowhere behind her vehicle. Her heart fluttered, as she couldn't get a good glimpse of the individual looking through the backup camera. She twisted her head and spotted an older man shuffling his way past the car.

She let out a massive exhale and continued to back out of the space, starting her trip back home. She turned her head from right to left, scanning the area, looking at all the moving vehicles in her immediate space. She didn't see anything of concern and continued out of the parking lot and onto the main road.

She glanced in the rearview mirror every few seconds, paying strict attention to any cars behind her. She tugged at her blouse, flapping it by her chest to try to dry the moisture accumulating on her skin. She eventually pressed her foot on the brake and came to a stop at a red light. She was centered in the middle lane as two cars pulled up along both sides. She gave a glance to her left, eyeing a black sedan with tinted windows, giving her no chance to view the occupants. She peeked to her right and saw an older woman staring straight ahead, paying her no mind. She looked once again in the rearview mirror as a dump truck pulled up behind her. Peering straight ahead, she waited for the light to turn green and paid the most attention to the vehicle with the tinted windows.

The light finally turned green, and she had the urge to press the pedal as hard as she could to get away from the other cars, even though there had been no immediate threat detected from these vehicles. Instead, she lightly pressed the pedal as the two cars on both sides of her moved ahead and eventually turned at the next intersection.

Amara did her best to calm her anxiety and mumbled what her therapist would always tell her, "Fear is nothing but false evidence appearing real."

She was amazed at how quickly her mind could take control of her body and launch her into a crazed frenzy of panic and dread if she fell into its trap.

She eventually approached her house, feeling confident she had not been followed. She pulled into the driveway and immediately exited her car before quickly walking to the door and entering. She shut off the house alarm and reset it once she closed the door. This gave her some level of comfort until Trevor was scheduled to arrive home.

"Thank you, God," she whispered.

She felt relieved being in the comfort of her own home, but frustration started to creep into her mind. She thought she'd conquered this crippling mindset that controlled her for the better part of ten years. She'd been hitting her stride and felt relaxed navigating the outside world with little fear of being watched. And now, all of those negative emotions started to float to the forefront of her mind.

In the past, she would use alcohol to get her through these difficult moments, but as she learned, this only made things worse. Besides, her home was an alcohol-free zone, and the only way she could get her hands on some was if she ventured back outside, which was not going to happen.

Trevor eventually arrived back home, and Amara embraced him like she hadn't seen him in a year. "So glad you made it back home."

He pulled away from her embrace and gently cupped his hands around both sides of her cheeks. "Are you okay? Did you see anyone following you home?"

"No, not that I know of," Amara said then winced. "I thought I had this thing beat. I was doing so well."

"It's okay. Don't beat yourself up about this. The therapist said relapses may occur from time to time."

"But it's been almost a year since my last attack."

Trevor hugged her again. "You'll get through it and before you know it, you'll forget this ever happened." He paused. "How sure are you this man was following you?"

"I . . . I don't really know. The store was crowded, and it could have been a coincidence I kept seeing him. I just had this strange feeling."

Trevor smiled in an attempt to lighten the mood. "You have been known to stop traffic with your looks. This isn't the first time a man followed you to get a better look. But I'm secure enough in my manhood to realize men are going to drool over you sometimes."

A hint of a smile developed along the corners of Amara's lips. "I tried the ol' Monistat trick."

Trevor laughed. "And that didn't work?"

"It didn't appear to. But maybe you're right; my mind could have been playing tricks on me."

Trevor gave her one last hug. "So I guess we're ordering out tonight since we still have no food in the fridge."

Amara shrugged. "I guess so."

# Chapter 10

Kayla gripped her backpack tighter than normal as she walked across Octagon Park. The picturesque campus setting did nothing to calm her anxiety, which spiked to abnormally high levels due to the presence of the mysterious car in the parking lot. She wanted to believe it was pure coincidence, but her mind outright refused that as a plausible explanation. She truly believed someone was watching, and it frayed every single nerve in her body that she couldn't identify who it was amongst the hundreds of people roaming the campus.

She continued her march across campus, being sure to pay attention to any individuals who might be staring at her a little longer than normal. She ignored several waves from a few friends, laser-focused on arriving safely back in her dorm.

She would normally feel comfortable walking on campus with just her pepper spray, but this unknown threat called for more protection.

She made a quick detour and headed to the dorm parking lot. She sidestepped her way around a group of groundskeepers setting up to trim hedges near the dorm. In her haste to maneuver around the men, she stumbled and dropped her phone. The phone landed in the grass and was quickly scooped up by one of the groundskeepers.

He inspected the phone, turning it from front to back. "Luckily for you, it looks like your screen didn't crack." He shook off a bit of dirt that had collected on the phone before handing it back to Kayla.

She forced a smile. "Thank you, sir."

"No problem," he said, waving as Kayla departed. "*Adios*, young lady."

She focused her attention back on the task at hand as she neared her car. These were the moments that validated her reasoning for keeping her car keys with her at all times. In her mind, time was always of the essence in any dangerous situation, and having the ability to jump in your car whenever necessary was extremely important.

She quickly observed the area before approaching her car and opening the door. She grabbed the pocket knife out of the glove compartment and then continued her walk toward the dorm room with this added self-defense insurance.

She was convinced Jordyn had to know something about this car, and it was of utmost importance she started talking. No more games, no more secrets. It was time she found out the truth.

Kayla arrived at her dorm room and opened the door, seeing Jordyn sitting at her desk in the middle of writing down some notes.

She dropped her backpack on the floor. "Sorry to disturb you, but we need to talk."

Jordyn turned to Kayla, appearing annoyed she'd interrupted her flow. "Can we talk in about an hour? I need to finish an assignment."

Normally, Kayla would have no problem complying with her wishes, especially when it came to completing any schoolwork, but this was an emergency in her eyes that needed to be addressed ASAP. So, without any respect for Jordyn's request, she said, "Is there any reason why the car we saw at the gas station a few days ago is now sitting in the library parking lot?"

Jordyn scrunched her eyebrows in confusion. "What are you talking about?"

Kayla walked over and showed her the picture of the car she took during their visit to the gas station.

"Why did you take a picture of this car?"

"For moments exactly like this. Since I had no clue what was going on or where you disappeared, I figured it was smart to take a picture of the other cars in the lot. At least I now know there's a good possibility we're being stalked."

"Stalked? Is that what you think?"

Kayla threw her hands in the air. "What else am I supposed to think?"

"How do you know it's the same car? There are plenty of dark-colored cars on the road."

"I don't think there are many dark cars with a red disco ball hanging from the rearview mirror. Also, I already compared the plates in the photo with the one in the library parking lot, and it's an exact match."

Jordyn sighed, twisting her legs from under the desk to face Kayla, and placed her hands on top of her head. "No one's stalking us."

Kayla's heart rate increased a few ticks, hoping and praying this was Jordyn's prelude to finally confessing about her weekend rendezvous.

"I sort of know who the car belongs to," Jordyn said before pausing as a few moments of silence elapsed.

Kayla opened her eyes wider than normal. "Are you freaking kidding me, Jordyn? You're just going to stop now and have me sitting here with my heart in my throat, waiting for you to continue?"

"It belongs to a man who works on campus."

Kayla stood puzzled, attempting to process what she'd heard. "Can you help me out a little more and narrow this down for me? A man who works on campus doesn't exactly help me out much," she said. But before Jordyn could answer, Kayla continued, "Wait, please don't tell me you have some type of freaky relationship going on with this mystery man on campus? Is that what this secret is all about?"

Jordyn vehemently shook her head. "Oh, heck no."

Kayla exhaled a huge sigh of relief. "Please, continue then. I'm all ears."

"The man is a regular at the station, and he dropped the car off for some repairs."

Kayla scrunched her eyebrows as if she'd eaten something horrible. "Are the car service centers that bad around here for him to choose possibly the worst-looking one he could find?"

Kayla sat on her bed and leaned forward. "Okay, here's what I need to know. Who told you all of this? Does this mystery man have a name? And do you have any idea of what he does on campus? Is he a professor?"

"I have my sources, and I don't know his name or what he does on campus."

Kayla dropped her head, rubbing her eyes before looking up. "Okay, now you're making it more difficult than it needs to be. Can you at least tell me if this man was at the station when I dropped you off? And if not, then who were you there to see? The only other person I saw was the gas station owner, and he acted like he didn't know you from a can of paint. Also, me and him were totally confused as to where you went, or at least he acted that way. And don't even get me started on what happened after I didn't find you in the bathroom."

Jordyn sighed. "I gave you all I could to help calm your fears and let you know we're not being stalked. But I . . . I don't want to say anything else about it right now."

Kayla stood with her arms folded. "Oh, hell no. We're not doing this, Jordyn. You can't leave me hanging like this. I have questions that need answers for my sanity's sake."

"Sorry, I'm just not ready to talk about it now."

Kayla bit her bottom lip, doing her best to control the urge to grab Jordyn by the shoulders and shake her like a rag doll to make her talk. "Okay, as much as it bothers me you won't tell me what's going on, I can wait until you're ready to talk," she said, knowing that was a massive lie.

# **Chapter 11**

Spring break couldn't have come soon enough for Kayla. The past few weeks of school had been an extreme challenge, keeping up with her studies while dealing with a roommate who continued to stand firm on her decision not to divulge what had happened during her secret weekend rendezvous. Her stress was further heightened by the C grade she currently had in her microbiology class. If she didn't pull this mark up to a B, her GPA would drop below the threshold to maintain one of her scholarships. This meant an additional ten thousand dollars would need to come from somewhere else to continue paying the yearly tuition. Not to mention her parents would be less than pleased since having extra money in their household was about as real as a rainbow-colored unicorn.

She pulled into her driveway after dropping Jordyn off at her house. She wasn't sure how she made it through the hour-fifteen-minute drive from school without addressing the elephant in the car, but she continued to temper her patience, waiting for Jordyn to finally reveal the secret that eluded an explanation for the past few weeks.

She was always happy to come back home, even if her enthusiasm was rather diminished during this spring break. Many of her friends were headed south, on their way to various beach destinations to enjoy a week of fun and sun. She'd been invited to a few parties taking place on Cape Cod during the week, but her parents didn't think it was a good idea. This left her with no choice but to stay home and lounge on her deck with a good book, which was not her idea of a memorable spring break.

She tilted her head against the headrest and sighed heavily before exiting the car. She immediately sneezed, as the high pollen count in the air started to trigger her allergies, which bothered her on occasion. It also didn't help she forgot to take her allergy medication. She frowned, knowing if this kept up, she could say goodbye to her aspirations of enjoying a good book outside on the deck.

She entered the house and shut off the alarm. She sat on the sofa in the living room and started to rub her itchy eyes. She blinked a few times before closing her eyes to help ease the discomfort.

Her lips curled into a small grin as she thought about Avery, who was probably laughing and enjoying the company of her family in San Diego. Kayla could only imagine what it looked like on the West Coast. Other than seeing images on TV or online, California seemed like it existed in another galaxy.

Her ultimate goal was to travel as much as she could once she graduated and had a full-time job. She was eager to experience the different foods, people, cultures, and ways of life that came with venturing to new places. She kept her eyes closed and began to drift off to sleep.

*****

Kayla was jarred out of her sleep with a nudge to her leg. She awoke to see Amara standing over her, smiling.

"Is this how you plan to spend your spring break?" Amara asked.

Kayla blinked several times to regain her focus. "I guess I didn't realize how tired I was."

Amara bent down to give her a hug. "Welcome home again."

Kayla tapped her phone, observing the time. "What time do you expect Dad to be home?"

"He should be home in the next half hour. Why are you asking?"

"I'm hoping he brings food home from the restaurant. I can use some good seafood right now."

"He didn't mention anything to me about bringing home food, but I also know how he likes to surprise you. We'll see what happens."

Amara noticed Kayla's duffle bag resting on the floor beside her. "Looks like you never even made it upstairs." Amara stared at the bag a little moure. "And when were you planning to switch this bag out for the nice rolling suitcase we got you for Christmas?"

"I know, Mom. But it's like those comfortable pair of shoes you don't want to get rid of no matter how busted they are."

"Okay, makes sense." Amara's smile suddenly relaxed with a more serious tone displaying on her face. "Are things going okay at school?"

Kayla shrugged. "I guess so. It's the usual stuff. Just looking to rest this week and get ready for the stretch run until the semester is over."

Amara placed her hand on Kayla's shoulder. "I hope you're still not upset at me and Dad for convincing you not to go to the Cape with your friends."

"I'd be lying if I said I'd rather be here than with my friends, but between gas for the car, sharing the Airbnb expense with the girls, and buying food, it was probably going to be too expensive, anyway."

Amara smiled. "I'm glad to see you thinking about this from a monetary standpoint. As you know, money—"

"Doesn't grow on trees," Kayla finished her mother's statement. "If you gave me a dollar for every time you said that, I wouldn't even—"

"Need a money tree," her mother said, returning the favor and finishing Kayla's statement.

They both laughed.

Amara extended her hand to help Kayla off the sofa. "Time to get up and get comfortable while we wait for your dad to come home so we can all eat together."

*****

An hour later, Kayla sat at the kitchen table, enjoying the fried whiting and hush puppies her father had brought from the restaurant.

"I don't think you can ever leave your job, Dad. You've spoiled me with all of this delicious seafood you bring home."

"Unfortunately, I can't work there forever, so these free dinners will need to end one day." Trevor took a sip of his sparkling cider. "So, how was the ride home? Any traffic?"

"Not really. Jordyn found a shortcut off the highway that avoids some of the traffic," Kayla said before realizing she should have kept her mouth shut about the shortcut.

74

"You need to be careful with those shortcuts. I'm not too comfortable with you straying too far away from the main roads," Trevor said, displaying a look of concern.

"Yes, you've told me before, but I'm only off the highway for about five miles."

"Plenty can happen in that small amount of time."

Silence followed as Kayla finished up her last forkful of food, all the while thinking of a way to divert the conversation away from her father's obsession with her safety.

"I found out one of my friends is on her way to San Diego for spring break to celebrate her grandmother's eightieth birthday."

"Sounds like a nice trip," Amara said.

Kayla wiped her mouth with a napkin. "Have either one of you ever been to the West Coast?"

"From what I've been told, I went to San Francisco as a child, but I honestly don't remember it," Trevor said.

Amara shook her head. "I've never been to the West Coast. Matter of fact, the farthest west I've been is probably Chicago."

"Oh, okay," Kayla said then remained silent.

Amara looked at her with an inquisitive glare. "Is that your way of telling us you want to venture out to the West Coast?"

"I guess you can say that. Honestly, I'd be happy to go anywhere outside of Rhode Island."

"I'm sure we can make that happen one day," Trevor said.

"My friends think it's weird I've never traveled outside of Rhode Island."

A few seconds of silence elapsed as Amara darted her eyes to Trevor before speaking. "It's probably more common than you think. I've had plenty of friends growing up who never left the state of Virginia."

Kayla chuckled. "Yeah, but Virginia is probably ten times the size of Rhode Island. And speaking of Virginia, don't we still have relatives there?"

Amara nodded. "We have a few. It's been so long since I've been in touch with them that I don't know if they're still living there."

Kayla drummed her fingers on the table, feeling more confident with asking questions. "Have we ever been invited to any family reunions or other family get-together where I may have had a chance to meet them?"

"I heard someone was trying to get a group of family members together a few years back, but I don't think it ever happened," Trevor said.

Kayla felt a hint of agitation rising, unsatisfied with the answers coming from her parents' mouths.

"Is it also weird I've never met any of my aunts, uncles, or cousins? Or, at least, I don't remember meeting anybody."

Amara and Trevor eyed one another, visibly uncomfortable with the conversation.

"As I've told you before, our family isn't as close as they should be, which I agree is not a good thing," Trevor said.

"But is that the case for both you and Mom's side of the family?"

"Unfortunately, yes," Trevor replied.

Kayla sighed and refrained from asking any further questions. She could feel the anger building inside and wanted to shut down this disruptive energy beginning to invade her mental space. She also didn't want to start her spring break off on the wrong note with her parents. She figured she could broach the topic another time.

# Chapter 12

Jordyn's nose caught a whiff of a familiar and pleasant scent, waking her out of her sleep. She sat up in bed and rubbed her eyes, attempting to clear her vision. She sniffed again and smiled. She could smell the aroma of her mom's famous French toast from anywhere in the house. This was no surprise, as her mother always enjoyed cooking an elaborate breakfast, especially now that Jordyn was home for spring break.

She stood on shaky legs before steadying herself and walking toward the window. She proceeded to pull apart the blackout curtains, preventing any hint of light from shining into her room. She squinted, attempting to adjust to the sudden wash of sunlight streaming in from outside. It had been a while since she'd been graced with the countryside view.

The rural setting invoked a wave of nostalgia as Jordyn smiled at the tire swing dangling from the massive branch of an oak tree standing in her backyard. The swing provided her with plenty of memories from her childhood and even up until her teenage years. She'd spent countless hours as a child swinging back and forth on that tire without a care in the world. As she grew older, the tire became a comfort place for her whenever she needed to get away from life's challenges and clear her mind. That tire had also played a part in her rather forgettable first kiss with Grover. *Who names their son Grover?* She'd always thought. She'd eventually realized her problem wasn't with the name, but more so with the chapped lips connected to the boy, who happened to be named Grover.

She closed her eyes for a brief moment then opened them, snapping herself out of her daydream. Her focus turned back to the scrumptious breakfast awaiting her in the kitchen.

She quickly brushed her teeth and washed her face before making her way downstairs as the aroma became stronger. Her mouth watered at the idea of sinking her teeth into the cinnamon-flavored French toast.

She rounded the corner and into the kitchen, expecting to see her mother sitting there, finishing breakfast, but she was nowhere to be found. Jordyn was elated to see the French toast and turkey bacon sitting in the middle of the table; however, she wondered where the cook had gone. She pondered momentarily before realizing there was only one place in the house her mother could be, especially on a warm sunny day.

She approached the front door and opened it, the front porch coming into view. The weather-beaten cedar floor planks had seen better days, but it was an important part of the rustic charm that came along with the one-hundred-fifty-year-old farmhouse.

Jordyn heard a creaking noise to her left and spotted her mother, Naomi, sitting and gently rocking on the porch swing with a book in hand. Jordyn had always thought it was amusing to see her mother sitting on the swing with her feet unable to reach the floor due to her short stature. She smiled, wondering if her mother owned anything other than the pair of faded blue jeans and cotton white T-shirt she wore every weekend. In addition to Jordyn looking to spice up her weekend wardrobe, she'd been fighting hard to try to convince Naomi to get rid of the curly bob cut she'd been sporting for the past few years. But she continued to fight a losing battle since Naomi believed her hairstyle took a few years off the half-century mark she'd reached on her last birthday.

Naomi focused her attention on Jordyn as she approached, and her lips curled into a wide grin. "I thought you were going to sleep straight through the morning."

Jordyn hugged her before sitting. "I probably would have, but my nose caught a whiff of your French toast. I don't need an alarm waking me up when I have your famous French toast kicking me in the nostrils."

Naomi laughed. "Did you eat yet?"

"No. I was trying to figure out where you were first."

"You know me. If it's a warm, sunny day on the weekend, I'm going to be right on this porch."

"That's what I figured."

Naomi gazed at Jordyn before rubbing the back of her fingers along her left cheek. "Your cheeks look a little drawn in; are you eating okay on campus?"

"Yes, Mom. We don't have Gordon Ramsay whipping up food in the dining hall, so the food is not the best, but it's edible."

Naomi sat with her arms folded and a smirk on her face. "Looks like I'm going to need to stuff you over spring break to get some meat back on your cheeks."

Jordyn smiled. "My cheeks are fine, but I won't push back on your idea of stuffing me." She paused and gave her mother a critical squint. "So, how are you feeling?"

"Outside of my normal aches and pains, I'm hanging in there."

"Does the new medication seem to be helping?"

"It's hard to tell. I've only been taking it for a few weeks, and I was told it could take a month or so before I may start feeling a little improvement."

"I hope it helps. This would be the second or third medication you've tried."

"Time will tell. But don't worry about me; I'll be fine."

A few seconds of silence passed as Jordyn looked around the porch. "Changing the subject; are you still planning to have the porch repainted?"

Naomi sighed. "I guess so. But I need to take care of the roof first. I saw a couple more water stains on the ceiling of my bedroom after the last rainstorm. I know we need a new roof, and I don't have the money to replace it now."

"Do you know how much it will cost?"

"More than I can afford."

"Do you have any money left over from the last loan you took out?"

"No, darling. That money is being spent on your tuition."

Jordyn's face grew pensive. "Maybe I'll take another semester off to help save money."

"We'll be okay. I still have overtime available to me during the next few months, and that extra money will be a big help." Naomi patted Jordyn on the leg. "I don't want you worrying about our finances. That's for me to figure out. I think it's extremely important you keep going and get that education so you won't be in the same position I'm in once you graduate and are on your own."

"Yes, ma'am," Jordyn said before displaying a broad smile. "So . . . how are things going with Mason? Has it been over a year now?"

"Yes, indeed it has. I honestly didn't expect us to be together this long after that disastrous first date, but things have turned around and seem to be heading in the right direction. He's thoughtful, reliable, and easy on the eye, which is probably something you don't want to hear me say."

Jordyn playfully nudged her mother on the knee. "Are we talkin' wedding bells in the future?"

Naomi laughed. "We need to pump the brakes on that one. I'm in no rush to get married again. Even though we've passed our one-year mark, we've still got a long way to go. Besides, I don't see him as much as I would like since he's consumed with running his business. I need to let the relationship marinate a little more and just take it one day at a time." She stopped and focused her attention on her Toyota Corolla in the driveway. "Speaking of Mason, I need to let him know the oil is starting to leak again. Found some oil stains on the ground yesterday."

"That car has been through a lot. Any chance of selling it and getting another used car?" Jordyn asked.

"Not at all. For one thing, I have a lawn mower in the shed that's probably worth more money than that car. Secondly, the last thing we need to do is add to our expenses with a car payment. And last but not least, it pays to have a boyfriend who's a car mechanic who can make repairs at a fraction of what it would cost if I went anywhere else."

"Okay, makes sense."

"I'll reach out to him later," Naomi said before pointing at Jordyn's stomach. "In the meantime, you should go inside and start feeding that belly of yours. I can't have my daughter walking around campus, looking like she hasn't eaten in days."

# Chapter 13

Mason looked out of the glass panel and noticed a familiar car pulling up in the lot. It was an unusually slow day for business at the gas station, and he welcomed the company to help pass the time.

He tried his best to contain a smile upon seeing his longtime friend from high school, Eva, exit the car and unstrap a rambunctious boy from the back seat. The seven-year-old started to sprint toward the door and, in his haste, tripped and crashed to the ground.

Mason jumped from behind the counter before exiting the store and jogging toward the boy, now in tears.

"It's okay, Owen," Mason said as he kneeled to observe the young boy's knee, which had suffered a small gash.

Eva approached, wearing black yoga pants and a beige T-shirt. Her mocha brown hair flapped in front of her face from the stiff breeze. "I knew this was going to happen. He gets so excited to see you."

"Hey, Eva. This is a welcomed surprise," Mason said, giving her a quick hug.

Mason scooped up Owen from the ground. "Let's go get you all patched up."

Eva followed Mason inside with Owen in tow.

"So, what do I owe the pleasure of seeing you both today? I thought Caleb mentioned you were all heading to the zoo?"

"That was the original plan until Caleb woke up with a sore back from working. He decided to stay home and rest. I figured, instead of wasting the day away, I would take Owen with me to run a few errands. And since we were near your shop, we decided to swing by so Owen could see Mr. Mechanic, as he calls you."

Mason placed Owen on a chair near the counter and wiped the few tears remaining on his cheek. He reached for Owen's belly and started tickling him in an attempt to change his mood. "Is that what you call me? Mr. Mechanic?"

Owen struggled to hold in his laugh.

Mason patted him on his head. "Okay, tough guy, let's see what we can do to get you all better."

Mason walked behind the counter and grabbed a small first-aid kit. He pulled out a bottle of peroxide, cotton balls, and a Band-Aid. He blotted the cotton ball with peroxide and then dabbed at the small abrasion on Owen's knee. Owen flinched for a moment, wincing as Mason gently pressed on the wound. After cleaning the cut, he placed a Band-Aid to cover the wound.

"You're good to go, champ," Mason said, raising his hand in the air for a high-five.

Owen laughed and jumped up to run around the store.

Eva smiled. "I swear, when he grows up, he's going to become a mechanic, just like you. I think Caleb gets a little jealous of you because Owen is always asking to come to your shop and watch you work on cars."

"Tell that husband of yours to relax. Besides, it's all Caleb's fault Owen likes watching me work on cars. He shouldn't have brought him here those few times when I was working. I also can't control what these kids take a liking to and, in Owen's case, if it's cars, then so be it."

Owen darted around the aisles before stopping in front of Mason and looking up. "Aren't you going to work on any cars?" he asked.

Mason laughed. "Sorry, kiddo, but business is slow today. I don't have any cars in the garage to work on right now. Maybe next time."

Eva glanced at her phone. "Speak of the devil. Caleb texted me. I need to run and pick up some pain medication for his poor back. Sorry for the quick visit, but hopefully we gave you a few minutes of company." She motioned for Owen. "Come on; we need to go. Say goodbye to Mr. Mechanic."

Owen frowned and eventually came around and hugged Mason.

Eva turned her head toward the refrigerated beverage section. "Let me grab a couple bottles of water before we go. How much do I owe you?"

Mason shrugged. "It's all yours. Free of charge."

"I can't do that, Mason. I need to pay you something."

"You already paid me by bringing the little fella here to see me." He reached over to hug Eva. "Now go on and get that pain medication for your ailing husband. I'll probably call him later tonight after work to see how he's doing."

Mason walked back behind the counter as Eva and Owen departed.

Seconds later, his cell phone rang.

"Hello, sweetheart," he said.

"I wasn't sure if I'd be able to get you on your cell since the service is so spotty at the station. I figured I'd try calling you first instead of texting."

"Ever since we changed carriers, the connection has been much better here." Mason hesitated for a few seconds. "Is everything okay?"

"Yes. Sorry if I scared you because I rarely call you at work, but while I was thinking about it, can you swing by the market and pick up some fresh fruit on your way home? It doesn't matter what kind—you know what I like."

"Oh, okay. I can do that. Do you need anything else?" he asked.

"No, that's it. See you when you get home."

Mason let out a sizable exhale after hanging up. The stress of keeping secrets from his wife was starting to take its toll, and every conversation was laced with tension on his side as he wondered if and when his infidelity would be discovered. Running around with Naomi on the side for the past year had been no easy feat. There had been a few occasions when he'd come close to slipping up but was able to recover and continue with the affair unscathed.

His problems were further compounded by his decision to withdraw one thousand dollars from a joint savings account behind his wife's back to help pay for some business expenses. But, since he handled the finances, he figured his wife would be clueless to notice it was even gone as long as he replenished it within a couple of weeks. But with the recent slowdown in business, he'd been unable to make enough to replenish the funds and needed to seek other options for obtaining the money before his wife found out. And if she caught wind of what he'd done, all hell would break loose since she'd been trying to get him to close down the shop and find another gig more profitable to help pay the monthly bills. This was the first time he'd resorted to such drastic measures to keep his business afloat, and time was ticking for him to replace every cent he'd withdrawn from the account and for him to decide if it was worth continuing with the affair before he was literally caught with his pants down.

# Chapter 14

"Stop. Leave us alone!" Amara mumbled before lurching forward in bed, clutching her chest.

Trevor woke up at the sudden movement. "Are you okay?"

Amara continued to breathe heavily, attempting to calm her senses from the dream jolting her awake. "I . . . I'll be all right."

Trevor rubbed his eyes. "Was it a nightmare?"

"Yes," Amara said, tugging on her T-shirt to peel the cotton fabric away from her damp skin. "I'll be back." She rotated her feet off the bed and then walked into the bathroom, where she grabbed a washcloth and doused it with cool water to dab her face and neck.

"I can't go through this again," she whispered.

It had been quite a while since she'd experienced a nightmare of this magnitude, which used to happen with much more frequency. She couldn't say for certain, but she imagined the nightmare could have been triggered by her recent scare at Trader Joe's. Her previous nightmare episodes all coincided with the panic attacks she'd experienced with much more regularity when she'd lived in Richmond.

After moving to Rhode Island, the panic attacks continued, prompting her to seek out help in the form of some lengthy mental health counseling sessions. It had taken a few years of therapy for her to get over the incident back in Richmond. Over time, she'd learned to cope with what happened, and not hold onto all of those negative thoughts that ravaged her mind. This allowed her to move on with her new life in Rhode Island, pushing the past far enough in the rearview mirror, which eventually resulted in the panic attacks and nightmares subsiding. However, the past sometimes had a funny way of catching up to you, and she understood from her therapy sessions that something as simple as a rogue thought or an unexpected incident could potentially nullify any progress she'd previously made. Based on her recent experience at Trader Joe's, she'd received confirmation her past trauma was still lurking in the shadows, stalking her, waiting for the perfect opportunity to strike.

# Chapter 15

Kayla pulled up in the driveway and spotted Jordyn sitting on the porch.

Jordyn walked to the car and placed her luggage carrier in the trunk. She opened the car door and said, "My mother wanted you to come in for a quick hello since she didn't get a chance to see you when you dropped me off."

Kayla shut off the car and followed Jordyn into the house. They walked into the kitchen, and Kayla was immediately greeted with a welcoming hug.

"So glad to see you, Kayla. It's been a couple of months since I last saw you and wanted to get my hug and wish you good luck for the rest of the semester," Naomi said.

"Thanks, Ms. Fisher."

"You're welcome to stay for dinner. I cooked up some baked ham, cabbage, and white rice."

"Sounds delicious, but I already had a bite to eat before I left home."

Naomi pointed to an apple pie sitting on the counter. "How about dessert?"

Kayla laughed. "No, thanks, Ms. Fisher. My stomach is too full."

Naomi grabbed a piece of foil. "Okay, but it would do my heart good if you could at least take a big piece back to school with you."

"All right, works for me."

Naomi cut a quarter of the pie and wrapped it in foil before handing it to Kayla. "I need you to do me a huge favor and make sure my daughter is eating at school. I can't have her coming back home again, looking like she hadn't eaten in days."

"Okay, I'll make sure she's eating like she should."

Naomi motioned for both Jordyn and Kayla to come close for a group hug.

"I don't want to hold you two up any longer. Time to make your way back to school. Safe travels, and text me once you get to your dorm room."

*****

Kayla pulled out of the driveway as they began their journey back to school.

"I'm so not ready to go back," Kayla said.

Jordyn nodded in agreement.

"Even though I didn't do much during the break, I was able to catch up on some sleep and lounge around like a couch potato."

"Yeah, me, too," Jordyn said.

Kayla turned on the wipers as a few drops of rain began to pelt the windshield.

"Would have been nice if the rain held off until we made it to school. "

Jordyn remained face forward and offered no response.

Kayla's eyes narrowed with suspicion. "Okay, did I say something wrong?"

Jordyn offered a cursory smile. "No, you're fine. And before you ask, nothing bad happened during my spring break."

"Are you upset about going back to school?"

"Nope."

"Okay, I'm all out of guesses."

Jordyn kept silent for a few seconds while drumming her fingers against her knee. "I've been thinking of telling you about what's going on."

Kayla did her best to control the excitement brewing at the notion of finally being privy to the secret Jordyn had been holding so close to her vest. She struggled to stay composed and offered her best poker face expression. "If that's what you want to do."

"I don't even know where to start," Jordyn said before stopping and giving Kayla a sidelong glance. "But before I begin, will you promise not to get mad at me?"

"That's not a great way to start this discussion. That just means there's something that's going to make me mad, and now you're expecting me to stay calm," Kayla said with her eyebrows raised.

"Maybe. But does that mean you promise?"

"So, now you're forcing me to say yes, and if I say no, you probably won't tell me what's going on." Kayla sighed. "Okay, I promise."

"The shortcut we took home a few weeks ago was all pre-planned. I never had any plans of going home that weekend. And I never had to go to the bathroom. I only needed an excuse to stop at that gas station."

Kayla continued to listen intently.

"Also, the gas station owner wasn't a stranger and was in on the plan. He knew what was going on because he's my mother's boyfriend, Mason."

Kayla's eyes widened. "Are you serious? You actually know that man?"

"Yup."

"I would have never guessed that. He definitely played his part well."

"And before I go on with the gas station story, I need to give you more information on why I took off last semester. Please keep this between you and me, but my mother was struggling financially and couldn't afford the tuition. I was working at a convenience store, trying to help, and not making much money. So, Mason had a connection at a nearby research facility and mentioned the option of volunteering in some medical clinical trial testing as a way to earn some extra cash."

Kayla's face softened a bit upon learning this information.

"So, after talking things over with my mother, I decided to move forward with his suggestion. And after researching, applying as a volunteer, and passing the eligibility requirements, they accepted me into a two-week-long clinical trial program."

"Whoa . . . that's deep." Kayla thought for a moment. "Do you mind if I ask you a few questions?"

"No problem. Shoot."

"Were you at the research facility for the entire time?"

"No. There were a couple of times when I did need to stay overnight for monitoring, but I was able to go home and sleep in my bed, also."

"Got it. What kind of testing did you have to do?"

"I was there to test medications for people suffering from digestive issues, mostly people with acid reflux."

"Not to get all in your business, but does that mean you have this problem?"

"No. The testing was for healthy people. We were testing the potential side effects from a new drug."

"And did you have any side effects?" Kayla asked before turning up the windshield wiper speed as the rain came down a little harder.

"Yes, but thankfully, it wasn't too bad, other than an upset stomach. The good thing is they gave me pills to take home to help me deal with the nausea and any pain I was feeling. But it was all worth it. Because of me and the other volunteers, we're one step closer to having medication approved that might help people suffering from this condition. Matter of fact, I know a few people who could benefit from this drug. And, not to mention I also got a nice healthy check as my reward for the testing."

"Wow! I'm sorry about all the questions, but this was far from what I expected to hear from you. I would have never guessed that's what you were doing during your semester off."

"And that brings us back to the night at the gas station. I volunteered for another clinical test, which was going to take place over that weekend. My mom didn't know about this round of testing. I wanted to surprise her with the money I was going to make to help with a few extra expenses she had. Mason made arrangements to take me, and he was planning to pick me up from campus after you left to go home. But something unexpected came up, and he wasn't able to get me and wanted to know if I could find a ride to the gas station. And since the station was located somewhat on your way home, it made sense for me to hitch a ride with you."

"Oh . . . okay. So that explains why you originally said you were staying on campus for the weekend and not coming home with me, but changed your mind at the last minute."

"Exactly," Jordyn said.

Kayla squinted through the windshield with the rain continuing to come down. "You know . . . it still would have been nice if you could have told me what was going on instead of keeping it a secret and sending me that mysterious text."

Jordyn buried her face in her hands. "Yes, I know . . . I know. To be honest, I don't know of too many people who like discussing their financial situation, especially if it's not good. So, I decided to remain quiet about it, and the only thing I could think of was sending you the text. I was actually thinking of telling you what was going on when I came back to campus that weekend. At least, that was the original plan until I found out you were going through my drawers. So, being the vindictive person I am, I decided to hold off from telling you and let you sweat it out some more."

"Oh . . . you little son of a—You got me good on that one. You definitely accomplished your goal of making me sweat." Kayla stopped at a red light and glared at Jordyn with a vertical wrinkle appearing between her eyebrows. "Now, can you please tell me where you went when I came looking for you in the gas station?"

Jordyn smirked. "When I first got inside, I went in the back hallway and tried sending you a text, but it never went through because I had no service. I tried walking around and even went outside behind the station to see if I could get a signal, which didn't work. I walked back inside, and that's when I heard you talking to Mason, so I quietly stepped back outside."

"And you couldn't have mercy on me at that point and fess up to what was going on?"

Jordyn shrugged. "Maybe, but as I said, I wasn't ready to go through a long explanation of what was happening."

"And because you chose not to say anything, your mother's boyfriend must think I'm a lunatic because I pulled a knife on him. I figured he was some strange man who kidnapped you and was going to come after me next."

Jordyn winced. "I know. He told me all about it after you left. He knew this was supposed to be a secret, and he didn't expect you to come in after you dropped me off, so that caught him off guard. I guess we didn't think about my text getting to you late because of the shitty cell service. It was all downhill after that. The funny thing is, he was just as nervous as you, trying to figure out how he could convince you to leave without me. He wasn't too happy with you pulling the knife on him. I'm sorry things got a little crazy for everybody."

"Apology accepted. By the way, did you tell him who I was?"

"I didn't give him your name. I only told him you were my roommate."

"All I know is I can't go through anything like that again." Kayla stepped on the pedal as the light turned green.

"And was that story true about this mystery man you refused to name?"

"Yes. Mason told me someone"—Jordyn proceeded with a dramatic pause, giving Kayla the side-eye—"someone punctured the front tires of this man's car and Mason had to replace them."

Kayla shrugged. "Hey, I was acting on my survival instincts. Wanted to make sure whoever owned that car wouldn't follow me. And can you now stop referring to this person as a man and finally let me know his name?"

"No can do, because Mason never told me his name or what he does on campus."

"Did you at least ask?"

"Yes, but he kind of went around the question and never told me his name. I didn't press him any further because I didn't think it was important at the time."

"Okay, so the mystery continues. And speaking of mystery, was it you who passed me on the road that night?"

"Passed you on the road? Not sure what you're talking about."

"There was a car tailgating me on the road after I left you. The car went past me, but I couldn't get a good look at who was in the car. There was someone with a hood in the passenger seat, and the driver had on a baseball cap."

"No, I can definitely say that wasn't us."

"Are you positive?"

"Yes, Kayla. I'm in confession mode now, so I'm not going to lie to you."

"Does that mean, any other time you're not in confession mode, you're lying to me?"

"Of course not. Well . . . maybe sometimes," Jordyn said with a smile.

Kayla laughed. "Okay, I'll believe you this time around."

That last bit of nagging anxiety living rent-free in the pit of Kayla's stomach for the past few weeks had finally been evicted. She felt a huge sense of relief with Jordyn finally revealing the secret to her voluntary disappearance. She was extremely thankful Jordyn had decided to spill the beans, which was the perfect way to start the second half of her semester.

Kayla continued to drive with a hint of a grin on her face and peered over at Jordyn, expecting to see a similar look of relief. However, Jordyn stared straight ahead, as if still bothered by something.

"Are you good? Or is there more to the story you need to tell me?" Kayla asked.

"Uh . . . yes. I have a favor to ask you."

"Oh, boy. Please tell me you're not going to ask me something that's going to spoil this moment."

"Since you know what's going on, I think you can handle the request."

"Okay, what is it?"

"The clinical test I participated in a few weeks ago was only part one. There's a part two, which means I'm hoping you can drive me back to the gas station so Mason can take me to the research facility."

"Are you sure it's safe to be doing all of this medical testing? I don't want you coming back to campus growing a second head."

"Yes, it's literally a second round of the trial medication I took the first time, and the side effects only lasted a day. I figured it would be more of the same this go around. Also, from what I've been told, this would be the last stage of testing, and if everything goes according to plan, it's a good possibility the medication could be available to the public within a year. It also means more money for me."

"So, when is the next round of testing supposed to happen?"

"Next weekend."

Kayla chuckled. "It figures you would request me to take you back to the scene of the crime. Wouldn't it be easier for me to take you to the facility since I know what's going on now?"

"It's not an easy place to find and, since Mason knows exactly where to go, he doesn't have to rely on the GPS, which sometimes won't work well due to the crappy service in the area."

"Okay, I'll take you back to the station. But I'm telling you right now, I'm dropping you off and not going inside to come face-to-face with Mason again. I can only imagine how awkward that would be."

# Chapter 16

The following weekend was upon them, and Kayla couldn't help feeling a strong sense of déjà vu as she pulled into the gas station parking lot. There were a few differences this time around, starting with the mysterious black sedan no longer parked in the lot. But the dilapidated pickup truck remained and was evidently a permanent fixture on the premises.

She looked through the gas station window and, from her angle, didn't see anyone inside. Although the reason for this second visit had been made clear, it did nothing to prevent a smidge of anxiety from creeping into the bottom of her stomach.

"Are you sure Mason is here now? Looks pretty quiet, and I don't see another car except for that truck, which looks like it hasn't moved since the day I was born."

"No. Mason is here. The lights wouldn't be on if he wasn't."

Kayla surveyed the lot further. "Where does he park his car?"

"He normally parks it in the repair shop garage."

Jordyn reached around and grabbed her knapsack from the back seat while smiling at Kayla. "Here we go again. At least, this time, you won't be receiving a mysterious text from me."

"Thank goodness," Kayla said.

The sun started to descend beyond the horizon as the daylight gradually faded away. Kayla surveyed the area with a look of concern on her face.

"Are you comfortable being alone with Mason without your mother around?"

"Yes. He's been like my personal chauffeur during the past year. He would sometimes pick me up from my job when I was working at the convenience store, and as I mentioned before, he drove me to the previous clinical trial appointments. So, I have no problems with this."

"Okay, thought I would ask." Kayla scanned the area once again. "Even though I know the situation now, this gas station still gives me the creeps."

"You'll be happy to know Mason is looking to make improvements to help liven up the place."

"Do you mean improvements to help raise it from the dead?"

"I can't argue with you on that. Anyway, I need to get going. I should be back on campus tomorrow night. No need for you to stay up worrying about me," Jordyn said.

"Good luck with the testing," Kayla said, reaching out for a fist bump.

She watched as Jordyn departed and entered the station. She was free to go, but she chose to stick around to see if Mason would finally reveal himself inside. After a minute, Mason appeared by the counter and started talking with Jordyn.

Kayla flashed back to the disastrous first visit to the gas station and couldn't believe she'd been so clueless as to what was going on. *As they always say, hindsight is 20/20.* A part of her understood Jordyn's reasoning for not telling her the situation at the time, but it would have made her life so much easier if she'd known.

She tried to look at the positive side of that uncomfortable interaction with Mason. That was the first time she'd truly felt threatened and pulled a knife on someone. She'd never known how she would react in that real-life situation but was proud of the way she'd remained composed under those high-intensity circumstances.

She was jolted out of her moment of self-admiration by a noticeable change in Mason's body language as he continued to talk. She squinted through the glass, focusing on Mason who appeared to be engaged in an animated discussion with Jordyn. She could see Jordyn vehemently shaking her head and Mason promptly raising his hand and pointing in Jordyn's face.

"What the hell is going on?" she whispered.

She reached over toward the glove compartment and grabbed her knife as panic began to set in. With a rush of adrenaline coursing through her veins, she exited the car and approached the building. She proceeded to walk, hunched over with her knees bent, trying her best to avoid being detected.

She neared a white metal icebox, positioned at the corner of the building, and crouched behind it to remain out of sight. She poked her head out from behind the icebox, peering through the glass to get a closer view. Mason had backed away from Jordyn and continued to act aggressively. She could hear him yelling but couldn't make out what he was saying. Jordyn appeared unafraid and continued to stand her ground as they both continued to argue.

Without warning, Jordyn reached out to a shelf near her, grabbed a bottle of water, and launched it in Mason's direction. He ducked and immediately ran toward Jordyn, grabbing her by the arm.

Without hesitation, Kayla bolted to the front door and yanked it open. "Get your damn hands off of her right now!" she yelled, firmly gripping the knife with her hand raised, ready to strike.

Mason continued to hold on to Jordyn's arm while she delivered several chops to the crook of his elbow, attempting to free herself.

Kayla gritted her teeth and marched toward Mason, coming within a few yards with her arm cocked back, holding the knife, ready to strike.

As she approached, Mason released Jordyn's arm, and Jordyn backed away with tears flooding her eyes, apparently startled and upset at the confrontation.

Mason's eyes narrowed. "Okay, so we gonna play this knife game again?"

Kayla swallowed hard. "Are you crazy putting your hands on her?"

"In case you didn't know, I wasn't the aggressor here. She threw a bottle at me, and I was just defending myself."

"That still didn't give you a reason to touch her."

"Of course it does. All bets are off once you start throwing things at me. And if you don't put that knife down, I have every right to defend myself against you."

Jordyn stood by Kayla's side and reached for something hanging on a shelf near them.

Kayla continued to stare at Mason and refused to take her eyes off of him. She heard a package rip open, and her peripheral vision allowed her to see Jordyn holding what appeared to be a small hammer she'd extracted from a tool kit. Mason remained near the counter, roughly ten feet away from both Kayla and Jordyn.

"I'd suggest you both put down your weapons before things get real ugly."

"It's already way past ugly," Kayla said, maintaining a vice-like grip on the knife. She fought hard to regulate her breathing and control her shaking hands in an attempt to hide the unrelenting fear flooding her body. She also didn't want to give Mason the satisfaction of knowing she was a nervous wreck and may or may not have the guts to stab him if necessary.

She took a peek over at Jordyn, who continued to stare at Mason with her arm in the air and the hammer raised high.

"You both have no idea what I could be hiding behind the counter. Now I'm going to give you to the count of three, and if you don't drop your weapons, I'm going to have to do something I don't want to do."

*Was this a scare tactic to get them to comply?* Kayla thought.

Mason had maintained a calm demeanor during the first interaction she'd had with him a month ago, but things were different this time. He was already riled up from whatever sparked the argument between him and Jordyn. Now it was up to Kayla to figure out if his verbal threats would escalate into something much worse.

She continued to stand firm and call his bluff. Jordyn followed suit and maintained a grip on the hammer.

"Three . . . two . . . one!" he shouted. Mason swiftly moved toward the counter and partially bent down behind it to grab something.

On pure instinct, Kayla lunged toward him and had her sights set on his right hand, which he had resting on the counter as he kneeled. She zeroed in on her target and, with all her might, swung down with the knife at about the same time Mason looked up and stuck out his arm in self-defense. She closed her eyes and could feel the knife stick into a soft, fleshy area of Mason's body. He let out a massive yell as Kayla opened her eyes and saw the knife sticking into his right forearm. She frantically dislodged the knife, resulting in a splattering of blood sprinkling her white sweatshirt. She backpedaled away and grabbed Jordyn by the arm. Without looking back, they both ran toward the front door and exited into the parking lot.

As they darted in the direction of Kayla's car, Kayla twisted her head back toward the station and saw Mason kneeling in pain, clutching his arm. She started the car and smashed her foot on the accelerator with the tires temporarily skidding on the dirt-covered surface. She drove onto the main road and completely ignored the speed limit, pushing the car faster than she ever had before.

Kayla's eyes watered, coming to grips with the horrific confrontation and the realization she'd actually stabbed Mason in the arm. She blinked several times, attempting to prevent any more moisture from accumulating in her eyes to help clear her blurred vision.

Jordyn sat face forward and wiped her eyes with the back of her shirt sleeve. "Thanks for coming in and helping me," she said, her voice cracking slightly.

"Of course." Kayla took a glimpse in the rearview mirror to make sure no headlights were visible. "I can't believe I just stabbed him in the arm. Was I wrong for doing that?"

"Hell no. We don't know what he had behind the counter. Could have been a gun. You were just defending yourself."

Kayla took a deep breath while attempting to control the involuntary shaking she was currently experiencing. "What the heck happened back there? One minute, you were both talking calmly; and the next minute, you were in a shouting match."

"He was asking if he could borrow some of the money I was going to make from the clinical trial test, and when I refused, it must have ticked him off. That was the first time I've seen him get upset like that." Jordyn looked down at her shaking hands. "He said a few things I didn't like, and I'll admit I lost my cool and threw a water bottle at him."

"Now what do we do? You think he'll try to follow us?" Kayla asked.

"I don't know, but I don't feel too comfortable having my mother home by herself. I'm assuming Mason will be making a trip to the hospital, but if not, I think the first place he'll try to go is my house to look for us. I say we go pick up my mom and take her somewhere else to be on the safe side."

"Maybe we can all go to my house. Mason has no clue where I live," Kayla said.

"Do you think that's a good idea? What excuse would you give your parents?"

"Don't know yet. I'll figure it out. Besides, there's safety in numbers, and if Mason finds out where I live, there would be two additional people he would need to deal with. Not to mention my father doesn't play around, and I'm sure would be able to handle Mason by himself."

Silence followed as Kayla continued driving, her senses heightened, paying strict attention to any headlights that might have presented themselves in the rearview mirror.

With all the chaos that had occurred, Kayla hadn't paid attention to whether or not she'd suffered any injuries. She didn't feel any different, but there was a good possibility her body had not yet registered any pain with the extreme amount of adrenaline coursing through her veins. She wiggled her fingers and grimaced, not from pain, but from the blood present on her right hand and smeared on the steering wheel. She flashed a look down at her blood-stained sweatshirt and struggled to fight off the sudden queasiness.

"I feel like I'm going to throw up. I need to get this blood off my hand," she said then pointed to the glove compartment. "I think I have wet napkins in there. Can you check?"

Jordyn opened the glove compartment and shuffled through several items before grabbing a few wet napkins. She tore open a few packages and motioned for Kayla to stick out her right hand. She proceeded to wipe off the blood as best she could, with the wet napkins eventually turning a dark shade of pink.

"Thanks," Kayla said. "Can you find another one so I can wipe off the steering wheel?"

Jordyn pulled out the last wet napkin and opened it for Kayla to wipe off the blood residue on the steering wheel. Once Kayla was finished, Jordyn collected all of the napkins, rolled down the window, and chucked them outside.

A few seconds of silence followed as Kayla continued to periodically look in the rearview mirror. She took a peep at her sweatshirt again. "Your mother is going to freak out if she sees this blood on my sweatshirt. What are we supposed to tell her?

Jordyn rifled through her bag and pulled out a long-sleeved Flagstone University shirt. "You can put this on once we come to a stop. It may be a little short on you, but this is the best I can do."

"I'll take it. Anything is better than wearing this. Thanks!"

*****

Thirty minutes later, Kayla slowed as she approached Jordyn's house.

"Any idea what you're going to tell your mother?" Kayla asked.

Jordyn frowned. "I have no clue. It's bad enough we're showing up at her house when we should be at school. And to make things worse, she didn't even know I was planning to meet up with Mason so he could take me back to the facility for another round of testing. I was going to surprise her and give her the money from the test to help pay for some home repairs."

"That sucks. This doesn't make things any easier. Whatever we decide, we need to do it fast. We have no idea where Mason is or if he's on his way to the house now," Kayla said. She pointed to Jordyn's phone. "I would block Mason's number in case he tries to call you."

"I'm already one step ahead of you and blocked his number."

That overwhelming feeling of angst that Kayla had been experiencing had subsided in her body. She was mentally numb from what had transpired back at the gas station, leading to a surprising feeling of calmness. She figured this was her body's way of dealing with the situation and preventing her from breaking out into a fit of mass hysteria. But the night was still young, and there were plenty of hurdles to jump over, starting with convincing Jordyn's mother to get out of the house so they could potentially avoid meeting up with Mason, who would no doubt be on a mission for revenge.

# Chapter 17

Jordyn focused her eyes on the second level of the house, the only window emanating a glow of light. "My mom's in the bedroom now," she said.

With the car parked in the driveway, Kayla took off the blood-stained sweatshirt and replaced it with Jordyn's long-sleeved shirt. Kayla held onto the sweatshirt, turning it inside out and rolling it up to avoid any direct contact with the blood that had settled into the fabric.

"And what are we supposed to do with this sweatshirt? I don't have anything to put it in, and I can't leave it sitting in the car, especially if your mother's going to be with us," Kayla said.

Jordyn pointed to her knapsack. "Guess we have no choice but to stuff it in my bag for now and figure out how to get rid of it later." Jordyn grabbed the rolled-up sweatshirt and proceeded to place it at the bottom of her knapsack.

Kayla sighed. "Now how the heck are we going to convince your mother to get in the car?"

"May just need to tell her the truth."

"Even the part about me stabbing Mason?"

"No, I'll do my best to leave that part out," Jordyn said before focusing on the road leading to the house to confirm no headlights were approaching. "I'll call my mother and give her a heads-up we're here."

Jordyn's heartbeat ticked up a few notches as she struggled to figure out how to explain the situation to her mother.

"Jordyn! This is a surprise. You rarely call me on a Saturday evening. Is everything okay?"

Jordyn struggled to keep her emotions in check. There was nothing worse than someone asking that question, and the answer was far from what that person could have ever imagined.

"I'm safe right now, but I need you to listen to me and trust what I'm about to tell you. I need you to put on some shoes, grab your wallet, cell phone, keys, and come outside."

"What are you talking about, Jordyn? This is making no sense."

"I know it doesn't, but me and Kayla are outside right now in her car." Jordyn gazed up at the window and saw her mother peeking outside.

"What's going on? You're starting to scare me. Why are you both not at school?"

"I promise I'll explain everything to you once you're in the car, but please trust me on this."

"You need to let me know what's going on now before I decide whether or not I'm leaving the house."

Jordyn let out a hefty sigh. "I had a disagreement with Mason, which didn't end too well. Kayla got involved, and let's just say he's not a happy man now."

"Why were you and Kayla with Mason, and what do you mean it didn't end well?"

"Mom! Please grab your stuff and come outside. I swear I'll answer all your questions once you're in the car."

"Okay, I'll trust you, and I'm coming outside, but you better have a good explanation as to what's going on."

Jordyn disconnected, leaned her head against the headrest, and said, "She's coming."

Kayla's eyes widened in alarm after seeing headlights approaching in the distance. "Oh, shit! Don't tell me this is Mason coming. Call your mother back and tell her to hurry up!"

Jordyn called. "Mom, please hurry. You need to get down here now!"

"I'm coming, Jordyn. Hold on!"

Kayla turned on the overhead light and frantically checked around the car cabin. With all the commotion of trying to flee the gas station, she couldn't remember where she'd put her knife. She twisted her body to get a glimpse in the back and saw the knife resting on the floor of the passenger side. She picked it up and flinched, feeling a sticky substance on the handle, realizing it must have been more blood. She hadn't thought of wiping off any blood from the knife after the incident, but this was no time to worry about it now.

She grabbed the knife and trained her eyes on Jordyn. "Do you still have the hammer?"

Jordyn tapped her phone to activate the flashlight and searched on the floor between her legs. "I don't see it. I guess I must have dropped it somewhere while we were running out of the gas station."

Kayla swiveled her head toward the rear window, eyeing the headlights creeping closer as Jordyn's mother exited the house.

Jordyn opened the door and stood, frantically waving her on. "Please hurry, Mom!"

Naomi approached at about the same time the mysterious car slowed by the driveway entrance before it proceeded to continue down the road, passing the house.

Kayla let out a huge exhale, not having realized she'd been holding her breath. She quickly dropped the knife on the floor between her legs before Jordyn's mother entered the car. Traces of blood were blotted around the palm of her right hand. Without anything to wipe it off on, she arched her butt off the seat, giving her a better angle to place her hand in her pocket and rub off the blood as best she could against the inside of her jean's pocket lining.

Naomi sat in the back, behind Kayla. "You both have some explaining to do. Now what's going on, and where are we going?"

Kayla put the car in reverse, backing out of the driveway and onto the road.

"To answer your last question, we're going to Kayla's house," Jordyn said.

"For what?"

"Um . . . for safety."

"Safety from what?"

"From Mason."

Naomi leaned forward. "Can I get more than a one or two-word answer? Why would you need safety from Mason?"

Jordyn closed her eyes to gather her thoughts. "Because me and Kayla had a disagreement with him at the gas station before he was planning to take me back to the research facility for more clinical tests."

"More tests? Didn't we talk about this before, and we agreed you wouldn't do any more testing after last semester?"

"I know. But . . . I wanted to surprise you and was planning to give you the money I was going to make from the test to help with some of the house repairs."

"Well, I appreciate that, darling, but I'll be able to get those repairs done on the house soon enough. We can talk all about it later. But what I want to know now is what kind of altercation did you get into with Mason?"

Jordyn and Kayla's attention was momentarily diverted to a vehicle approaching from the opposite direction. Kayla swallowed to wet her parched throat. She gripped the steering wheel tighter as the vehicle passed and kept going. Both Jordyn and Kayla twisted their heads as the car went by, attempting to get a good look at the occupants inside.

Naomi followed suit and swung her head to catch a glimpse of the car. "What's so special about that car?"

"Thought it may have been Mason. This is why I wanted to get you out of the house. I wasn't sure if he'd be looking for us there," Jordyn said.

"How serious was this disagreement that you both think he's looking for you? Did one of you do something to piss him off that much?"

Both Jordyn and Kayla eyed one another.

Jordyn shifted in her seat, contemplating the best way to respond. "Um . . . it got a little physical at the end."

Naomi tilted her head up and closed her eyes briefly before focusing back on Jordyn. "JoJo, you know I have all the patience in the world, and there are very few moments when I might lose it. And I'm telling you right now, this is one of those moments. Now, I'm going to take your vague answers as a sign something serious occurred, and I need you to stop playing games with me and tell me exactly what happened!"

Jordyn cringed at the sound of hearing her nickname. Her mother only referred to her by that name whenever she'd reached her boiling point. There were plenty of moments in Jordyn's childhood when her mother had chastised her using this nickname, but it had been quite a while since that name had spewed from her mother's lips. Jordyn knew she was treading on thin ice, and cracks were forming on the surface. Although her mother displayed a calm and pleasant demeanor on the outside, if you pushed her too far, most people would be in for a rude awakening on how quickly her temperament could switch from cool to hot within a matter of seconds. It was time Jordyn fessed up or risked being embarrassed in front of Kayla by her mother, whose patience was about to exit stage left.

"He was asking to borrow the money I was going to make from the clinical trial. I refused, and he got mad. Things got a little heated, and Kayla came in to help me. He threatened us with something behind the counter, and when he reached for whatever it was, me and Kayla ran out."

Naomi sat with a puzzled expression. "I didn't expect that answer."

"You said you wanted the truth, and there it is." *At least most of it.*

"I'm glad you both are all right. I've never seen him aggressive like that before. And why would he be asking you to loan him money?"

Jordyn shrugged. "I have no clue."

Naomi turned her attention to Kayla. "How are you holding up, sweetheart? Are you okay?"

Kayla put on a forced smile. "Okay, I guess."

A few moments of silence followed as another car approached in the opposite direction, but like the first instance, this vehicle passed without any incident.

"Based on your story, I don't think you girls are in any danger of Mason coming after you. I also don't think you two needed to pick me up from the house. I would have been fine staying home. But I'm concerned about what he was reaching for behind the counter. He never mentioned anything about owning a gun, and I would find it extremely hard to believe he would pull a gun on you two, even if he did own one. He was probably trying to scare you both. Maybe I should give him a call."

Both Jordyn and Kayla vehemently shook their heads.

"No, Mom! Please don't call him. I'd feel more comfortable if we just let him calm down for now. I'd also feel more comfortable if you don't see him for a while or answer any of his calls."

"Why not? Don't you think you're going a little overboard with your reaction? It sounds like it was a simple disagreement that got a little out of hand. I'm sure I can talk to him and help smooth this all over."

"I don't think that's a good idea after seeing him mad like that for the first time," Jordyn said.

"There isn't much I can do if he shows up at the house when I'm home. But know I can handle myself if he stops acting like the respectable and pleasant man I've been dating for the past year."

# Chapter 18

Kayla felt a serious headache coming on as she neared her house. The past couple of hours seemed like a horrible dream she couldn't wake up from. Showing up at her parents' house unexpectedly would have been bad enough, but with the knowledge of a bloody knife out of view on the floor, a blood-stained sweatshirt hiding in Jordyn's knapsack, and the sickening realization she'd stabbed Mason in the arm, it all made this visit indescribably unsettling.

The thoughts flew back and forth in her head as to what to tell her parents. With Jordyn's confession to her mother, Kayla knew she couldn't flat-out lie. She had to go along with the same story Jordyn had told her mother. This also meant she and Jordyn needed to be in complete sync with their attempt to hide the most graphic part of the confrontation with Mason.

Pulling into the driveway and parking, she closed her eyes for a few seconds to gather whatever strength she needed to get through what was to come. Then she momentarily locked eyes with Jordyn, hoping she was equally up to the task of getting through this second round of deceptive confessions.

"It's been a while since I've been to your house, Kayla. I love the landscape lighting. Is that new?" Naomi asked.

"Yes, we had it installed recently."

Kayla glanced at her right hand, which still contained traces of dried blood. She also imagined the rubber floor mats between her legs and the one in the back, on the passenger side might have been stained with blood. But, there was just enough darkness inside the car to prevent anyone from visibly seeing any traces of blood on the floor mats, which Kayla hadn't thought about until now. She was thankful Jordyn's mother had chosen to sit in the back seat of the driver's side. If she sat behind Jordyn, there would have been a good possibility traces of blood could have collected on the soles of her shoes.

Kayla opened the door and was careful to keep her feet from kicking the knife where it remained on the floor. She figured it was safe to leave it there for now until she had the opportunity to pick it up and wash off any traces of the incident.

As she stood and observed her surroundings, her answer to clean off the knife presented itself in the form of the garden house resting on the side of the house. This would also give her the chance to wash off the floor mats. She kept this in mind for later as she focused her attention back on the daunting task of attempting to explain to her parents why she was showing up at the door unannounced, along with Jordyn and her mother in tow.

As she proceeded down the stone-paved walkway, the door opened and Trevor stood with a look of confusion. "What are you all doing here? Is there a party at my house I don't know about?"

Kayla made a feeble attempt to smile. "I wish."

Trevor reached out his arms for a hug. Kayla made it a point to keep her right hand balled into a fist as she hugged him.

"And I see we also have some special guests," he said then proceeded to hug Naomi and Jordyn.

Trevor yelled up to Amara, "We have visitors."

They all walked into the family room as Amara joined them.

After all the initial hugs were done, Kayla said, "Give me a minute to go to the bathroom, and when I come out, I'll tell you all about why we're here."

She immediately excused herself and entered the bathroom. She closed the door and jubilantly washed her hands free of any remaining dried blood that had embedded itself on the outer layers of her skin. She gazed in the mirror, looking surprisingly fresh considering what she'd been through these past couple of hours. She rotated her head from side to side, carefully focusing on the skin along her face and neck, making sure no blood splatter could be found. She took out her ponytail, sliding her fingers down her shoulder-length, ebony hair to confirm no blood droplets were present.

If it were any other time, she would have laughed at the shirt Jordyn had given her to wear, which barely reached her waist. The sleeves were also an inch or so short of touching her wrists. *Beggars can't be choosers.* She rolled up her sleeves and figured that would be a better look. Then she closed her eyes and started running her version of the story she was planning to tell through her head, attempting to get up the nerve to communicate with confidence.

She placed her ear against the door after hearing various voices outside. She heard Trevor ask, "So, what brings you all here on a Saturday night?"

Kayla grimaced, not surprised Trevor didn't have the patience to wait for her to exit the bathroom and tell her rendition of the story.

Before Kayla could react, Naomi responded, "The girls had a disagreement with a friend of mine and got a little spooked that he might end up at my house to cause trouble. They felt more comfortable getting me out of the house so we could all come here until things simmered down. I don't think it's necessary, but the girls are pretty adamant about it, so . . . here we are."

Kayla shrugged, not expecting Naomi to take the reins and explain what happened. *That was a lot easier of an explanation than what I was thinking.*

She welcomed Naomi speaking up since it took the initial pressure off of her attempting to explain the situation. Therefore, she remained in the bathroom, waiting to hear how it all played out.

"Was this a simple argument, or are we talking about something beyond that? And did it happen on campus?" Trevor asked.

Kayla knew this was too good to be true as the pressure was quickly reapplied by her father's question. She knew she had to be the one to answer, and with careful consideration of the words she chose to explain what had happened.

She promptly exited the bathroom and said, "I can answer that."

Kayla momentarily paused, thinking she wanted to respect Naomi's and Jordyn's privacy, not knowing how much details she should be providing, regarding the cause of the confrontation and how it ended. Yet, there was no more time to think since all eyes were on her.

"We were off campus, and as Ms. Fisher said, there was a disagreement that turned into a little shouting. But me and Jordyn ran away before things got out of control. We were just worried this person would follow us based on the way things ended."

She stopped talking and wanted to bury her head in the sand. Her delivery wasn't as smooth as she would have liked, and her explanation opened her up to more questions from her father. She desperately wanted to clean up what she'd said and cut Trevor off from asking the next obvious question. *How did things end?*

Before Trevor could speak, Kayla blurted out, "It ended with me losing my cool and throwing a bottle of water at this person, and then we ran."

She couldn't help but glance at Jordyn to see if she had any reaction to this twisted version of the story. However, her face remained expressionless. She also had the urge to take a peek at Naomi but refused since she could only imagine the look on her face since it would have been the first time she'd heard this scenario.

Amara chimed in, "It's not like you, Kayla, to react that way unless this person did something that really ticked you off."

Kayla shrugged. "I was just sticking up for Jordyn."

"So, do you know if you were followed at any point?" Trevor asked.

"Not that we know of," Kayla responded.

Trevor stroked his goatee. "This just put a jolt of excitement into my quiet evening. I could be here all night asking questions, but I'm going to leave it alone for now. As long as you and Jordyn are physically okay, I'd say we enjoy this unexpected time together and find something to eat for dinner unless, of course, everyone already had dinner." He didn't get an affirmative response from anyone and continued, "Since we didn't expect company, we'll need to order some takeout." He eyed Naomi and Jordyn. "You're welcome to stay here for the night if you want. Or if not, just let me know whenever you're ready to go, and I can take you back home." He then looked over at Kayla and said, "And when the time comes to take them home, I'd suggest you come along for the ride, also."

# Chapter 19

Kayla finished her second slice of pizza from the pies Amara had ordered to help feed everyone. She'd thought of an excuse prior to the pizza being delivered to run outside and clean off the knife, as well as the floor mats with the water from the garden hose. After finishing, she temporarily placed the knife back in the glove compartment and, for psychological reasons, had every intention to switch it out for a new one.

*****

Later in the evening, Kayla and Jordyn hopped in the back of Trevor's SUV with Naomi sitting in the front passenger seat. It was close to midnight, and Naomi had declined the invitation to stay overnight. Plans were made for Kayla to pick up Jordyn at her house the following day and make their trip back to campus.

Jordyn had grabbed her knapsack from Kayla's car before they departed and placed it safely on the floor between her feet. Kayla shuttered at the thought of having the blood-stained sweatshirt sitting at the bottom of Jordyn's bag as a reminder of the violent confrontation with Mason. She prayed Jordyn could successfully get rid of the evidence once she arrived home.

Kayla felt a trickle of sweat run along the side of her face. She was initially concerned with the idea of running into Mason somewhere along the trip. But once she thought about it more, she realized Mason was unfamiliar with

Trevor's car, and the tinted windows provided all the cover they needed. Her next concern involved the trip back home after dropping off Naomi and Jordyn. She knew Trevor wanted her to tag along so he could have every opportunity on the way back home to continue his interrogation to find out exactly what had happened during the confrontation, which scared Kayla more than anything.

It was at this point she regretted not telling Naomi and her parents the entire story. They were all completely unaware the confrontation was much worse than falsely advertised, and she needed them to be on high alert and ready to respond in case Mason decided to retaliate.

Kayla began to furiously type, resulting in a text coming across Jordyn's phone.

Kayla: *I think we should tell them exactly what happened so they can be prepared for whatever Mason's planning to do.*

Jordyn: *You sure you want to do that? They're going to kill us for lying.*

Kayla: *Better to fess up now than wait till later. Besides, once Mason gets in contact with your mother, he's going tell her what happened, anyway, and he'll have the injured arm to prove it.*

Jordyn: *I should have listened to you and had you take me to the research facility*

*for the testing, then none of this would have
ever happened.*

Kayla: *My heart is racing now. I'm
trying to get up the nerve to confess.*

A few minutes had passed, and Kayla still hadn't said anything. Her anxiety was getting the better of her, and she had trouble forcing the words out.

Jordyn: *Well . . . are you going to do it?*

Kayla: *I'm scared shitless right now. Don't
know if I can do it.*

Jordyn: *Do you want me to tell them?*

Kayla: *No! I'm the one who stabbed him,
so I need to be the one to tell them. I just need
a little more time to get up the nerve.*

They eventually approached Jordyn's house as Trevor slowed and turned into the driveway. Kayla had kept quiet the entire trip and never found the courage to confess.

Looking at the house, Naomi raised one eyebrow in a questioning slant. "The front porch light should be on, but it's completely out." She noticed the lone streetlight on the country road running parallel to the house was still lit. "Looks like the power is still on in the area." She angled her head toward the back seat. "Do you girls remember if I turned off the porch light when we left earlier?"

"I wasn't paying attention if you did," Jordyn said.

Trevor pulled up behind Naomi's Toyota Corolla in the driveway and shut off the engine. "If it will make you feel any better, I can walk you to the door and make sure everything is okay."

"Works for me," Naomi said with a smile.

Everyone exited the car except for Kayla as she scanned the yard, looking for anything out of the ordinary. She eventually opened the door to follow behind the rest of the group as they walked to the front porch.

Without the porch light on, the front area of the house was shrouded in darkness. The streetlight was too far away from the entrance to provide any assistance with illuminating their path. Trevor turned the flashlight on his cell to provide a hint of light to the area.

"I can see why you need the light on the front porch. Can't see much without it," Trevor said.

"Guess that's the price you pay when living outside of the city limits. I prefer the peace and quiet of country living, anyway," Naomi said.

Kayla wasn't too fond at the moment with the country atmosphere. She peeked over at Jordyn who appeared equally uneasy with the situation. Although, Kayla did find relief in knowing Trevor was leading the way.

They proceeded to walk up the porch steps as the wood creaked under their footing. Both Kayla and Jordyn had their cell phone flashlights on, rotating the light beam from right to left and, on occasion, behind them.

Trevor approached the front door and attempted to twist the knob to make sure it was still locked. He focused his attention on Naomi and said, "Before you go in, do you mind if I check around the house perimeter, to make sure all the windows are secure?"

"Sure, no problem," Naomi said.

Trevor walked back down the porch steps and then stopped before turning to Naomi. "I want to make sure you don't have any pets, specifically dogs I need to worry about."

"Outside of the goldfish we have swimming around in our tank in the living room, we don't have any other pets."

Trevor nodded then disappeared around the corner of the house.

Naomi focused on Kayla and Jordyn. "You two were exceptionally quiet on the ride over here. I hope you're still not spooked by the incident with Mason?"

Jordyn glared at Kayla with her eyes a little wider than normal. Since Kayla couldn't find the courage to say anything in the car, she knew this would be the perfect opening to start her confession, but without Trevor present, she hesitated and didn't want to be forced into blurting out her confession twice. She chose not to offer any response.

Jordyn stepped in and replied, "I'd be lying if I said it still wasn't bothering me."

Naomi eyed Kayla. "And don't worry, sweetheart; I'm not holding anything against you for throwing a bottle of water at Mason."

Kayla forced a halfhearted smile. *Would driving a knife through his forearm change your decision?*

Naomi walked to the porch swing and sat as she waited for Trevor to return. Kayla continued to rotate her flashlight around the front, bothered by the deafening silence. It was still early in the spring, and the weather was a touch too cool at night for the crickets to start their incessant chirping that normally occurred during the summertime months. She closed her eyes to search for that moment of Zen to help bring about some internal peace and calm down her thoughts furiously circling in her head.

Trevor eventually returned to the front. "Everything seems secure with your windows," he said.

"Thanks for checking. I'm assuming I just need to replace the light bulb on the porch," Naomi said.

"I can take care of that if you want before I leave."

"Thanks, but I can handle it from here. You did more than enough for tonight."

Jordyn gave Kayla a frigid stare, adding more pressure for her to finally move forward with the confession.

Trevor reached out and hugged Naomi then Jordyn. "You ladies should be good now. Glad we could catch up with one another, even if the circumstances were a little weird."

Kayla meekly waved goodbye as Naomi turned the key in the front door lock and pushed the door to enter the house.

"Wait! I have something to tell you both," Kayla blurted out.

# Chapter 20

All eyes were on Kayla as she stood on the porch. She could have never imagined the paralyzing fear she was currently experiencing would rival the fear that consumed her during the violent confrontation with Mason. Flashbacks of the knife harpooning Mason in the arm played furiously in her mind. She fought to control her hands from shaking and struggled with making solid eye contact with Trevor and Naomi.

"I . . . I wasn't completely truthful about the way things ended with our confrontation earlier." She stopped and puffed out her cheeks before exhaling. "Ms. Fisher's friend was acting pretty aggressive with Jordyn, and I was worried, so I pulled out my knife. And when he threatened us with whatever he had behind the counter and went to grab it, I guess I panicked and reacted by swinging the knife at him and ended up stabbing him in the forearm. And that's when we ran out."

Even though there were only a few seconds of silence, Kayla felt like it lasted for an eternity. She could clearly hear her heart beating inside her chest and felt like a criminal on trial for a serious crime, waiting to hear a verdict from the jurors.

Both Trevor and Naomi started to talk at the same time, but Trevor deferred and let her speak first.

"Okay, I'm having trouble processing all of this. First off, how aggressive was Mason acting that you had to stab him in the arm? Did he physically touch either one of you?"

Jordyn chimed in, "Yes, he grabbed my arm after I threw a bottle of water at him."

Naomi stood with her arms folded, looking completely confused. "I thought Kayla threw the bottle?"

"No, it was me. She said that to try to protect me from getting in trouble."

Kayla gave Trevor a sidelong glance, noticing he looked surprisingly calm, considering the circumstances as he waited his turn to speak.

"I won't even ask right now why you threw a bottle of water at him. Did he hurt you when he grabbed your arm?" Naomi asked.

"He was holding on pretty tight and only let go when Kayla came at him with the knife."

Kayla's eyes began to water. "I swear I was just acting in self-defense when he went behind the counter. I didn't know if he had a gun or what," she said, wiping the tears rolling down her cheeks.

Trevor approached Kayla and gave her a hug. "It's all right. I'm sure you were scared and weren't sure how to react in that situation." He turned to Naomi. "Not that I'm trying to get in your business, but how close of a friend is this person to you?"

"He's someone I've been dating for the past year. He's always been kind and considerate around me and Jordyn, so I'm completely stunned he would act this way. Now I feel like a complete fool. I can't believe that bastard put his hands on Jordyn."

Trevor's eyes narrowed. "Um . . . please don't take this the wrong way, but what was Kayla and Jordyn doing alone with him, anyway, without you around?

"That's a legitimate question, and the answer is I didn't know Kayla was taking Jordyn to meet up with him. He's the owner of a gas station in the next county over, and she was meeting him there to take care of some personal business that would eventually benefit me. She wanted it to be a surprise." She stopped talking momentarily and focused her attention on Kayla. "Do you know how badly his arm was injured? Was this a little puncture of his skin?"

Kayla cleared her throat and attempted to compose herself before speaking. "I don't know how deep it went in, but it was more than a puncture. Everything happened so fast, and we ran right after it happened, so I don't know how bad the injury was."

Naomi let out a large exhale. "Wow, this is a lot to take in. I'm grateful you girls are okay. Now I'm worried about Mason retaliating. He knows where you go to school, and he knows where we live. We can't live our lives constantly looking over our shoulders and wondering when he might show up and what he might do."

"You're welcome to come back to our house and stay overnight to play it safe," Trevor said.

"I hate for you to keep taking us back and forth between our house and yours."

"It's no problem, especially knowing what I know now. I wouldn't feel comfortable at all leaving you and Jordyn here by yourselves."

"Okay, I think I'll take you up on that offer."

# Chapter 21

Trevor opened his eyes after hearing the toilet flush in the bathroom. He rubbed his eyes to help clear his vision and noted the empty bed beside him. Amara was awake, and Trevor had to gear himself up to deliver the shocking news Kayla had confessed to last night.

By the time they'd arrived back home, after midnight, Amara had been sound asleep. He also needed to make her aware of the two extra guests who'd slept over, which meant additional mouths would need to be fed for breakfast.

Trevor propped up the pillows and pushed himself up in bed. Amara eventually came out of the bathroom.

"Good morning! Did your snoring wake you up?" she asked.

"Nothing like some Sunday morning humor. To answer your question, I woke up after hearing you in the bathroom."

"What time did you get back last night?"

"It was close to one in the morning. You were knocked out."

Amara sat on the edge of the bed and smiled. "No kisses for you until you brush your teeth."

"I'll brush them when I can get the energy to get out the bed."

"So, were there any issues with the drop-off last night?"

"Yes and no. We made it to Naomi's house with no problem, but they ended up coming right back here."

Amara scrunched up her eyebrows. "Okay, now you have me totally confused. She didn't want to stay over when we initially asked her last night. What changed her mind? "That's because your daughter wasn't so truthful last night when she explained what had happened with Naomi's friend."

"How so?"

"Just to give you a little more context, I found out Naomi's friend is actually a man named Mason, who she's been dating for the past year, and he owns a gas station in the next county over. Apparently, Kayla took Jordyn to meet Mason at the gas station; she was working on some type of surprise for Naomi. And, as you know, things got a little ugly for whatever reason. But what Kayla declined to tell us was the altercation turned physical, and she ended up stabbing this man in the arm before they ran away."

"Whoa, wait a minute. Did you say she stabbed him in the arm?"

"I did."

"How could she forget to tell us that part?"

"It's not that she forgot. She was scared to tell us."

"I can't believe this. And where did she get the knife from?" She paused for a moment. "Or is this the same knife you gave to her?"

"I'm sure it was."

"I told you giving her that knife was bad news. Now she used it to mangle this man's arm. Do we know how serious his injury was?

"No clue because they didn't stick around to see."

Amara folded her arms. "And how come you're so nonchalant about this?

"I wasn't exactly happy when I heard the news, but it was a matter of self-defense. He was going for something behind the counter, and she got scared and reacted."

"She didn't have to get violent and stab the man. They could have run away from him."

"That's probably true, but you never know how you're going to react in a situation like that until it happens. You most certainly know I can speak to that from experience."

Amara shook her head. "Now this brings about a whole new set of problems. We have this man, who is beyond pissed at Kayla, and I'm sure now looking for revenge. We don't know if he's some lunatic with access to a gun. And it doesn't help that Kayla is on her own, over an hour away at school." She stopped as her eyes glazed over with moisture. "I can't have anything happen to my baby girl."

"We're going to make sure nothing happens to her. I think we first need to start with keeping her home this week. I'm going to suggest Naomi do the same for Jordyn. I'm sure they can complete their assignments online."

"They're going to need to go back to school sooner or later, and we have no clue if or when this man may try to show up on campus looking for them."

Trevor rubbed his goatee. "We can contact the campus police department and alert them to the situation. Also, both Kayla and Jordyn should save the campus police phone number as a favorite on their phones. It also helps their dorm is pretty secure—no one can gain access to the building without passing the security booth and having a student ID to unlock the door."

"They can't be trapped in their dorm room forever."

"That means they need to be smart when they're walking on campus. No more walking with their faces buried in their phones. No more roaming around the campus at night or walking solo if they can help it. They need to stay among crowds as best they can. As I always told Kayla, there's safety in numbers." Trevor twisted and planted his feet on the floor before standing. "And this also means the knife and pepper spray will need to be with her at all times. I'm going to suggest Jordyn get her hands on these items if she doesn't already have them."

Amara sat back down on the bed with her head tilted up and eyes closed momentarily. She then opened them and glared at Trevor. "How come you're so calm? I would expect you of all people to be going crazy right now, worrying about Kayla's safety."

"That's a fair question. For one thing, based on how Kayla handled things at the gas station, I trust she would have the courage to do what she needs to do to protect herself if she's physically threatened. And second, staying calm helps me avoid thinking of what I would do to this man if he ever put his hands on Kayla."

# Chapter 22

A couple of days later, Naomi sat at her kitchen table, eager to dig into the stir-fry chicken she'd prepared for dinner. She'd arrived home a short while ago and welcomed some peace and relaxation after spending the last eight hours as a home health aide, caring for one of her clients. Even though the work could be demanding at times, she enjoyed taking care of her older generation of clients, who might have been past their prime physically yet had the most amazing life experiences and words of wisdom to share.

This passion for taking care of the older generation stemmed from her time spent as a young adult caring for her mother who'd suffered from dementia. She'd been by her mother's side from when the first signs of this horrible disease had surfaced. Periodically forgetting names eventually progressed into misplacing items on a daily basis and gradually culminated with her mother being unable to recognize Naomi as her daughter.

The moment this first happened shook Naomi to her core. She'd felt angry, not with her mother but with this unforgiving disease that ate away at her mother's memory until there was nothing left.

Naomi took the first few bites of her meal and closed her eyes while enjoying the food, which had eluded her since the noon hour. This was her second evening back at home after spending a couple of nights over at Kayla's house. At the insistence of Trevor, she agreed to keep Jordyn off campus and let her stay with Kayla for the remainder of the week to be extra cautious. Jordyn protested against Naomi for wanting to stay at the house by herself, but she refused to be inconvenienced with her daily routines because of the potential threat of Mason showing up on her doorstep in a bad mood. She hadn't mentioned anything to Jordyn regarding several calls she'd received from Mason during the morning that she ignored. He'd left a voicemail, followed by a few text messages, which Naomi refused to acknowledge. Her blood was still running hot from the incident, and she wasn't sure how she would react if she interacted with him in any way. She also knew there was a good possibility he could show up at the house unannounced, but she would be ready for him if he did.

Her phone chimed once more after taking a sip from her wine glass. She could see this was another text from Mason. But, unlike the previous text messages that she swiped to immediately clear from her screen, her eyes caught a glimpse of two words she hadn't expected to see.

*"I'm sorry."*

"I'm sorry? What's he talking about," she whispered.

Her curiosity was piqued and she reluctantly went down the rabbit hole to read the previous text messages that she's initially ignored, starting with the first one.

Mason: *If you have a few minutes I would like to chat about what happened on Saturday night. Give me a call when you can.*

Mason: *I'm guessing you probably don't want to talk to me but I would like to give my side of the story. Please call me.*

Mason: *It's been a few hours and I haven't heard from you. I'm not mad if that's what you're worried about. I really would like to talk to you.*

Mason: *Not sure if an apology will help but I'm sorry.*

Naomi struggled to interpret these messages. This was far from the angry tone she would have expected Mason to have, considering what had happened. *Is this some sort of trap? Is he baiting me to reach out to him?* As much as she didn't want to admit it, these messages did soften her attitude. This was the kind and considerate man she'd always known him to be.

Then she shook her head as if fighting against these words attempting to sedate her feelings of anger. *Oh no, you don't. Not today.*

She shifted her focus and thought about Mason putting his hands on Jordyn. That was all she needed to rouse her anger once more and prevent her from falling for any manipulation tactics Mason might have been trying to perpetrate.

A short while later, Naomi's head dropped every so often as she nodded off while lounging on her couch, attempting to watch the news. This had become her nightly ritual during the week after eating dinner and finishing off a glass of wine.

She was startled awake by the doorbell ringing, followed by three hard knocks.

Naomi's eyes widened with intrigue, as she knew there could only be one answer as to who was knocking at the door. She was extremely thankful she'd closed the curtains earlier, which kept the living room out of view.

She shut off the TV and contemplated what to do. She'd previously convinced herself she would be ready if Mason showed up at the house, but sometimes reality could make even the most prepared person feel ill-equipped to handle a situation. She also felt extremely uncomfortable knowing there was another side of Mason that had surfaced during his altercation with Jordyn and Kayla. That was a side she hadn't known existed and one that would forever change how she interacted with him moving forward.

She stood and tiptoed her way toward the stairs, doing her best not to disturb any squeaky floorboards. She ascended the stairs as a few more knocks followed in succession. She entered her bedroom and reached under the bed, pulling out an aluminum bat. She hated guns and felt this was the next best order of protection for her. And being a former high school softball all-star, her ability to swing a bat was still second to none.

It was quite possible she was overreacting and Mason hadn't shown up to cause any trouble. But, she didn't want to take that chance and let her guard down. She heard another knock, along with the sound of muffled talking. She tightened her grip on the bat, exiting her bedroom and stepping into the hallway to listen a little more closely.

"Can we please talk, Naomi? I'm not here to cause you any trouble. Just want to give you my side of the story and, hopefully, we can patch things up between me and Jordyn," Mason yelled from beyond the door.

Naomi stood still. She contemplated whether to go with her first instinct and not answer the door. She let out a nervous laugh, wondering where the big bad mother had gone. The same one who was going to give Mason a piece of her mind if he ever showed up at her doorstep. And there he was, delivered to her on a silver platter, waiting for the verbal ass-whooping she'd planned for him.

"I know you're definitely in there. I can see the lights on, and your car is in the driveway."

She jumped at the buzzing sensation from the phone in her hand. She looked to see Mason's name appear on the screen. She thought about his persistence in attempting to contact her throughout the day, along with this unexpected visit to her house, raising enormous red flags in her mind. If he was truly sincere and apologetic for what had happened, there should be no reason why he was making such a determined effort to track her down in the span of one day.

A part of her wanted to answer the phone and tell him to go to hell, but she refrained from carrying through with the idea. Instead, she patiently waited in the hallway, hoping he would get the hint and leave.

She remained motionless as the phone stopped buzzing and she no longer heard his voice. She also didn't hear a car door slam or engine start, so she figured he hadn't left.

She approached the stairs and took a few steps down, listening closely for any indication Mason was still lurking outside.

Naomi listened intently, hearing the wood flooring on the porch creak ever so slightly, giving her the confirmation she needed that Mason was still present outside. She imagined he might have been listening for any movement inside the house, but she refused to lose this cat-and-mouse game and allow any squeaky floorboards from giving away her location. She stood perfectly still, knowing she had the advantage because any step Mason took on the porch would cause the antique wood flooring to groan in protest and allow her to track his every movement.

She heard the wood creak in succession as the sound traversed across the porch. She didn't know if he would be brazen enough to try to open a window, but she took comfort in knowing Trevor had inspected her windows a few nights ago, confirming they were all locked and secured.

She took a moment to catch her breath and hadn't realized she was gripping the bat with such force that her fingers started to lose feeling.

She followed the sound of his footsteps as they moved back and forth along the porch, indicating he might be pacing. After a few more moments, she heard the creaking stop and a car door eventually slam, followed by an engine starting. She made her way downstairs and peeked through the curtain to see him reversing out of the driveway and disappearing down the road. She was elated to see him finally leave and, at the same time, kicked herself for being such a coward. However, she'd learned from previous experience it was better to listen to your instincts and not follow your ego, which had the power to remove all rational thoughts and could convince someone to walk off a cliff without a parachute, just to prove a point. She wasn't interested in participating in any suicide cliff diving this evening and made peace with herself knowing, at this particular moment, she'd made the right decision by following her instincts.

She couldn't help but wonder whether Mason was being sincere and truly wanted to make amends with Jordyn or if he had the will to forgive Kayla for stabbing him in the arm. But the one thing she did know was this wouldn't be his last visit, and she had to be better prepared for his eventual return.

# Chapter 23

Trevor closed the bedroom door and locked it. He sat on the edge of the bed and took several deep breaths to help calm the agitation steadily growing. It had initially started a few weeks ago with Amara's scare at Trader Joe's. He was proud of the way he'd reacted at that moment, with the possibility of her being followed. While he had felt some anxiety at that time, he'd never dwelled on the situation and honestly believed Amara might have been overreacting to what was probably pure coincidence and not remnants from their past lives. The second and most concerning event adding fuel to his fire of agitation came after Kayla admitted to the physical confrontation with Naomi's boyfriend, which did present more of a challenge with him attempting to control his actions and keep his mind at peace. He'd initially taken the news better than he'd thought he would, but now that he had more time to think about it, his concern blossomed.

He took pride in knowing Kayla had stood up for herself and hadn't backed down, while truly acting in self-defense when she'd stabbed Mason in the arm. But actions had consequences, and he knew Kayla now potentially had a target on her back after what had happened. It also didn't help for him to know both Kayla and Jordyn were three days into being sheltered at the house for safety reasons in case Mason went looking for them on campus.

Trevor's ability to remain calm had reached a breaking point. He stared at the closet door and wondered if the mental exercises he'd previously learned from his therapist would be enough to avoid what he believed to be the best solution for keeping his family and friends safe.

He clenched his fists and stood before approaching the closet. One final thought entered his mind. *Even a hurricane is calm in the center.* This was a phrase he'd chanted during many difficult times in the past, which had allowed him to overcome some challenging moments during his lifetime. But it wasn't going to work this time, knowing Kayla was smack dab in the brunt of this storm.

He opened the closet and reached up onto the shelf, pushing aside a few items until he spotted the metal safe in the corner. He punched in the code and opened it, placing his hand on the compact Glock G19. He promised himself he would only carry the gun if he or his family felt threatened. And this hadn't been the case since they'd left Richmond when Kayla was only a baby.

Amara was never fond of having this gun in the house, but she understood the reason for its presence. Trevor made it a point to refrain from acknowledging the gun even existed in any conversations with Amara. And there were plenty of times he almost forgot it was tucked away in the corner of the closet shelf since there had been no need to even think about carrying it. Now, with this recent event, there was no longer just a temptation to hold the gun. It had become an absolute necessity in Trevor's mind.

His thoughts were interrupted by a knock on the bedroom door.

"Trevor? Are you in here?" Amara asked.

Trevor hesitated to answer. His initial instinct was to place the Glock back in the safe, close the closet door, and not even acknowledge to Amara he'd gone looking for it.

But as his therapist always said, it was best to be truthful about your feelings, especially to your spouse. This was something Trevor had struggled with throughout their relationship. It made him feel much more vulnerable if he displayed any feelings of anxiety, frustration, or fear. And, at this moment, all three of those feelings were swirling in his mind. He could no longer act like he was calm and unbothered by this recent event.

He placed the Glock back in the safe and didn't bother to shove the box back in the corner. He left the closet door open and proceeded to let Amara into the bedroom. After she entered, he closed the bedroom door and locked it. Without saying a word, he sat on the edge of the bed.

Amara observed the opened closet door. "So, is this what it's come to?"

Trevor shrugged. "I guess so."

Amara's face tightened. "You know how I feel about this."

"I do, and that's why I can honestly say this is the first time I touched the safe since we moved here."

Amara focused her eyes back on the closet. "I hope you weren't planning to carry this thing around with you all the time like you did in Richmond."

"Can't say I didn't think about it."

"Now you know that gun isn't going to resolve anything. It could only make things worse."

"It made us feel safe in Richmond, didn't it?"

"Yes, but that was a completely different situation."

"Not in my eyes. If you're coming after my family, I have every right to defend us by any means necessary."

"And I'm not completely disagreeing with you. I can just tell you're a little on edge now, and when you get that way, I just get a little nervous if you're carrying around this gun at the same time. Being angry and holding a gun is usually a recipe for disaster."

Trevor kept his head down and didn't provide any eye contact to Amara.

Amara approached and began massaging his shoulders. "Let's keep a level head about this and see how things play out."

Trevor let out a small laugh as he was caught off guard by his knee-jerk reaction.

"What's so funny?" she asked.

"It's funny how things turned around in a couple of days. You were the one so frantic about the situation, and I was the calm one."

"I guess that's why we're married. When I'm struggling and worried about something, you keep me calm; and when you're in panic mode, I can keep you calm. I think the million-dollar question would be: what happens if we both end up in panic mode at the same time?"

Trevor thought for a moment. "I guess that's when all hell breaks loose."

# Chapter 24

Mason gripped the steering wheel with his left hand and rotated his arm to complete the turn. The front wheels from his 2020 Dodge Charger wobbled making the turn, responding to his impaired ability to control the car with one good arm. His decision to drive to Naomi's house at night with an injured right arm had not been the brightest of ideas; however, that had been his best opportunity to visit her before his wife arrived home the following day. She was scheduled to return home from a weeklong conference in Atlanta, and he had to be ready to explain the injury, which was technically the result of a workplace accident, in his mind.

He underestimated the difficulty of attempting to drive with his left hand on the wheel and his right arm resting on his thigh. He periodically balled his right hand into a fist and gently squeezed, attempting to shake the pins and needles feeling radiating throughout his hand. This tingling resulted from a combination of the internal damage caused by the knife, in addition to his forearm, which was tightly wrapped to protect the wound. He was thankful the trip to the hospital hadn't revealed any major nerve damage, but his right forearm muscle had taken a good hit from the blade. He was also extremely grateful he had a first-aid trauma kit on hand at the gas station to help control the bleeding, allowing him to drive to the hospital without passing out from blood loss. After having the wound cleansed, receiving antibiotic treatment, and a fair number of stitches, he was released from the hospital with instructions to rest his arm for at least the next week. Yet his ability to follow through with the doctor's orders was never the greatest, which prompted him to move forward and make the questionable decision to drive to Naomi's house.

He'd regretted his decision to attempt to scare Jordyn and her friend. He did have a hunting knife resting on the shelf behind the counter, but it had never been his attention to grab it during the altercation. Truthfully, he was startled and somewhat scared at the weapon-wielding young ladies and hadn't expected the situation to escalate like it did. He figured they would run away as soon as he threatened them and darted behind the counter.

He could tell Jordyn's friend had been nervous during the confrontation, yet he hadn't expected her to lunge at him with the knife. He should have known better after his first interaction with the young lady when she'd thought Jordyn had disappeared and proceeded to pull out a knife. He believed the knife was only for show, but she obviously had no problems using it.

Now he had a serious problem. Because of the injury, he was limited in what tasks he could perform at the gas station, and this included working on any car repairs. The other mechanic, who worked at the shop, was out of town for the week, which put a halt to any possibility of generating income from car repairs. This didn't bode well since his business was already teetering on the edge financially. This also meant, that since his plan B option of borrowing money from Jordyn hadn't worked out as planned, there was no way he could replenish the funds in the joint savings account before his wife found out. And on top of everything else, he was on the hook for some expensive medical bills since he still hadn't reached the deductible for his wife's healthcare plan.

This all didn't sit well with him, and he needed to respond. He had to be strategic about his response and didn't want to immediately react like a complete madman out for revenge. He figured he could use his nice guy persona to get back in good graces with Naomi and Jordyn. And if he played his cards right, there would still be a chance he could wiggle his way into their pockets and get the money he felt he deserved. As for Jordyn's knife-wielding friend, he needed some extra time to think of an appropriate response.

# Chapter 25

Kayla drove under the Flagstone University sign and entered the campus grounds for the first time in a week. She looked over at Jordyn, who maintained a stoic facial expression as they proceeded toward Dario Hall. Kayla peered into the rearview mirror to confirm Trevor continued to follow them to their final destination. She would have normally declined his offer to chaperone them back to campus, but based on the current circumstances, she'd welcomed his suggestion.

She pulled into the dorm parking lot. It had only been a week, but it seemed like an eternity since she'd been back on campus. The cloudy skies had given way to a light mist, which was a perfect match for her underwhelming mood. Most of her focus no longer revolved around her school projects; prioritizing her and Jordyn's safety was the name of the game. Being aware of their surroundings, limiting distractions, and being ready for the unexpected had become the new norm.

Kayla and Jordyn exited the car, with Trevor approaching. Kayla could tell he was attempting to conceal his gun with the untucked, oversized shirt. She could still see the slight bulge on the side of his right hip. He'd previously mentioned there was a gun in the house, but she never knew where it was hidden. Now, with these recent events, she wondered how often he would be carrying the gun.

Kayla hugged Trevor. "Thanks for following us."

"I wouldn't have it any other way. I'm sure I don't have to tell you both again, but please be aware of your surroundings at all times. This means keeping your phones in your pocket while you're walking on campus and trusting your intuition if something doesn't feel right. And please try staying amongst crowds if possible and not walking around at night."

Kayla tried to force a smile. "Yes, we get it."

He focused his eyes on Jordyn. "And what are you going to have with you at all times?"

"My pepper spray and box cutter," she said.

"Perfect. I trust you two will look out for one another. I also trust the campus police will do what they need to do to keep you both safe. And I'm only a phone call away." He observed the dorm entrance. "Do you need me to walk you both to your room?"

"No, Dad, we're good. You've done more than enough. I'll make sure to reach out to you if we're having any issues."

He motioned his arms for both Kayla and Jordyn to bring it in for a group hug.

Kayla grabbed her duffle bag and walked into the dorm lobby with Jordyn trailing behind. She had comfort knowing the safety measures in the dorm building were above standard with the security desk monitored twenty-four-seven and a student ID needed to open the door and gain access to the lobby. This was, in fact, the safest place to be on campus.

Her anxiety level subsided once they entered the lobby and eventually approached the dorm room. They walked into the room and, in unison, both collapsed onto their respective beds.

Kayla stared up at the ceiling while lying on her back and felt like she could immediately drift off to sleep. She was exhausted mentally, emotionally, and physically from the events that had occurred during the week.

She pulled herself up into a seated position and noticed Jordyn, who was sitting with her head down, looking just as exhausted.

"I think we can use some words of encouragement. Can you do us both a favor and look at your calendar to see today's positive affirmation?" Kayla said.

Jordyn grabbed the calendar, flipping to the appropriate date. "I can transform problems into challenges, weaknesses into strengths, and fear into action," she said with conviction.

"Sounds like great advice for both of us," Kayla said with a slight bit of optimism rising from hearing those words.

"I'm struggling to figure out how we got to this point. Everything seems so surreal," Jordyn said.

"I feel the same way." Kayla closed her eyes and shook her head. "No matter how hard I try, I can't keep that image out of my mind—me stabbing Mason in the arm. I've never been anywhere close to being that violent with someone. I had a few shoving matches with people in my younger days, but that was way beyond what I thought I was ever capable of doing. It's kind of scary for me to think I could actually do what I did."

"Please, don't let this drive you crazy. I told you it was a matter of self-defense. What if we both stood there while he was reaching behind the counter and he pulled out a gun? We don't know what he would have done in that scenario. I would like to think he wouldn't have pulled the trigger if he was holding a gun, but then again, I've never seen him mad before, so I have no idea what he's capable of. The way I see it, it was either him or us. And I choose us all day every day."

A slight chuckle escaped Kayla's mouth. "Wow, I didn't know I could laugh at a time like this, but what you said makes sense." Kayla stopped talking for a moment, glancing down at her long-sleeved shirt. "And thanks for getting rid of that bloody sweatshirt. I don't need anything else to remind me of what happened."

"Oh, yeah. No problem. I'm sure that thing is somewhere sitting in a landfill by now."

"I would have suggested burning it, but I can live with you tossing it out with the trash."

Jordyn stretched out her arms and yawned. "I don't know about you, but I think we've spent enough time talking about Mason. Do you mind if we change the subject?"

"Absolutely not. So, what else is there to talk about?"

Jordyn rubbed her chin. "You ever wish you could be a kid again? No adulting necessary. Those times when your parents took care of everything for you. Those were the days. Knowing what I know now, I'd go back to that in a heartbeat."

Kayla shrugged. "I guess."

"What do you mean *you guess*?"

"Don't get me wrong; I did enjoy that part of being a kid. I just feel my childhood could have been a little more . .

. exciting. I was always stuck in the house, and it would have been nice to get out, go on vacations, attend family reunions. Do things normal families do."

"I'm sure a lot of people would be jealous of you for growing up in a nice house in the suburbs, with a big yard to run around in."

"Yeah, but doing that day after day when you're the only child gets tiring quickly. And the strange thing is my parents always act weird when I ask them about my childhood and why I never met any of my relatives."

"I'm not going to lie, that does sound a little suspect."

"I try not to think about it too much, but the older I get, the more it seems to bother me. It was like I was living in a black hole during my childhood—very empty. I feel like I don't know who I am or where I come from."

"Are you thinking—"

"Can't say I haven't thought about it before."

Jordyn smiled. "Do you even know what I was going to say?"

"Yes, I've known you long enough that we can finish each other's thoughts and sentences."

"Okay, so what was I thinking?"

"Being adopted."

"Damn, you're good. I would have hoped if that was the case, your parents would have told you by now."

"That would have been the nice thing to do. I've never brought up the topic but have been thinking about doing it a lot more." Kayla sighed. "I'm not sure if this change of topic helped ease any of my anxiety."

"I'm sorry I brought it up," Jordyn said.

"No need to apologize. My parents are going to need to address it sooner or later." Kayla reached into her duffle bag and started to unpack. "Since we can't seem to find anything to talk about that's going to help improve our moods, we might as well get some rest and let's see what tomorrow brings."

# Chapter 26

Mason entered his modest two-bedroom apartment, looking forward to the day he could become a homeowner again. He'd been forced to sell the three-bedroom ranch he'd owned with his wife when she'd temporarily lost her job and they could no longer afford the mortgage on the money he was making from the gas station business. They'd only lived in the house for a few years, so there wasn't much equity generated when they'd sold it. Now that his wife was working again, they'd planned to rent for a few years while attempting to save up money for a down payment on a new home.

Mason's stomach grumbled as he entered the kitchen. The granite countertops and stainless steel appliances provided somewhat of a luxurious feel to the apartment.

He opened the refrigerator and eyed the two Chinese takeout boxes sitting alone on the top shelf, which were the only options for dinner. He'd intended to swing by the market to pick up a few groceries after leaving work, but his laziness had won over, and he'd chosen to come straight home instead.

He opened the box of vegetable lo mein and sesame chicken and grimaced. There was barely enough food for two people, and he expected his wife, Leah, to be home at any moment. He started to regret his choice of foregoing the trip to the market because now he had to deal with a wife who would no doubt be hungry and not happy with eating these leftovers. In fact, her mood had been sour ever since she'd arrived home from her business trip to Atlanta a few days ago and he told her his best fabrication of how he'd been injured on the job. This added more fuel to the fire as she continued to recommend he sell the business and find something more lucrative from a financial standpoint.

They'd been at odds about the gas station for quite a while. Mason had inherited the business from his father, and he'd promised to continue running it after his father had passed away. Decades ago, business had been booming for the Last Chance gas station, back when his father was the owner. The area was still in its infancy, and there were plenty of mom-and-pop businesses thriving. The gas station was also helped by its unique name, which garnered plenty of attention from curious travelers as they drove by.

Mason could remember, at one point, his father had sold T-shirts with the name of the gas station embroidered on the front, helping advertise the business to those who might have never heard of it. But as the population of the area grew, so did the commercial infrastructure, leading to corporations with deep pockets building these large brand stores that eventually choked out the client base for many family-owned establishments.

His father had eventually become sick and could no longer run the business, wanting Mason to take over and see what he could do to restore the gas station to its former prominence. This had been an extreme challenge in Mason's mind, and he was initially reluctant to move forward with his father's request. But he'd felt the right thing to do would be to honor his father's wishes while he was on his deathbed.

Mason sat at the kitchen table after microwaving his leftovers. He rotated his right wrist and clenched his fist to test out the pain levels in his forearm. It had been over a week since the incident, and his arm had shown improvement. He felt a smidge of excitement whenever he could use his right arm without feeling too much pain. Simple tasks like holding a fork in his hand to feed himself or grabbing the steering wheel with two hands had become a cause for celebration. He had also reveled in the fact he could now perform some light car repair work without struggling. Although he was happy to see these moments of progress, the signs of the financial damage caused by this incident had already begun to surface. He had to completely shut down the business for a couple of days as he continued with his recovery. In addition, the first hospital bill found its way into the mailbox, and he was presented with a payment due hovering a smidge over five hundred dollars.

His moments of joy and pain were interrupted after hearing the front door open to the apartment. He sighed as he prepared himself for the inevitable bickering about to commence.

Leah entered the kitchen and quickly bent down to kiss him on the cheek. She sported a navy blue business suit, hugging her natural curves. Several strands of her jet-black, wavy, shoulder-length hair jutted out in different directions, struggling to stay in place after a long workday. A mild scent of passion fruit infiltrated Mason's nose.

"Hope your day was better than mine," she said.

"Depends on how bad your day was?"

"I thought I would have a break from traveling for the next week, but my manager wants me to travel to Charlotte to help consult with a team that's been having issues with one of our construction projects."

Mason shrugged. "I told you from the beginning it probably wasn't a good idea to accept this job because of all the travel. We barely see each other. It's like we're two ships passing in the night. Is it too much for me to ask for some quality time with my wife?"

"Yes, I know. It was just hard to say no with the salary they were offering. And we needed the second income, so here we are. But, to be honest with you, after two years of traveling, it's starting to get old fast."

"Glad to hear you feel that way. I don't know what to tell you other than to look for another job if it's bothering you that much."

She took out her phone and said, "And speaking of salary, I was trying to log into the online banking on my phone to confirm if my paycheck was deposited after the issue I had last time, but I'm unable to get in with the password. Are you having the same issue?"

Mason paused for a moment. "Uh . . . yes. I was having a problem, also. I'm planning to call customer service to see if they can help us out. I'll keep you posted once we have access to view the accounts again."

Leah nodded as she hung her leather tote bag over the kitchen chair. She looked at Mason's plate. "You decided to eat leftovers?"

"This was the only real option in the fridge."

Leah furrowed her brow. "I thought you were going to the market after work?"

"I was tired and wanted to come home."

"Thanks for letting me know. I could have swung by and picked up some food on my way home. And now I'm tired and don't feel like going out again." Leah shook her head in disgust. "What's wrong with you? Are you allergic to communicating properly?"

"Don't start with your smart-ass comments."

"I can't help it, Mason, because you bring me there sometimes." She reluctantly grabbed a plate and sat at the table. "I honestly don't have the strength to even start another argument now. Just know, I'll remember this, and we'll see how you like it if I forget to communicate something that negatively affects you."

# Chapter 27

It had been almost a week since Kayla and Jordyn reappeared on campus. They both followed the extra safety measures as outlined by their parents, and there had been no sightings of Mason. By all accounts, everything appeared normal, but Kayla refused to let her guard down. She knew being consistently vigilant was crucial to maintaining her and Jordyn's safety.

With her attention so focused on the potential threat that loomed every time she set foot on campus, her studies suffered immensely. She struggled to concentrate long enough to complete her assignments and pay enough attention during her class lectures to make any sense of what the professor was trying to teach. This new norm, as she called it, had become much more than just a distraction. It had completely turned her college way of life upside down. She'd become a complete recluse, as her social life was reduced to only conversations with Jordyn in their dorm room. This was no longer a healthy and sustainable way for her to function, and she knew something had to change.

At times, she wondered if she was overreacting, and this was only a byproduct of her chronic worrying habits and a simple case of submitting to her fears. She knew she needed to get a grip and find a way to push through. She never realized Jordyn's positive affirmation calendar would play such a pivotal role in keeping her mind focused and allowing her the chance to rise above these anxiety-inducing moments. Turning weaknesses into strengths and fear into action was profound advice to follow at this time. She just needed to trust and believe enough to speak those words into existence.

*****

The next morning, Kayla was startled awake by hearing the chorus to the Bruno Mars song "24K Magic" blaring in her ear. She reached over and shut off her phone alarm. Then she rubbed her eyes and tilted her head toward Jordyn's bed, which was unoccupied. She imagined Jordyn had already left for her morning class. Kayla's schedule on Fridays was light, with only two classes. She normally looked forward to getting through her classes on Friday and planning out her weekend activities. But these were not normal times, and she needed to adhere to her parents' instructions to lay low for these next few weekends, which meant staying in the dorm room and binging on her favorite shows.

After showering and throwing on nylon sweats and a T-shirt, she opened the blinds and squinted as her eyes momentarily adjusted to the sunshine. This would be the first day during the spring season when the temperature was expected to reach eighty degrees. She could only imagine how crowded Octagon Park would be with all of the students milling around to soak in the sun. She figured there would be no harm if she joined the festivities on the lawn since she would be amongst a crowd, as her father always drilled in her head.

These were the times she wished she had a premium view of the campus, overlooking the park. Instead, her dorm room window faced the opposite side, which only provided a view of the parking lot. She tried looking at the bright side of the view and thought having a visual of her car in the parking lot wasn't such a bad thing.

She quickly realized the parking lot view would pay dividends this morning as she eyed from a distance what appeared to be a slip of paper under her windshield wiper blade. She hoped it wasn't a parking ticket. She did have her dorm parking lot permit proudly displayed on her windshield, and it hadn't expired.

With her curiosity piqued, she made her way outside to the parking lot and approached her car from the passenger side. She noticed the front of her car leaning abnormally closer to the ground before discovering her passenger side front tire was completely flat. She walked around to the driver's side and immediately stopped, her eyes widening.

The handle of what appeared to be a pocket knife was stuck into the top of her driver's side tire. With both of her front tires flattened, her stomach tightened from the immediate rush of tension enveloping her body.

She reluctantly walked over to the front windshield as her hands trembled. She lifted the wiper and extracted the note.

*An eye for an eye.*

Kayla flung the note to the ground as if it was burning her fingers. She took in several deep breaths to try to handle this unexpected gut punch. She twisted her head from right to left, scanning for anyone who might have been within her view. She knew she couldn't leave the note on the ground, as this would be the physical evidence the campus police would need to begin their investigation in an attempt to identify the guilty party. She also thought it would be a good idea not to further contaminate the note with her fingerprints by touching it again.

She immediately dialed the campus police and reported the incident. When she disconnected, she proceeded to take pictures of the scene with her phone. She was unsure of how long it would take for the campus police to arrive and didn't feel comfortable staying outside near the car. She figured she could wait back in the dorm.

Before leaving, she surveyed around and spotted a rock in the grass. She picked it up and placed it on top of the note resting on the ground to help prevent the wind from carrying it away.

She scanned the parking lot once more, noting a few individuals getting in or out of various cars on the other side of the lot. She observed the time on her phone and cautiously began walking back to the dorm, intending to return once the campus police arrived.

Upon approaching the dorm, she caught a glimpse of a campus police officer walking toward the car. She pivoted around and made her way back to the car.

"Hi, this is Officer Woods. Are you the one who made the call regarding this car?"

"Yes. Thanks for getting here so quickly."

"No problem. I was in the area when I received the call from dispatch."

He studied the tire with the knife sticking out. "I guess my first question is: do you have any idea who could have done this?"

"Not exactly sure." She was reluctant to explain the entire story to the officer and decided to keep things simple for now.

"Did you see anyone suspicious around your car recently?"

"No."

Officer Woods observed the note pinned on the ground by the rock.

"Is this how you found the note?"

"No. It was originally under my windshield wiper. I dropped the note on the ground after I read it and placed the rock on top of it to keep it from blowing away. Didn't want to get any more of my fingerprints on it."

"Smart move." He approached the flattened tire to get a closer view. He rotated his head around, scanning the back perimeter of the dorm. "We do have cameras mounted to the building, but I think your car may be too far away for us to have captured any footage of what may have happened. We'll most certainly review the camera footage to see what we can find."

"Okay, thanks."

Officer Woods stood with his arms folded, looking at the tire, and then back at Kayla. "I'm sorry, I never got your name."

"My name is Kayla."

"Nice to meet you, Kayla. I'm sorry we had to meet under these circumstances."

Officer Woods slowly walked around the car. "I think this may be the first instance of a car being vandalized on campus since I've been working here these past couple of years. I don't get how some people could be so heartless and damage other people's property and not even think twice about it."

Kayla focused her attention on two more officers arriving. The officers proceeded to ask Kayla more questions, and she filed an official campus incident report. The officers carefully extracted the knife from the tire using gloved hands and put it in a plastic bag, along with the note.

Officer Wood approached Kayla. "Unless you happen to have two spare tires in your trunk, which I'm guessing you don't, we're going to need to call a tow truck to take your car to the nearest auto center and get those tires replaced. And don't worry; depending on your insurance, you may be able to get them to reimburse you. Are you able to catch a ride with someone to follow the tow truck to the auto center? If not, you can hop in my car, and I can take you. I believe there's a tire repair place only a few miles away."

Kayla noted the time. "I have class in about a half hour, but I can miss it if necessary and get my assignments online." She paused and looked at Officer Woods. "And thanks for the offer, but I can reach out to a friend to see if they can take me."

*****

A short while later, a tow truck appeared and Kayla's car was loaded onto a flatbed. She sat in the passenger side of Avery's car, who was kind enough to give her a lift to the auto shop for the tire repairs.

Kayla watched the tow truck driver secure the last cable to the underside of her car. She turned to Avery. "Thanks again for helping me out."

"No problem. This is what friends do. And it worked out; I had a few hours' break between my classes."

Avery pressed her foot on the gas as her Mazda 3 jerked forward to follow the tow truck out of the parking lot. "I know you probably don't want to say too much about it, but can you at least let me know if this has anything to do with that car you saw a few weeks ago?" Avery asked.

"It's a good possibility."

"Do you have a picture of the car or the license plate number?"

"Yes."

"That's all we need. We can hunt down the car to see if we can find it on campus and stalk it until the owner shows up."

"I already tried that, but it didn't work. The owner never came back to the car after I waited for over two hours. Besides, I don't know for certain if this is the same person who flattened my tires. There's a good possibility it could be somebody else."

"I don't get it. You're the sweetest person in the world. Who would even think about doing something like this to you?" Avery asked.

"I can think of somebody."

"I'm almost afraid to ask what you did to piss somebody off."

Kayla grimaced. "It's a long story. Tell you about it another time. All I know is there's someone on campus who knows my car and knows what dorm I live in. I just need to watch my back." She began rubbing her forehead. "I would have thought I'd be more scared right about now. Guess I'm just tired and feel numb about the whole situation."

Avery sped up to close the distance between her car and the tow truck as it exited the campus grounds. "We're not going to let anything happen to you. If somebody's messing with you, then they're messing with me. You helped me out last year when I was going through all my boyfriend drama, and I owe you big time for that. Just know I have friends in low places who would have no problem scaring the hell out of someone if that's what it takes for this person to leave you alone."

Kayla showed a glimmer of a smile. "I don't know how you do it, but no matter what's going on, you can always make me smile. I appreciate that."

*****

A short while later, Avery followed the tow truck into the auto center parking lot. Kayla entered and completed the necessary paperwork for the tire replacements. Then both Kayla and Avery sat in the waiting area.

"You don't have to wait here with me. I'll be okay by myself," Kayla said.

"Leaving you here by yourself was never an option. Besides, I still have a couple of more hours before my next class."

Kayla observed the TV mounted on the wall as the midday news broadcasted the normal chaos going on in town.

"So, how was your trip to San Diego?"

"It was fun up until the normal family drama started. I have an uncle who always puts his foot in his mouth when he has a few drinks. And he had more than a few, so I can't even begin to tell you the nonsense that was coming out of his mouth. But he shut up once my grandmother got involved. She's can get real feisty in her older age."

Kayla laughed. "Outside of that moment of family drama, it sounds like you had a good time."

"I guess you can say that. I hope your break was okay."

"Nothing special. I hung out at home, talked to my parents, and read a good book."

Avery displayed a frown. "Oh, boy. We need to put some spice in your spring breaks going forward. We should start making plans for next year's spring break. Maybe a few days at the beach, or a trip to New York City."

"Sounds good to me."

A few moments of silence passed as Kayla looked at her phone. She contemplated reaching out to Trevor, knowing he might be on his lunch break. She'd promised him that she would call if anything concerning happened. And this most certainly fell under the category of concern. She excused herself and left the waiting area to make the call.

# Chapter 28

Naomi pressed her foot on the brake to stop at a red light, wincing in discomfort. She gently rubbed her right knee, attempting to massage away the pain. She dreaded working on the days her joint pain flared up. She was able to endure the discomfort for the most part and was grateful to be on her way home. Her knees had always given her the most trouble, but she'd learned to cope with the pain over the past couple of years. She was convinced all those years of playing softball in her youthful days had become the eventual catalyst to the pain she now experienced. The wear and tear on her joints might not have been evident when she'd been in her prime, but her body was now complaining and intent on being heard through the various aches and pains she currently felt.

She turned onto Colonial Woods Drive and approached her house. She fantasized about having dinner, a glass of red wine, and a hot bath to help soothe her aching knee joints.

She made the last turn into her driveway and hoped what she saw on her front porch was simply a figment of her imagination. She was aware of the most common side effects from the new drug she was taking, which did not include hallucinations as far as she could remember. She put the car in park, squeezed her eyelids shut for a second, and then opened them, hoping what she'd seen would have disappeared. Much to her dismay, the image of Mason sitting on her front porch swing, staring at her, was completely real.

She struggled mightily to make sense of his presence, especially with his car nowhere to be found. She'd imagined he would most likely show up again, but not under these circumstances. And like his first visit, she was completely caught off-guard. But, she refused to give him any visual indication she was surprised by his presence. Although her mind and body were far from operating at optimum capacity, she had to suck it up, put on her big girl pants, and get ready for whatever was to come from this interaction. And this time, her instincts implored her to commence with the verbal ass-whooping.

She grabbed her tote bag from the passenger seat and exited the car, approaching the porch. Mason sat quietly with a hint of a smile forming on his face.

"Surprised to see me?" he asked.

"Yes, especially since I don't see your car anywhere."

"I figured that would be your reaction. Since you refused to answer my texts, calls, or previous knock at the door, I had to get a little more creative." He pointed toward the road. "In case you're wondering, my car is parked up the road. I apologize for deceiving you, but I needed to speak with you and figured this was the only way to get you to talk to me."

*Sneaky bastard.*

"I guess your plan worked, and here I am. So, what do you have to say that's so important?"

"I first want to truly apologize for the incident that happened with Jordyn and her friend. I'm sure she told you all about it, but I wanted to give you my side of the story."

Naomi positioned her tote bag over her shoulder and folded her arms. She leaned to the left, taking pressure off of her right knee, which continued to ache. "Okay, I'm listening."

"I admit I lost my cool during the conversation with Jordyn, which unfortunately spiraled out of control, and before I knew it, I had a knife sticking in my forearm," he said as he raised his forearm, showing off the Ace bandage wrapped around the wound.

"Is that supposed to make me feel some type of sympathy for you?"

"No, I wasn't expecting that. I was just showing you the results of my careless decision to try to scare them."

"So, if you don't want any sympathy, what do you want from me?"

"I was hoping you could accept my apology and know that I realize the way I acted that night was truly uncalled for."

Naomi peered at Mason with furrowed eyebrows. "You're damn right about that. And what makes you think it was okay for you to put your hands on Jordyn?"

Mason stood as Naomi stepped back, reacting to his sudden movement.

"There's no excuse other than I wasn't in my right frame of mind, and I regret doing it."

"Right frame of mind? That's a sorry excuse. Does it make sense to you why I would be upset?"

"Absolutely, and I don't blame you."

"And what would have happened if her friend wasn't there to intervene? Would you have done something more than just grab her arm?"

"I was only trying to calm her down. I didn't want her to grab anything else to throw at me."

Naomi sighed. "This entire situation is a damn shame. Things were going so well between us, and you had been the perfect gentleman up until this point. This is why I'm a firm believer in taking your time to get to know someone. You need to see how someone reacts in every situation before you can truly say you know them. And I can clearly see you failed miserably when it came to keeping your emotions in check when faced with something that didn't go your way." Naomi gritted her teeth as, the more she talked, the angrier she became. "And how dare you ask Jordyn for money. What makes you think that was okay? You're a grown man with a business, and if you're having financial difficulties, there are plenty of other ways to figure things out. And asking my daughter for money should damn sure not be part of the plan."

"I agree and regret every bit of asking her for money. It was stupid and unprofessional."

"Glad to see you realize the error of your ways. Now, what's next? What else are you hoping to get out of this other than professing your apologies?"

"I'm hoping you accept my apologies and we can patch things up and move on."

"This isn't a patch things up situation. You must be out of your mind if you think a simple apology is going to undo the anger I'm feeling now. Your trust card has been revoked and shredded, and when that happens, there's nothing you can do or say to get it back. I agree with your comment about moving on, but know you'll be moving on without me."

Mason shrugged. "You're just going to end everything like that? All the good times we had don't mean anything?

All the help I gave you and Jordyn with the clinical trial testing doesn't mean anything? All the money I saved you with the car repairs don't mean anything?"

"It meant the world to me at that time. That's when I thought I was dealing with a real man with true values. But now that your mask is off and I see the real you, none of those things in the past matter to me. So, I suggest you walk your way back to your car and leave."

Mason stood quietly for a moment, looking confused at Naomi's suggestion. "Ain't this a bitch? Here I am, coming to you to apologize and being a man about the situation, and you're dismissing me like this past year meant nothing to you."

"That's what happens when you put your hands on my little girl."

Mason displayed a wry smile. "Boy, if you only knew."

"What does that supposed to mean?"

Mason rubbed his hand against the stubble on his cheek. Then he put his hands up in the air as if he were surrendering. "Nothing. It means nothing. I'm leaving."

He slowly walked past Naomi as she moved a few steps to the side to give him room to exit the porch. She had her right hand balled into a fist as it rested on her thigh. Since she knew he now had issues controlling his emotions, she had to be ready for any subtle moves of aggression from him.

He proceeded down the walkway and onto the driveway. He briefly turned, giving eye contact, before continuing his way out to the road.

Naomi let out a massive exhale, feeling relieved he'd exited her property without doing anything stupid. But she also had a good hunch this wasn't the last time she would see him.

# Chapter 29

Trevor sat in the family room, in deep thought, waiting for Amara to arrive home from work. Kayla had relayed the news to him earlier in the day regarding the incident on campus with her car. He'd contemplated letting the campus police handle the situation; however, his patience was wearing thin. He could no longer see himself sitting idle and letting Kayla be threatened while on campus. He believed making his presence known to Mason might be all that was needed to stop any future incidents.

Amara arrived and walked into the room. She gave him a quick peck on the lips then stepped back with a puzzled look. "If I know my husband, I would say you either had a bad day at work or something else is bothering you."

"I talked to Kayla. Someone flattened her front tires in the parking lot on campus and left a knife sticking in her tire."

Amara stood with a look of concern. "Did she report the incident to the campus police?"

"Yes, but I'm not waiting for them to complete their investigation."

"What does that mean?"

"I'm planning to pay this Mason guy a visit tomorrow and let him know I don't appreciate what he's doing."

"Hold on a minute. Don't you think we should let the campus police do what they need to do before you start getting involved? Besides, we have no clue if he was even the person who did this."

"I don't think this is some random incident. In my eyes, he's guilty, and we need to nip this in the bud before it gets out of control."

"I don't think that's a good idea. I can tell you're on edge, and the last thing we need is for you to go up there with your gun, get in an argument, and God knows what could happen. And how do you even know where he works?"

"Kayla told me the name of his business. And I can tell you there's only one location coming up on Google Maps with the name Last Chance gas station."

Amara shook her head. "I can't let you do this."

"So, you're comfortable letting this man taunt and threaten Kayla and we just sit here and do nothing about it?"

"That's what the campus police are for. They're aware of the situation, and I trust they'll do their job."

"I guess that's where you and me differ. No one's going to look after Kayla like I do, and sitting back, waiting for the investigation to be completed, is giving this man more time to figure out his next plan. And what would happen if we wait and then God forbid he comes up to campus and tries to physically harm Kayla or Jordyn? I'll tell you right now, that's not happening on my watch."

"I get it, Trevor. I know you're anxious and upset—so am I—but there are better ways to handle this."

Trevor sighed but remained quiet.

"Give yourself time to relax, calm down, and clear your head. You're letting this situation get the best of you, and we don't need you making any rash decisions. I think if you show a little more patience and trust the campus police to handle this, I'm sure everything will work out fine. Can you do that for me?"

"Can't make any promises."

*****

Trevor awoke the next morning, about an hour earlier than normal. The room remained dark as the sun had not yet risen. He was physically tired as a result of his overactive mind keeping him up for a good part of the night.

He rotated his head toward Amara, who was sound asleep. It would be another two hours before her alarm went off. He thought about what Amara had said and tried his best to see things her way, but he couldn't fathom the idea of sitting back and waiting for Mason to make his next move. He imagined the knife sticking into the tire was only a warning shot, and if they continued to wait, things could get progressively worse.

Patience was not his virtue at the moment. He couldn't wait any longer, and inaction was no longer an option.

He'd previously mapped out the distance between his house, the gas station, and his job. If he timed everything right, he could leave the house an hour earlier than normal, allowing him time to have a chat with Mason at the gas station, and still arrive to work on time. He also realized his plan would ultimately hinge on whether or not Mason would even be at the gas station this early in the morning. He thought he would give it a try, and if Mason wasn't available, he could always swing by after work.

He looked over at Amara again to ensure she was still sleeping. If he played his cards right, he could leave the house before Amara awoke, and not even mention this extra stop on his commute to work. He knew Amara wouldn't be happy if she ever found out, but this was a chance he was willing to take.

He gently pulled back the covers and gingerly walked to the bathroom for a quick shower.

Moments later, he peeked out of the bathroom door to confirm Amara wasn't awake. He momentarily stood still as she shifted in bed, but with only a sliver of light coming from the cracked bathroom door, he struggled to see if her eyes were open. He waited until she stopped moving then continued getting ready, hoping she hadn't noticed him stirring around. He proceeded to get dressed and eventually exited the bedroom, making his way into the kitchen.

After eating breakfast, he sat quietly in the chair, second-guessing his plan. Maybe Amara was right and he was overreacting. Maybe he should let the campus police do their job. Maybe confronting Mason would be the absolute wrong thing to do. He wavered back and forth, weighing his options.

He reflected on his therapy sessions and the initial struggles he had dealing with the events back in Richmond. His therapist had always discussed the importance of recognizing whenever these anxiety-inducing thoughts invaded his mental space and not letting them be the driving force behind his actions. He could sense the impatience and agitation floating in his head, which were no doubt fueling his decision to want to interact with Mason. But the temptation to carry out his plan was too great to ignore. He couldn't see harnessing the kumbaya energy that Amara and his therapist believed in and forego his visit to the gas station. He would never forgive himself if he sat back and did nothing and something awful happened to Kayla or Jordyn.

He decided to push forward and pay Mason a visit. He contemplated how the interaction would play out. Without knowing anything about Mason, he figured this could go several ways. He knew it was important for him to have patience and practice restraint to prevent any chance of escalating his chat with Mason. But if Mason became aggressive with their chat, he couldn't promise his patience would stay intact.

He set his sights back on Amara who continued to sleep peacefully. He planned to send her a text, informing her that he'd left earlier than usual to prepare for an upcoming catering event. If his timing was perfect, he could leave shortly before Amara awoke and arrive at the gas station when it was scheduled to open.

# Chapter 30

Trevor examined his GPS to confirm how much more time was left before he arrived. He tried his best to envision having a nice and easy discussion. He had to find that delicate balance of not being too aggressive in his approach but still getting his point across so Mason was aware any further threats would not be tolerated.

"Last Chance gas station," Trevor said as he approached.

He pulled into the dirt-covered parking lot and immediately noted the station needed a serious facelift. He couldn't imagine this business getting many customers with the way things appeared on the outside. He focused his attention on two other vehicles in the lot. One was a dilapidated pickup truck parked to the side, and next to it was a black Chevy Impala.

He turned off the engine and sat for a moment. He heard a chime on his phone and saw Amara react to the text he'd sent earlier, indicating he'd left early to go to work. A part of him felt guilty for lying, but this was the only way to accomplish his plan without Amara getting worked up into a nervous frenzy.

He pushed the button to open the glove compartment, confirming the Glock was still resting inside. He figured he would leave the Glock in the glove compartment for now to make the situation a little less threatening. He then focused his sights on the oversized windows in the front of the building giving him a clear view of the inside. He noticed a few aisles of snacks and other miscellaneous items, as well as a counter with a register, but no one was present from his vantage point.

He double-checked the time and noted the station should have opened. He did see an open sign hanging on the glass front entrance door, so he imagined someone had to be inside.

"Let's see how this goes," he said before exiting his Tahoe.

He approached the door and entered. He surveyed the area and did not see anyone in sight. He walked to the counter and searched for a bell, or anything else to indicate his presence.

"Hello?" he called out as he knocked on the counter.

After a few moments, he heard a toilet flush in the distance, and then a gentleman eventually walked from the back hallway and greeted Trevor with a smile.

"Hello, sir. How can I help you?"

Trevor scrutinized his appearance, surprised at how far off the mark he'd been when he'd imagined what Mason would look like. He was shorter than he'd imagined and did not have a head full of hair or a beard like he'd envisioned. He was also much younger than he'd expected.

"Hi, I'm looking for Mason."

The gentleman looked at the time. "If you can hang out for about half an hour, he should come walking through the door. My name's Noah. I'm a mechanic here at the shop that works with Mason."

Trevor accepted the fact this initial trip was already a failed meeting attempt since he couldn't afford to spend any additional time waiting for Mason.

"Is it something I can help you with, or is your business strictly with Mason?"

"It's some personal business I need to handle with Mason."

"If you give me your name and number, I'd be happy to let him know you stopped by and have him reach back out to you."

"What time do you close?"

"We're open until nine p.m. tonight. You can swing back around later if you want. Mason will be here late to close up the shop."

Trevor noticed a few faded red blotches scattered around the wood-grained countertop. If that was traces of blood, he imagined this was where the confrontation between Kayla and Mason might have taken place. He also couldn't imagine a place of business would continue to interact with customers while blood residue stained the counter where transactions were taking place.

He quickly broke away from his trance, realizing he was holding his gaze a little too long at the counter. "Okay, I think I'll take you up on that offer and swing by later."

Noah gave him a questioning stare. "Is this about any recent work he did on your car?"

"Oh, no. He didn't do any work on my car. It's about something else."

"Okay, then I guess we'll see you sometime later today. Any idea what time you think you'll be back?"

"I would say sometime in the evening."

"You got it, boss. I'll let Mason know to expect you. But I still didn't get your name."

"Just let him know TJ stopped by."

# Chapter 31

Leah typed on her phone, responding to a text from one of her business partners. She was in the back seat of an Uber, coming home from T.F. Green International Airport after a two-day business trip to Charlotte. She worked as a construction consultant and met with stakeholders to determine the project feasibility of a potential commercial worksite. With a master's degree in civil engineering, she was more than capable of handling the job, but the travel demands were becoming too much to bear. She had aspirations of retiring early and living her best life, traveling the world. Yet, she knew this was nothing but a pipe dream. Since she was the breadwinner of the household and Mason's business continued to struggle, she had no choice but to keep working and pray each day their financial situation would improve.

She closed her eyes, thinking about what Mason had said a few days ago. She agreed with his observation that they hadn't spent much quality time together recently. She struggled to think of the last time they'd enjoyed a night out on the town. Her constant traveling did not help the situation and proceeded to drive a deeper wedge in their relationship. This was evident by the constant bickering that normally took place when they did spend time together. She did her best to think about the good times they had early on in their relationship. She'd hoped it would spark something and reignite the flame that now dangerously flickered and threatened to be extinguished completely.

She'd always given him some grace after the passing of his father, which had no doubt put a damper on his once vibrant personality and stripped away his zest for life. She understood this was part of the problem, but his attitude had recently changed for the worse during the past year, and she couldn't exactly pinpoint the reason why. Although, she did have her theory as to what might been going on and had a lead she was planning to follow. He'd always shown flashes of grumpiness during their marriage, and she'd noticed it was getting out of control lately. She did her best to remain patient and deal with the shift in his attitude.

The car slowed on the highway, momentarily jolting her out of the relationship concerns. She looked up ahead to see plenty of brake lights flashing on and off, indicating a build-up of traffic. She was surprised by the traffic since there were still a few more hours to go before the normal evening rush-hour frenzy.

Her mind drifted once more, thinking of what she could do in an attempt to add some spice back into her relationship with Mason. With their anniversary coming up in a few days, she thought a dinner date would be a great opportunity for them to reconnect, strengthen their relationship, and celebrate their marriage vows. She double-checked her calendar and confirmed her next travel date wouldn't be until late the following week. This would also be perfect timing from a financial standpoint, as she was expecting her bonus to come through in the next couple of days. She figured they could splurge a little with the extra money and make reservations at one of the steakhouses in town.

Even though these plans sounded good on the surface, her excitement was tempered by her hunch that Mason might not even be aware of their approaching anniversary.

During their five years of marriage, there was one other instance when he'd forgotten the date. And with Mason's recent attitude shift, she wouldn't be surprised if this year would make it the second instance of him forgetting. She was intrigued at how this would all play out since she had no intentions of tipping him off to the upcoming date. But if he did forget again, she was ready to give him a piece of her mind.

# Chapter 32

Trevor pulled back into the gas station parking lot after work for his second attempt at meeting up with Mason. It was nearing the eight o'clock hour, and the sun was beginning to set.

He surveyed the area and noticed the black Chevy Impala that was parked during the morning was no longer there, and in its place was a white SUV. He parked and squinted through the oversized glass windows and noticed a customer talking to a gentleman at the counter in the rear. The individual behind the counter looked nothing like the young man assisting him during the morning, so there was only one other option of who this could be.

Unlike the morning, the impending darkness brought about a whole new set of circumstances when it came to safety precautions. He wasn't sure if the young mechanic was still somewhere on the premises to help Mason if things did go sideways, but he needed to be extra cautious. Trevor was fully aware it would be much easier for Mason and his mechanic to pull off an ambush against him during the cover of night if things became heated. For this reason, he reached into the glove compartment and grabbed the Glock. He holstered it to his hip and pulled out the tucked shirt from his pants to help conceal the weapon as much as possible.

He stopped for a moment, thinking about Amara. It was bad enough that he'd lied to her twice during the day—once in the morning, and a second time in the evening when he'd told her he would be working late.

He tilted his head against the headrest and sighed. "Damn, Amara. You're not even here and have me second-guessing what I should do."

He knew if things did get out of hand and a physical altercation did break out, he would no doubt be extremely tempted to pull out the Glock, but he stopped short of thinking that he could actually use it. He couldn't picture coming back home and fessing up to Amara that he'd gone against her wishes, confronted Mason, and something terrible had happened.

He held his hand against the Glock on his hip and looked back at the glove compartment. He shook his head. "Okay, you win, Amara," he said before taking the Glock off the holster and placing it back in the glove compartment.

Without the Glock, Trevor's ability to protect himself had diminished significantly, but his days as an amateur boxer were not forgotten, and he was still adept at using his fists as a second line of defense.

Trevor snatched his head up as a flurry of movement caught his eye. An older gentleman exited the station and waved at Trevor as he approached the white SUV. Trevor focused his attention back inside and saw whom he believed to be Mason, sitting all alone by the counter, unaware his quiet evening was about to experience a shot of adrenaline.

Trevor exited his vehicle and contemplated how he would start the conversation. He knew this would be a critical part of attempting to keep the chat with Mason civil. He also understood the wildcard in this interaction would be dependent on how Mason responded to his request to stay away from Kayla and Jordyn. Trevor was mentally prepared to hold onto his patience for as long as possible and not be the aggressor.

He opened the door as a chime sounded. The gentleman looked up from the counter and locked eyes with Trevor, offering a friendly smile.

"Good evening, sir. How can I help you?"

On pure instinct, Trevor was about to smile but refrained and simply nodded. He wanted Mason to understand from the beginning this was no joyful matter and the normal pleasantries between a business owner and customer did not apply in this instance.

Trevor quickly surveyed the store layout, looking for any cameras that might be mounted on the walls.

"I'm looking for Mason."

"Wow, this is a first. Haven't had a customer come in and immediately ask for me by name." Mason eyed Trevor more carefully. "My business partner mentioned someone was in here earlier looking for me. Would that be you?"

"That's correct."

Mason's smile eased. "I don't believe we ever met before."

"No, we haven't. You can call me TJ."

"Nice to meet you TJ. So, I'm very curious as to how you know me by name and I don't know you."

"Let's just say I'm a friend of one of your friends."

Mason's eyes narrowed with suspicion. "I have plenty of friends and don't know which one you're talking about."

"Does Naomi ring a bell?"

Mason's demeanor shifted, and any joyful energy he was giving off immediately came to a halt. "How do you know Naomi?"

"As I mentioned before, she's a friend."

"What kind of friend are we talking about? Just an acquaintance? A close friend? Or something else?"

"To be honest, I don't think that's important. What you have going on with her is none of my business. But my concern is with my daughter."

Mason stood from his chair behind the counter as Trevor calmly shifted his feet to solidify his balance.

"May I ask who your daughter is?"

"I doubt you know her by name, so it doesn't matter."

"It matters to me. You have me totally confused, and I'm trying to make heads or tails of the situation."

Trevor rubbed his goatee. "Have you been up to Flagstone University recently?"

Mason furrowed his brow. "I've been there before, but it's been a while. Why are you asking?"

"Because my daughter's car was recently vandalized on campus and her front tires were flattened with a knife. Does that sound familiar?"

"Sorry to hear, but if you think I had something to do with it, you're completely wrong. And why would you even accuse me?"

"Based on what I know, you two have a history together."

Mason let out a small laugh. "Okay, I think I see where you're going now. So let me take a guess. The young lady who gave me this permanent forearm tattoo is your daughter," Mason said, looking down at his forearm.

Trevor simply nodded.

"I must admit I wasn't happy when she poked me, but I recognize it was probably my fault. I guess I got what I deserved, and I've been paying for it the past couple of weeks with my injured arm."

Trevor relaxed his stance as the explanation at least indicated Mason wasn't looking to pick a fight at this time.

"But I will say, I don't appreciate you accusing me of driving up to Flagstone to vandalize her car. I can definitely tell you it wasn't me."

"So, what else am I supposed to think? You said you weren't happy she stabbed you. So, who else would be looking to harass her? My daughter doesn't have any enemies that would do something like this that I'm aware of."

Mason put his hands up in the air. "Sorry, TJ, but I'm not the guilty party in this situation. And maybe you don't know your daughter as well as you think."

Trevor's hope for a peaceful and pleasant discussion was on the verge of going off the rails. He tilted his head up at the ceiling and closed his eyes momentarily to regain his composure. He then turned his attention back to Mason with an intense stare.

"Unless you know something I don't know about my daughter, we're about to have a problem."

Mason smirked. "I don't know if your daughter mentioned anything to you, but she was here a while back, before she jabbed me with the knife and flattened one of my customer's front tires in the parking lot."

"What are you talking about? Why would she even come here in the first place? And what would make her do something like that?"

"It's probably best you get those answers from her."

Trevor thought for a moment. "So, if this is all true—and that's a big if—do you have any idea who owned the car?"

"Unfortunately, no."

"Is there maybe some surveillance video on that date showing the customers who visited your business or maybe some paperwork you can reference?"

"I would love to say yes, but as you can see, my business is not too tech-savvy, and we don't have any cameras mounted on the walls. This is all part of my wish list."

"Was this a repeat customer? Have you seen this person before?"

"It's possible, but I'm not certain. Not sure what else to tell you."

Trevor placed both of his hands on the counter, in deep thought, before snatching them off after being reminded of the potential traces of Mason's blood that may have soaked into the wood countertop.

"Give me one good reason why I should trust what you're telling me is the truth."

Mason laughed. "I've been called many things in my lifetime but a liar isn't one of them."

Trevor kept his eyes trained on Mason. "I'm not sure what's going on now but if you're lying to me and had any intentions of getting even about the situation, I would implore you to steer clear of my daughter. Because I'll tell you right now if something happens to her, you can expect a second visit from me, and it won't be a pleasant one."

# Chapter 33

Kayla's leisurely walks on campus were a thing of the past. She stepped with some authority as Jordyn struggled to keep up with her long strides. They agreed to walk as a team as much as they could while shuttling back and forth to their classes. It was the middle of the afternoon, and the campus bustled with activity as students roamed around to get to their various destinations.

It'd been a few days, and there had been no further incidents since Kayla's car had been vandalized in the dorm parking lot. She'd been instructed by the campus police to park as close as possible to the dorm to keep her car within the security camera's view. The campus police were also on high alert and stepped up their patrols to help look out for any suspicious individuals or activity.

Kayla rotated her head from side to side, highly dependent on her intuition to help recognize anything out of the ordinary. "Were you planning to stay after class for your study group?" she asked Jordyn.

"No. We're planning to Facetime each other tonight instead of meeting in person."

"Yeah, that's probably a good idea. And speaking of classes, how are things going? Are you able to keep up with your work?"

Jordyn shrugged. "Doing the best I can I guess."

"Same here, but my best is pretty horrible right now. I'm struggling big time trying to keep up with everything and concentrate in class. The way things are going, I may lose one of my academic scholarships, and my folks won't be happy if that happens."

"I'm hoping the school will have some sympathy with everything that's gone on this month. Maybe there's some type of hardship circumstances you can qualify for to help keep your scholarship."

"That would be nice," Kayla said before thinking for a moment. "Um . . . I wasn't going to say anything because I'm a little embarrassed, but I signed up for mental health counseling on campus."

Jordyn's facial expression remained stoic. "I'm not surprised with everything going on. At least you have the courage to reach out for help. I probably need some counseling, too, but don't know if I'm ready to do that right now."

"Don't get me wrong, it wasn't an easy decision. I always felt I could handle things on my own and figured the tough times wouldn't last for long. But now I can barely sleep, I'm dozing off in class, having nightmares about me attacking random people with a knife, and being chased by a masked man. I'm getting tired of waking up with my heart racing and sweating through my clothes. I just feel agitated at every little thing. I'm not in a good headspace right now."

"I get it, and I don't blame you one bit for reaching out for help. This may sound cheesy, but if more people could have your courage to ask for help, then maybe this world would be a better place," Jordyn said.

"Yeah, you're probably right."

"By the way, when is your first session?"

"Tomorrow morning. I'm nervous about how things will go."

"Don't worry. These counselors are professionals, so I'm sure they'll do their best to make you feel relaxed."

"I sure hope so."

They both stopped upon coming up to a fork in the walkway.

"This is where we split. Forgive me if I'm about to sound like a parent, but text me once you make it to class," Kayla said.

*****

The next morning, Kayla's eyes shot open as another nightmare disrupted her sleep. She focused on the time, which read a few minutes before six. She touched her chest, feeling her heartbeat racing at an abnormally high pace. She took a few deep breaths to help relax and soothe her body's visceral reaction to the latest frightening scenario spawned from her mind. She glanced over at Jordyn, who was sound asleep.

Although she was nervous about the upcoming mental health session, she knew it was much needed, and she prayed it would help limit these night terrors, which seemed to be occurring more frequently.

She eventually dozed back off until her alarm startled her awake an hour later. She envied Jordyn at that moment since she didn't have any morning classes to attend, free to sleep most of the morning away if she wanted.

She pulled herself off of the bed and proceeded to get ready. She had to first attend her psychology class before her counseling was scheduled to start.

*****

A couple of hours later, her class had ended, and she was proud she'd stayed awake during the entire session. She knew the nervous anticipation for what was to come had kept her awake.

She grabbed her backpack and could feel her heart rate picking up as her counseling session was scheduled to start shortly. She didn't have far to go since the counselor was located in the same building. But, she wouldn't have complained if the session was farther away, which would have allowed her time to gather her thoughts and psych herself up enough to enter the room without letting her anxiety get the best of her. Instead of taking the elevator down two floors, she decided to walk the few flights of stairs and concentrate on controlling her breathing.

Minutes later, she approached the door to her destination before gently knocking. A female voice on the other side requested she enter. Kayla stepped into the office and immediately spotted a woman sitting behind a mahogany wood desk.

The woman smiled. "Welcome. I take it you must be Kayla?"

Kayla offered a smile in return. "Yes."

A small hint of relief enveloped Kayla as her first fear of seeing an intimidating older gentleman behind the desk did not come to fruition. She was pleasantly surprised as the more she stared at the woman, the younger she began to look. With her ebony micro braids falling on both sides of her face, smooth skin, and a dimpled smile, she could have possibly passed for a student on campus. Kayla continued to stand, not realizing she was gazing at the woman longer than she probably should have.

"Hi, I'm Ms. Crawford. You can have a seat," she said, pointing to the chair on the other side of the desk.

Kayla blinked a few times, waking herself up from this moment of surprise, and sat in the chair. "I'm so sorry. I'm a little nervous about the meeting."

"No need to apologize," Ms. Crawford said before glancing at some documents on her desk. "So, did I tell you, along with being a counselor, I'm also a psychic?"

"Um . . . no," Kayla said with hesitation.

"I bet I can read your mind right now."

Kayla shrugged. "Okay."

"I bet you're sitting here, thinking, how in the world is this woman, who looks like my classmate, going to be able to counsel me."

Kayla laughed. "I guess I'm thinking something like that."

"Don't worry. I get that shock and surprise look all the time from other students." She stopped and pointed behind her. "See these certificates plastered on the wall behind me? These all say I'm qualified to not only be your friend and classmate, if that's how you want to think of me, but also someone who's here to listen and offer you some sound advice to help you get through whatever problems you may be having."

Kayla nodded.

"I can also tell you I'm someone who suffered from anxiety and depression when I was in school, so I know the struggle firsthand. And this is what motivated me to get my bachelor's degree in psychology and a master's in mental health counseling. I want to help as many people as possible avoid going through what I endured."

Kayla smiled but did not offer to speak.

"So, is there anything else you want to know about me before you tell me a little about yourself?"

Kayla desperately tried to think of a question so Ms. Crawford could continue talking. She wanted to delay the attention about to shine on her for as long as possible. She was extremely tempted to ask Ms. Crawford what year she'd graduated from college, but the words were stuck in her mouth and refused to come out.

"No, I can't think of anything else right now."

Ms. Crawford leaned forward. "Okay, so let's get started on why you're here. Now, most of the students coming into my office imagine lying on a couch and confessing to their various issues and darkest secrets while I sit with a serious look on my face, taking notes. Is this how you pictured it?"

"I've seen that in plenty of movies but can't say I thought much about how it would go."

"I can assure you what you see in the movies is nothing like how I handle my sessions. Matter of fact, don't even think of it as a session. We'll just call it a casual talk between two people looking to figure out how to get through this obstacle course called life and avoid all of the self-inflicted pitfalls we create during our journey."

Kayla struggled to keep a smile from forming. She was conscious of the frequency in which she was smiling and imagined it would seem weird if every reaction she had to Ms. Crawford's talking ended with her smiling.

"I first want to start by saying I know this isn't easy asking for help, and I give you my utmost respect for having the courage to do this in the first place. So, if you have any anxiety about our talk, you should find comfort in knowing the hardest part for you is already done, and it was walking through those doors."

"I hadn't thought about it that way, but I guess you're right."

"On that note, tell me why you decided to give me the privilege of meeting you and starting our new friendship?"

"Well . . . I'm not sure where to begin."

"I'll make it easier for you. Tell me at what point did you say enough was enough and you realized you needed help?"

Kayla nervously tapped her heel against the floor, thinking of an answer. "I would say after waking up three nights in a row from nightmares."

"Okay. Now we're getting somewhere, but let's build on this a little. Were these your normal nightmares we all have from time to time, or was there some type of theme associated with these dreams? Or was there an event triggering these nightmares that you're aware of?"

"Yes, I would say from an event. Um . . . I had an uncomfortable confrontation with someone recently, and it kind of shook me up."

"Now, when you say uncomfortable confrontation, did this translate into something physical?"

"Yes."

"Are we talking about something physical falling in the category of being a criminal offense? Or something reported to law enforcement?"

It was at this moment Kayla regretted leading the discussion directly to the confrontation with Mason. She'd been trying with all her might during these past few days to avoid the mental images of the knife sinking into Mason's forearm and the blood splatter on her sweatshirt that followed. Discussing the situation forced her to relive the anxiety-inducing moment, which would most likely be etched in her mind for the foreseeable future.

She began to doubt her decision to reach out for help and schedule this session. She figured she could handle this all on her own like she'd done in the past, and not get a total stranger involved.

"I don't think I can continue talking about this. I'm so sorry I wasted your time. I should probably go now."

Ms. Crawford offered a sincere smile. "Please know my time is never wasted, especially when it comes to a conversation, which I know can have a positive impact on both of us. Most people would think this is a one-way street where the person being counseled is the only one benefiting from the talk. But I'm here to tell you that's so far from the truth. Allowing me to help you validates my decision to become a mental health counselor and would do my heart a world of good knowing I can potentially get rid of any stress and anxiety weighing you down. It could be a win-win situation for both of us. Now, with all that said, I would be extremely honored if you allow me the opportunity to help you as best I can. But I can't do that if you choose to leave now."

Kayla lowered her head for a moment. *She's really good at her job. Now I'll feel guilty if I walk out the door.*

She did her best to hold in a smile. "I see why you have your degree in psychology. You made it a lot harder for me to leave now."

"I don't want you to think you're trapped here. I'm not trying to hold you against your will. You can still leave if you're truly feeling uncomfortable with the situation. I won't take it personally."

Kayla puffed out her cheeks and closed her eyes before proceeding with a large exhale. She couldn't trust herself enough to return if she did decide to leave at this moment. The thought of what could have been would forever be etched in her mind if she didn't dig deep down and find the courage to stay and talk through her situation.

Her heart rate began to slow, along with her feelings of self-doubt. The spike in her anxiety leveled off enough for her to think with a clear mind. She suddenly felt more comfortable with the notion of staying put and seeing what help Ms. Crawford could offer. She'd said all the right things up until this point, and Kayla had a good hunch she was dealing with a more than reputable counselor.

"Okay, you win. I'll stay."

Ms. Crawford clapped softly. "Bravo. I think you made a wise decision. I'll leave it up to you on how you want to proceed. We can go in another direction if you don't feel comfortable talking about the confrontation you had."

"No, I can speak about it a little. Without going into too many details, I was trying to defend my roommate from an argument she was having with someone she knew and things got out of hand, which led to me injuring this person in self-defense."

"Are we talking about a serious injury?"

"It was serious enough that I'm sure this person needed to go to the hospital."

"I apologize for all the questions in advance, but did this incident happen on campus? Did this involve another student? And have you seen this person since the confrontation?"

"No, it was off campus, and it wasn't another student. And I haven't seen this person since the incident, but my car was vandalized on campus a few days ago, and I'm thinking the person that did this is the same person involved in the incident."

"I'm assuming you reported it to the campus police?"

"Yes, and they're doing what they can to keep me safe, but I'm still struggling to get over what happened and not feeling good at all knowing someone could potentially be coming after me and my roommate."

"Okay, and I imagine this is what's prompting those nightmares you talked about earlier."

"Yes. And it's not only affecting my sleep, but I'm struggling in my classes now—can't concentrate at all. I'm probably going to lose one of my academic scholarships, and it's been really rough trying not to think about what happened. It keeps playing through my head. And not to mention my social life has completely ended since I'm not going anywhere except to my class and back to my dorm."

"Does your family know about this?"

"Yes, my parents know and are doing what they can to help keep me safe, but it's a little hard when they live over an hour away."

"I'm so sorry to hear about all of this. Sounds like you're suffering from a little PTSD because of the incident."

"I guess so. Me and my roommate are constantly looking over our shoulders on campus to make sure we're not being watched or followed. I've never been in this situation before, and I'm having trouble dealing with it."

Ms. Crawford leaned back in her chair while delicately rubbing her hands together. "It sounds like you're doing all you can to protect yourself. I would continue to stay vigilant and be fully aware of your surroundings. I trust the campus police will do all they can to keep you both safe.

"Now, as for your nightmares and any anxiety you're feeling about the situation, just know this is a completely natural reaction to a traumatic event. It will take time to conquer any negative thoughts or feelings you may be experiencing." Ms. Crawford folded her hands together as if in prayer. "I will first and foremost say to give yourself some grace and don't beat yourself up whenever you're struggling with your mood or if you're feeling any fear. Can you promise me you'll do that?"

"I'll try."

Ms. Crawford stopped to take a sip from a bottle of water she had resting on her desk. "I'm going to talk about something that took me some practice to master, but I think it will help get you going in the right direction. Let me start with this question. Have you ever noticed when you're worried or upset about a situation that it not only brings your mood down but all those around you?"

"Yes."

"That's all a byproduct of negative energy. When you're under the influence of negative energy, it can completely drain your body and be felt by those around you. Most times, it leaves you feeling irritable, impatient, scared, and downright mad at everything and everybody. And the scariest thing about negative energy is it's a chameleon, which can shift and change form to disguise itself so you wouldn't even know you're under its influence. The longer this energy has a hold on your mind, the harder it becomes to even recognize it exists within you. Then the million-dollar question becomes: how do you fight an enemy that many times you can't even recognize?" Ms. Crawford paused. "I want to make sure I didn't lose you before I continue."

"No, I'm still with you."

"Good. Now, the answer to this question is simply being aware. When you become aware of negative energy, you can acknowledge its presence and act accordingly. This allows you to know it's attempting to take control of your mind and cause you mental harm. But a funny thing happens when you become aware and can see an enemy coming. In this instance, you can prepare and choose not to follow any negative thoughts seeping into your mind.

"It's like the old cartoon with the devil on one shoulder and the angel on the other. You become aware when the devil is attempting to talk and influence you, but you can simply choose to ignore him and not follow any self-destructive thoughts. You must know you have control of your thoughts at all times, meaning you can choose to think of all the good things going on in your life and all of the blessings you do have. I know I'm making this sound much simpler than it probably is, but it's the easiest way I can explain it.

"As I mentioned previously, it will definitely take some practice to figure this out, and I promise you it will make a world of difference when you're struggling with your mood by simply being aware when negative energy has a hold on you." Ms. Crawford stopped momentarily and smiled. "I know that was a mouthful, and I'm hoping it all made some type of sense to you?"

"Wow, that was deep. I admit I do have times when I'm not in a good mood, and it stays with me for a while. It's almost as if I just accept it as normal. So I can see how being aware may help me get out of that mood quicker." Kayla stopped talking and let out a small laugh. "Where have you been all my life? I could have used this talk a long time ago."

"I guess I was working on me first. I needed to get myself straight before I could provide you with any useful information."

Kayla peeked at the time. "So, what do we do now? Is the session over?"

Ms. Crawford laughed. "We've only been talking for about five minutes. I would like to make this session worth it and give you more than five minutes of my time. I don't know about you, but I'm just getting started. I have plenty of time to talk some more. Is there anything else on your mind you want to discuss? Or are you even satisfied with the bit of advice I've given you so far?"

For a hot second, Kayla pondered mentioning her family situation and her concerns about being adopted. But she felt that would be too personal of a conversation to have with a counselor she'd just met. And she also wasn't exactly sure how she would even broach the topic.

"No, I think I'm good for now. In this short amount of time, you gave me plenty to think about."

Ms. Crawford stood, and Kayla followed. Kayla's eyes widened, as she was not only surprised at Ms. Crawford's youthful appearance but also by her height, as both of their eyes were about level with one another.

"I see we have something else in common," Ms. Crawford said.

She reached out to shake Kayla's hand. "Please be safe out there on campus, and if there's any time you want to talk about something else, let me know."

# Chapter 34

Mason tapped his fingers on the steering wheel, wondering what was taking Leah so long. He'd been sitting in his car for a while, waiting for her to return from the apartment. She'd taken heed of his comment regarding spending more quality time together and had recommended they go out to dinner. He'd initially pushed back on going out on a Friday night after work since he didn't have the energy, but she wouldn't take no for an answer. He also didn't put up too much resistance to the idea since this was going to be her treat based on the extra money coming into the household from her bonus. Although, he was surprised she'd chosen one of the rather fancier steakhouses in the downtown area.

He leaned his head against the headrest. She promised she'd only needed a minute to go back to the apartment and grab something she'd forgotten.

While waiting, he shuffled through his phone, looking at the last text he'd sent to Naomi. He'd attempted to contact her one more time after she'd kicked him off her property, but she never responded. He figured he would wait until she calmed down to see if she maybe had a change of heart about getting back together. However, that hadn't been the case.

He'd enjoyed the year-long connection he had with Naomi, but the breakup wasn't all bad, since it had lifted a huge weight off his shoulders, and he no longer had to worry about sneaking around behind Leah's back.

As he was holding his phone, he realized this was the first time since the stabbing incident he didn't feel any pain in his forearm. He rotated his wrist and squeezed his right hand into a tight fist and noticed only a smidge of pain, which was a huge improvement from the last couple of weeks. He was relieved at his progress but still held a grudge against Jordyn's friend for causing him the physical pain he'd endured, along with the financial stress. And now he had the added bonus of her friend's protective father coming to the job and asking questions. He was content with the way he'd handled the visit to prevent anything from escalating, but Mason was completely aware if something did happen to the young lady, he could expect a second visit from TJ. Although, he wasn't going to let this deter him from doing what he felt was right to get even.

He began typing on his phone.

*We have a little fly in the ointment. I'll call you later to—*

Mason abruptly stopped typing upon hearing Leah tug at the door handle, which was locked. Mason put down his phone and unlocked the car door.

"Any reason why the door was locked?" Leah asked as she sat.

Mason shrugged. "Just for safety reasons."

Leah shifted her eyes at Mason's phone in the cup holder before looking back at him.

"Did you get lost in the apartment?" Mason asked, jumping at the chance to quickly change the subject.

"I received a call from one of my business partners to discuss a project we're working on."

"Does this mean you have another unexpected business trip to go on?"

"No, at least not in the short term. I'm free from traveling until the middle of next week."

Mason shifted the car into gear and pulled onto the street. "So, have you had any more thoughts of looking for another job where you don't need to travel as much?"

"I think about it on occasion, especially the times when my flights are delayed and I'm stuck at an airport. But I'm still trying to figure things out." She looked at Mason intently. "And what about your situation? Any thoughts of selling the business and moving on to something you're passionate about?"

"I am passionate about the business."

Leah raised one eyebrow in a questioning slant. "Oh, come on. You gotta be kidding me. I guess you've never seen the look on your face when it's time for you to leave for work in the morning."

"Do you expect me to leave with a smile on my face? I'm pretty sure the majority of the working population would rather be doing something else instead of going to work."

"Yeah, I can't argue with you there."

A few moments of silence followed before a small grin developed on Leah's face. "Do you approve of our night out?"

"Of course. Why would you even ask?"

"I want to have this on record that I heard what you said about us not spending any quality time together."

"Yes, and I do appreciate that."

Leah's eyes glazed over for a moment in thought. "I'm thinking back to the first time we met. Who would have thought a sudden flat tire on my car would have led me to your gas station looking for help? And the funny thing is, I would have normally not taken that way, but the highway was backed up, and I followed the GPS for an alternate route. You need to be thankful there was traffic that day or you would have never met me."

"I think you also need to thank the nail that went into your tire. I guess it was fate we had to meet that day."

"And here we are, six years later," Leah said while staring in Mason's direction.

The car cabin fell silent for a brief moment.

Leah grabbed her cell phone resting in the cup holder. "I don't know about you, but I'm looking forward to a nice meal instead of our normal leftovers."

*****

A half-hour later, they arrived at a local steakhouse and sat at a table in the far corner of the restaurant, away from the other patrons. This suited both of them well, as this allowed for a bit of privacy. The restaurant resembled an old-fashioned cabin with various wooden beams fixated along the walls and the ceiling. A dull glow of light radiated from a fireplace set on the adjacent wall to their table. The air was sprinkled with a scent of cedar, providing the finishing touches to the cabin-like décor.

"I like the ambiance," Leah said.

Mason nodded. "Hopefully, the food is as good as the nice setup."

Leah rotated her head, scoping out the area. "Doesn't this feel good for a change? Instead of us staring at the four walls of our kitchen while we eat?"

"I completely agree. This is exactly what I meant about us spending some quality time together."

A waiter came by to take their orders.

"I can't remember the last time I ordered surf and turf," Mason said. "I want to thank you and your bonus for allowing us the opportunity to enjoy this treat."

"I don't know how often this will be happening, so you better enjoy the hell out of your meal."

The waiter returned, delivering two glasses of red wine on the table.

Mason grabbed the glass and was about to take a sip before Leah put her hand in the air.

"Aren't you going to lead with a toast before we take a sip?"

"Ah, yes. Of course," Mason said as he raised his glass. "Congrats on your wonderful bonus that's allowing us this night out on the town, and cheers to us for finally spending some quality time together." Mason touched glasses with Leah, and they both took a sip.

He focused on Leah's facial expression, which, from his vantage point, had suddenly lost some exuberance.

"What's the matter? Is it something I said?"

She took another sip, staring at Mason with questioning eyes. "It's more about something you didn't say."

Mason eyed her, visibly confused. "I'm at a total loss. How did we go from having a great time together to you flipping the switch and acting like you're mad at me for some reason?"

"You haven't seen mad yet, but I'm about to be."

Mason put down his glass. "You got me on this one, Leah. I have no clue what's going on."

"And that's the problem. Isn't there something you should be telling me now?"

From the look on Leah's face, Mason quickly realized he had a serious dilemma brewing. He guessed she'd either discovered the missing money from the account or uncovered a clue that might confirm he was cheating. Then again, he couldn't have imagined Leah being so cheerful leading up to this moment if she'd previously known about one of those secrets, unless it was all an act.

Based on her stone-faced expression, he struggled to determine which skeleton in the closet she might have discovered. If he was going to admit to something, he figured he would choose the least hurtful confession and go with the missing money. But, for the moment, he decided to continue to play dumb to see if she might provide him a clue as to what she was talking about.

Mason grabbed his wine glass and took a large gulp. He proceeded to tap the glass with his index finger and struggled to maintain solid eye contact with Leah. He let off a nervous laugh. "I need a lifeline here. Can I phone a friend?"

Leah maintained a ferocious stare without a hint of a smile forming on her face. She remained quiet, not the least bit amused.

"Don't make me say it before you do," she said.

Mason was trapped in a corner and had the unenviable position of taking a wild swing at what Leah was thinking and hoped he guessed right. "Is this about the money?"

Leah's stoic facial expression morphed into a look of total confusion. "Money? What the hell are you talking about?"

Mason felt a rush of heat flush his face. Based on Leah's initial reaction, he realized he'd stepped into a massive pile of shit with no shoes or socks on. His wild swing had been nowhere near the target.

His mind attempted to concoct a lie about what he meant regarding the money, but Mason was never good at thinking on his feet, and any ideas he had of attempting to make up a story on the spot would only put him deeper into the hole. He decided it was time to put on his big boy pants and admit to what had happened.

"I thought you were talking about the money I needed for some business expenses."

Leah's eyes narrowed in speculation. "Do you mind giving me some more information?"

"I fell a little short last month on some expenses at the gas station and borrowed some money from our joint account. I had every intention of paying it back, but things didn't go as well as I hoped for the business from a financial standpoint."

An eerie silence followed. Mason felt like a suspect in the middle of an interrogation room, admitting to an unsolved murder. He'd never seen this look of exasperation on Leah's face.

Leah surveyed around the restaurant at the nearest occupied tables before leaning forward. "I'm speechless for many reasons," she said in a whispered but menacing tone. "First of all, I'm shocked and dumbfounded at your decision to go behind my back and steal money from our joint account to pay for a business expense and figured you could just replenish the money and act like it never happened. Now, I'll admit, I'm partly to blame for letting you handle our finances and pay our bills while I've been on the road, but that won't be happening anymore. Second of all, if you truly cared about me, our relationship, and our marriage, you would have realized today is our five-year anniversary. I was hoping this would occur to you at some point today, but I see I put too much faith in you remembering." She stopped and began typing something on her phone. "And last but not least, I hope you brought your credit card because I requested an Uber to bring my ass back home, and you're going to pay for this food we have yet to receive. And I'd appreciate it if you could wrap my food up and bring it home when you get there." She stood and took a swig of her red wine. "Happy anniversary and enjoy eating solo!"

# Chapter 35

Kayla sat on her bed, thinking about the advice she'd received from Ms. Crawford. She fought with all her might to be aware of the negative energy continuing to linger around her. Her efforts to replace any negative thoughts with positive ones were extremely challenged by a conversation she'd had with Trevor a short while ago.

He hadn't said how he found out, but he'd questioned her about the initial visit she'd made to the gas station when Jordyn had voluntarily disappeared. She'd thought that was a thing of the past, buried in the closet and safe from having to explain to anyone about what had happened that night. But she should have known that was too good to be true and found herself under a barrage of questions from Trevor.

She'd been caught off guard when he'd called and she struggled to explain what had happened at the gas station while trying to keep Ms. Fisher and Jordyn's situation private. She powered through her explanation as best she could and made sure Trevor understood the only reason she'd flattened the car tires was for safety concerns, to make sure no one would follow her as she fled. The discussion ended on a decent note, yet she couldn't help but feel like she was being judged for her lack of ability to be truthful with her parents. This was completely unfair in her mind, especially since she had a good hunch they were hiding something about her childhood and not forthcoming with whatever they were trying to keep secret. She'd made up her mind to sit with them in the near future and have a serious chat in the hopes of finding out more about her family history.

In the meantime, she did her best to avoid thinking about how, on a Friday evening, she and Jordyn were confined yet again in their dorm room and not taking part in any of the various weekend activities happening on campus.

She looked over at Jordyn, who had fallen asleep on her bed. She had ideas of following Jordyn's lead and closing her eyes until her phone buzzed.

Avery: *Whatcha doing now?*

Kayla: *No surprise, but I'm in my dorm, doing absolutely nothing.*

Avery: *I know you're trying to lay low, but there's a party going on in the campus center, and I really think it would be good if you could come with me to the party.*

Kayla: *You know I shouldn't be roaming around on campus in the evening.*

Avery: *I already thought about that and have it figured out. I can meet you at your dorm, and we can walk together to the campus center. There are still a lot of people on campus now, so we should be good walking there. Besides, no one is going to try and mess with you when I'm around.*

Kayla: *Lol. Are you my bodyguard now?*

Avery: *You can call me that if you want, but I swear if someone tries to approach us, I can burst their eardrum and scare them away with the loudest scream they ever want to hear.*

Kayla: *How can I resist that method of protection? But seriously, I'm more concerned with coming back to the dorm after the party since it would be later and not as many people would be on campus. And no offense, but I'm not sure how safe we would be even with your super scream.*

Avery: *No problem. I got it covered. We can call the campus police and schedule for them to escort us back to our dorms after the party. I've used the service before and had no problems.*

Kayla: *This sounds tempting, but I don't know if it's a good idea.*

Avery: *I promise you'll be thanking me if you decide to go.*

Kayla: *. . . I'm thinking. If I decide to go, what about Jordyn? She's sleeping right now.*

Avery: *She can come if she wants.*

Kayla: *I don't want to wake her up.*

Avery: *So let her sleep. You can just text her so she knows where you are. Does this mean you agree to go?*

Kayla: *I guess so.*

Avery: *YES!!! I'll be there in a half-hour.*

## Voluntary Silence

*****

Kayla secured the pepper spray and knife in her jeans pocket. She glanced over at Jordyn, who was still asleep, and sent her a text to confirm where she was going. Based on Avery's recommendation, she also called the campus police and requested an escort back to the dorm at 10 p.m. She was told to wait in the lobby of the campus center and an officer would arrive to accompany her on the walk back.

She did what she could to control her nerves, as this would have been the first time she ventured outside of her dorm building during the evening since she arrived back on campus after the incident. Although nervous, there was also a sense of excitement to attend the party. Even before the incident, it had been a while since she'd experienced a party at the campus center. And now this was her opportunity to add a little spark to her recent lackluster social life.

She made her way downstairs to the lobby to look out for Avery. She did notice a decent amount of students roaming around on campus, offering her relief to know they would not be alone on their fifteen-minute walk to the center.

She spotted Avery approaching the building with some pep in her step. She exited the dorm to greet Avery.

Avery opened her arms wide for a hug. "Look at you, all ready to party. I'm so happy to see you out on campus, besides going to your classes. I feel like I'm picking you up from jail after paying your bail," Avery said with a laugh.

They both embraced each other.

"Thanks for calling and inviting me." Kayla stopped and looked around. "I'm not going to lie, I'm still a little

230

nervous, but I trust you. I also never thought about using the campus police escort service, so that was a good idea."

Avery smiled. "You know me. I'm all about good ideas. Now, let's ease on down the road to this party. And don't worry; my vocals are warmed up and ready to break some glass with my screams if anybody we don't know approaches us."

"Okay, I'm counting on you."

They began to walk as Kayla gazed up at the night sky as if it were a rare occurrence. The stars were out in full force on the crystal clear evening. The temperature was a touch cool, but Kayla didn't mind. She was elated to be out after the sun had gone down.

"I heard some fellas from the basketball team were supposed to be at the party. Are you interested in meeting one of them?" Avery asked.

Kayla giggled. "I told you before that I'm not a part of that groupie life. I'm not chasing after anyone just because they're popular on campus."

"I get it. You did tell me before, but I figured this would be your best chance to snag a boyfriend with some height." Avery pointed to herself. "Now, me, on the other hand, I'll talk to almost any boy as long as he smells clean, his teeth are straight, his breath is fresh, and he's not dressing like a clown."

Kayla laughed. "Well, that knocks out about eighty percent of the dating pool here on campus."

"You're not lying. And that number may be closer to ninety percent," Avery said before displaying a more serious look on her face. "I know we're out here to have some fun but wanted to see how you're holding up with everything that's been going on."

"I'm hanging in there. Doing what I can to survive."

"So, have you had any more incidents with your car?"

"Thankfully, no. Things have been quiet—knock on wood. But I can't let my guard down."

"I hear ya. I'm happy I can add a little spice to your social life tonight and you can hopefully forget your worries and enjoy this party."

"Yup. That's the plan."

*****

They arrived at the campus center without incident. Kayla's stress levels had subsided, knowing she'd survived the walk and made it safely inside, amongst a large group of partygoers. She felt a sense of accomplishment and hoped this would convince her to venture out more frequently but still maintain a watchful eye on her surroundings.

The campus center was a popular gathering place for students. The main floor consisted of several lounge areas with various neon-colored sofas scattered about and positioned in front of large flat-screen TVs affixed on the walls. The lounge was no doubt a hot spot for students to come and watch the different varsity sports games taking place away from campus. There were a few rooms scattered against the walls of the campus center designated as quiet areas for students to study or take naps if needed. In addition, there was a mini food court, consisting of a coffee shop; a food market, containing an assortment of drinks and snacks; and a fast food restaurant with an all-inclusive selection of burgers, fries, and pizza.

Kayla and Avery ascended the stairs to the second level, housing several conference rooms and the grand ballroom where the large campus parties normally took place.

Kayla tried her best to relax as they approached the ballroom, yet she couldn't help but notice a few stares from students making her slightly uncomfortable. She wanted to believe her mind was overreacting to the situation based on her heightened awareness. There was also a good possibility this extra attention was due to her height, as there weren't many girls on campus listed at nearly six feet. She'd become accustomed to these stares during her teenage years, but because of the recent events, she had to consider eyes might have been on her for different reasons.

She felt a tap on her shoulder. "Loosen up, Kayla. You're looking a little nervous. I promise you're safe in here, so take a deep breath and smile," Avery said.

Kayla could hear the rumbling bass from the music reverberating against the walls before they even entered the ballroom. She took a deep breath as Avery suggested and flashed a smile.

They opened the door to a busy scene of students dancing, hanging against the walls, participating in large group chats, and enjoying the start of the weekend. The party atmosphere was exactly what Kayla needed as her mind drifted away from all the chaos of the past month and into a normal world of college students living life to the fullest on a Friday night.

Avery grabbed Kayla by the arm as they entered the fray and became engulfed by the dancing crowd.

*****

Two hours later, Kayla and Avery left the ballroom and descended the stairs to the main level. Kayla tugged on her cotton shirt clinging to her skin from the sweat produced by her dancing. They made it to one of the lounge areas and sat on a sofa to rest.

She extended her arm to reach out to Avery for a fist bump. "I want to thank you for getting me out of my dorm room. You were one hundred percent right when you said I'd be thanking you. I really needed that."

"I told you, girl. I knew what I was talking about. And maybe next time, we can bring Jordyn along, because I'm sure she needs to get out of that dorm room also."

Kayla observed the time. "It's almost ten, but I don't see any campus police yet."

"Don't worry; I'm sure someone will be walking through the doors shortly."

Immediately after Avery finished her sentence, two campus police entered the center.

Kayla and Avery stood and walked toward them. As they neared, Kayla noticed the taller of the two was the same officer who'd first responded when her car tires had been flattened. The other officer did not look familiar.

"I'm guessing you're the two young ladies who called for a campus police escort back to your dorms."

Kayla and Avery both nodded.

The taller of the two officers eyed Kayla. "I thought you looked familiar. You're the young lady I helped a while back with your car. Is it Kayla?"

"Yes, that's me," Kayla said.

"I see we meet again. If you don't remember my name, it's Officer Woods."

"Yes, I remember."

"Have you had any issues with your car since the incident?"

She shook her head. "No issues. Hopefully, that continues."

"Good to hear. If you're ready, I can escort you back to the dorm, Kayla." He pointed to Avery. "I'm sorry, but what's your name, young lady?"

"It's Avery."

"Nice to meet you, as well, Avery. You can go with Officer Campbell."

Kayla reached out to Avery for a quick hug. "We'll talk soon. Thanks again."

Kayla left the campus center with Officer Woods by her side.

"Did you say we're going to Dario Hall?"

"Yes."

"I see you're one of the lucky ones to be in one of the newest dorm buildings. And not to mention next to the main campus cafeteria."

"Yeah, that's what I've been told."

"So, tell me a little about yourself. What year are you, and what are you studying?"

"I'm a junior, studying biology."

"Good for you. I give you credit for being a biology major. Sounds like it's a lot of hard work."

"Yes, it can be tough at times."

"Are you local to the area or out of state?" Officer Woods asked.

"Um . . . I live in New York."

"Oh yeah? What part? I have family from Brooklyn."

"I live in Upstate New York, near Albany."

"Okay, that's far from Brooklyn. I've never been up there before. But you can ask me anything about Rhode Island because I've been here my entire life."

"How far do you live from the school?" she asked

"About a forty-five-minute drive. I live in Warwick."

"That's a long commute."

"Yes, but I've done it so many times that it doesn't feel too long of a drive anymore."

Kayla squinted up ahead as they approached Octagon Park. The area appeared entirely different at night, with only a handful of students roaming the landscape. The walkways leading through the park were illuminated in small stretches by dull yellow lights coming from the campus lampposts scattered throughout. Even though she had the benefit of the campus police escort, she remained vigilant with her eyes opened wide, scanning the area.

"Seems like it can get a little lonely out in this park at night," Kayla said.

"And this is why we offer police escorts, especially at night," Officer Woods said. "Even though this may be the most beautiful outdoor area of the campus during the day, it looks completely different at night. But don't worry; I can tell you we do a good job of patrolling the area once the sun goes down, and I'm not aware of any reported crimes occurring in the park since I started working here two years ago."

The talking stopped momentarily as only the sound of distant laughter from a few students in the park echoed in the night.

"Have you had any issues walking around on campus?"

"No, I've been okay."

"Good to hear. I'm assuming you're aware of the blue emergency call buttons set up around various places on campus if you ever need help?"

"Yes. Thankfully, I haven't had to use it, but I know what to do if the time ever comes."

They eventually arrived in front of the dorm entrance.

"Looks like the end of the line for you, Kayla."

"Thanks for walking me back here."

"It was my pleasure to escort you safely back to the dorm. I'm sure I'll probably see you around campus another time. Enjoy the rest of your evening."

# Chapter 36

Kayla entered Dario Hall, feeling invigorated by the unexpected night out with Avery. She hadn't realized how much she'd needed that outlet to help push her concerns aside for even just a few hours.

She approached her dorm room and wondered if Jordyn was still asleep. She opened the door, spotting Jordyn sitting up in bed while scrolling through her phone. She felt a sudden sense of guilt for not waking Jordyn to see if she wanted to attend the party.

"How was the party?"

"Not bad. It felt good to get out. I'm so sorry, but I should have woken you up to see if you wanted to go."

"I was tired, anyway, and probably would have said no."

"That makes me feel a little better." She stopped and peeked over at Jordyn's desk. "What's today's positive affirmation?"

Jordyn reached over and grabbed the calendar. "I'm a force to be reckoned with—strong, capable, and unstoppable."

Kayla smiled. "I'm loving these affirmations. They're always exactly what I need to hear and when I need to hear it."

"Yeah, I need to do a better job of reading them every day. I'm always a day or two behind."

Kayla sniffed under her arm. "I'm sorry if there are any unpleasant smells coming from me now, but all of that dancing made me sweaty. Let me take a quick shower, and then we can talk some more.”

*****

A short while later, Kayla sat on her bed, feeling refreshed from the shower. She waved to get Jordyn’s attention, whose face was buried in her phone. “I’m thinking about going home for the weekend for a change of scenery and to finally have the talk with my parents.”

Jordyn’s eyes widened. “Does this mean you’re going to ask them about the ‘A’ word?”

“Yes. I’ve been doing a lot of thinking, and it’s about time I know the truth.”

Jordyn sat on the edge of her bed and leaned forward. “Do you think you’ll be able to handle the truth if they tell you something you don’t want to hear?”

“I hope so. I’m kinda bracing myself for the worst.”

Jordyn put up her hands in prayer. “I hope it works out well for you.”

“I need to keep remembering all of these great positive affirmations to help get me through whatever happens.”

“What time are you planning to leave?”

“In the morning, after breakfast. I’m hoping you want to come along so I can drop you off at home?”

Jordyn laughed. “Hell yeah! You’re not leaving me behind to stare at these four walls.”

*****

The next morning, Kayla dropped Jordyn off at her house. She rubbed her eyes, attempting to wipe away the sleep she couldn't seem to shake off. She struggled to get a decent night's rest, which had become the norm.

Her mind drifted from one concern to another and gave her no shot at a peaceful slumber. With tired eyes, she continued driving and rehearsing how she planned to bring up the subject to her parents. They were aware she was planning to come home for the weekend but had no clue about Kayla's main intentions.

A short time later, she pulled into the driveway. She closed her eyes, attempting to slow her heart rate. They say don't ask questions you don't want to know the answer to. Kayla also realized if she didn't move forward with confronting her parents about this topic, she could never be whole. She could never truly believe in who she was without knowing her family history. She'd always felt like a garden plant without roots to anchor it to the soil. Now it was time she found out what kind of roots were hiding beneath her soil.

She grabbed her duffle bag and exited the car, her anxiety ticking up a notch as she approached the door. She'd planned to sit and chat for a couple of hours before blindsiding her parents with the conversation. A small part of her did fear she might get cold feet and not have the courage to even bring up the subject when the time came.

She sighed before entering the house. The family room was quiet, and she didn't hear anyone upstairs in the kitchen, indicating they could still be in bed. Her parents were normally early birds who rarely stayed in bed past 10 a.m., and it was already close to the noon hour.

She ascended the stairs and into the kitchen before she heard muffled talking coming from the deck outside. She opened the patio door.

"There's our baby girl," Trevor said while standing to give her a tight hug.

Amara followed with a hug of her own. "Did you eat breakfast yet? I cooked some pancakes and sausage links."

"No, I'm good. I had something before I left campus."

Amara patted the patio chair next to her. "Have a seat. As you can see, we're outside enjoying the nice weather."

Kayla sat and waited for the inevitable questions regarding school.

"How are things going on campus? Any more safety concerns or incidents we should know about?" Trevor asked.

"No, it's been fine since the tire incident. But I'm still not letting my guard down. When we're not in class, me and Jordyn are normally sitting in our dorm room, staring at the four walls."

Amara leaned over and gave Kayla another hug. "I'm so sorry you have to go through this but, hopefully, you understand it's for your own safety."

"Yes, I understand."

"You're home now, and we can go wherever you want. How about a movie or miniature golf and a nice dinner to cap off the evening? It's your choice. Just let us know," Trevor said.

"Okay, I'll let you know."

Silence followed, and Kayla wondered if she should abandon her plan to wait for a couple of hours and move forward with the questions now since they were both in a talkative mood.

*There's no time like the present.*

"Can I ask you both a question? Am I adopted?" Kayla said, cringing as to why she'd let this thought swirling in her mind fly out of her mouth so quickly and without warning.

Both Trevor and Amara looked at her with total confusion. They then eyed one another, as if to figure out who was going to respond to the question first.

Amara cleared her throat. "Why would you even ask?"

"I've been thinking about it for a while. I know we talked a little about it before, but I don't know much about my childhood, other than some memories here and there I can remember. I've never met any family, which I think is pretty odd for someone my age. I kind of went along with whatever you two would tell me, but it's been bothering me lately, and I think it's time for me to know more."

Trevor leaned forward in his chair. "I mentioned before we unfortunately aren't close with our family members and have very limited contact with anyone—"

"But why? Why are we not close to family? Did something happen to pull us all apart?" Kayla asked, feeling her agitation brewing.

Trevor grimaced. "It's . . . it's just a little complicated, and we . . ." He paused, glancing at Amara. "I thought it was best to let the past be the past and not burden you with any old family drama."

Kayla's eyes narrowed. "I appreciate you looking out for my best interest, but now that I'm older, I think it's only fair I know more about my family history." She looked back and forth between Trevor and Amara. "And I still didn't get an answer on whether or not I'm adopted."

For the first time in Kayla's life, she could see Trevor struggling with a conversation and being unsure of how to respond. He'd always had that air of invincibility while displaying supreme confidence in any conversation he'd been a part of and knew what to say no matter the circumstances . . . until now. On the flip side, Amara's reluctance to enter the discussion didn't make things any better in Kayla's mind. They were both walking on a tightrope with no more safety net. And Kayla had no plans to let them safely get to the other side without telling her the truth.

"No," Trevor finally responded.

Kayla tilted her head to the side. "Is that your response to if I'm adopted?"

Trevor nodded.

She let out a large exhale. She'd been setting herself up for the worst and was happy to at least hear she wasn't adopted.

Kayla focused her eyes on Amara as her choice to be silent remained a cause for alarm. "Do you have anything to add, Mom?"

Amara let off a series of quick blinks. "I hope you're relieved to hear you're not adopted."

"Yes."

"So, are we good now that you know the answer to that question?" Trevor asked.

Kayla shifted in her chair, clearly aware of Trevor's attempt to abruptly end the talk.

"And what about the family drama you mentioned?"

Trevor sighed. "It's probably best we don't go there."

Kayla clenched her teeth. In the past, she would back down and not push further with questions, but enough was enough; she needed answers—and needed them now.

"Sorry, Dad, but I'm done with brushing this subject to the side. I'm at the point now where I feel like I don't even know who I am. I feel like a complete idiot when talking with my friends and the subject of family comes up, and I have nothing to contribute. I have no experiences to share about family reunions or funny stories about my uncles, aunts, or cousins."

Trevor sighed. "Just so you know, you're not alone. I didn't know much about my family growing up—"

"But this doesn't mean I need to follow in your footsteps, especially if you have information to give but refuse to speak about it." Kayla set her eyes on Amara. "Come on, Mom! Aren't you going to say something? Don't you understand how I feel?"

Amara simply nodded but remained silent. Her eyes began to fill with moisture, and she blinked several times to hold back the tears threatening to crest her eyelids.

Kayla sat completely flustered at the voluntary silence being delivered by her parents. With the onset of Amara's tears, Kayla couldn't imagine what was hiding behind the curtain her parents refused to pull open. She was tempted to walk away for fear of knowing the truth, but she couldn't carry on with this enormous burden of not knowing about the family drama her parents refused to divulge.

Kayla closed her eyes, feeling the unrelenting negative energy stalking her and filling her mind with all sorts of ominous thoughts about the truth. However, she knew she had to find the strength to push forward with the conversation.

She focused her attention back on Trevor, locking eyes with him, no longer intimidated by his title of father and his role of being the protector of the family.

Trevor looked away and put his head down.

Kayla focused her attention on Amara, who sniffled periodically and dabbed her eyes with the back of her hand to help control the tears from flowing down her cheek.

Trevor eyed Kayla once more. "Why do you want to do this, Kayla? Can't we leave this alone?" he asked, sounding more desperate than confident with his words.

Kayla slowly shook her head while maintaining a cold stare and didn't offer to say anything further.

Trevor placed both hands on top of his head and let out a long exhale. He closed his eyes and mumbled something under his breath, as if in prayer. Then he opened his eyes and took a quick glimpse over at Amara before leaning forward in Kayla's direction.

"There was an incident that happened while we were living in Richmond. I was at work and received a call from your mother about somebody threatening her at the apartment we were living in. You were with her at the time, but just a baby, maybe a little over a year old. I left work and drove back to the apartment to find a man outside in the building courtyard, pointing a knife at your mother while she was holding you."

Trevor stopped talking momentarily and gathered himself. "I jumped out of the car and stood in front of you and your mother to protect you both. The man kept yelling and making all kinds of threats before he lunged toward me.

He cut me on the hand, and we both fell to the ground, wrestling for the knife. I was able to get a grip of the knife and . . . and in self-defense, I jabbed him in the stomach. I stood while he was on the ground, holding his stomach. I told your mother to call 9-1-1, and by the time an ambulance arrived, he bled out and was dead on the scene."

This was far from the story Kayla had expected to hear. She could only imagine the trauma her father must have felt after killing someone. She also knew if he hadn't stepped in, it could have ended much worse for her and Amara.

She stood and rubbed Trevor's back as he sat hunched over, looking straight at the ground. Kayla looked over at Amara, who continued to tear up and rub her watery eyes. She struggled to understand why there was such a strong show of emotion between Amara and Trevor if he'd done something heroic and saved them from a complete stranger threatening them. And it suddenly became evident to Kayla that there might be more to the story.

She sat back down on the patio chair. "I'm so sorry you had to go through that, but based on your story, it sounds like you were a hero to me."

Trevor raised his head and, for the first time she could remember, Kayla noticed a hint of moisture in his eyes. He eyed Amara as they stared at each other for a few seconds before Trevor turned his attention to Kayla.

*This can't be good.*

"I get a sense there's more to this story."

Trevor peeped over at Amara once more and cleared his throat before speaking. "After the incident, I was cleared of any criminal charges because it was considered an act of self-defense and there were witnesses to back up my side of the story. But soon after I was cleared, we started getting death threats from this man's family and friends. We couldn't leave the apartment without worrying about someone following us. It got so bad that there was one time when someone almost ran us off the road after tailgating us. I decided to purchase a gun to keep us safe and carried it around with me everywhere we went."

Trevor shook his head. "Even though I was cleared of murder in the eyes of the law, it led to a strained relationship with the rest of our family who lived in the area. I could tell they were mostly sincere about the situation, but I couldn't help but notice how uncomfortable they were whenever they were around me. Those few moments we did hang out with family eventually faded away to virtually nothing. I'm sure I was partly to blame because I wasn't the easiest person to be around. I was traumatized and depressed about what happened, and who would want to be around somebody like that? We eventually decided to move out of state to get away from all of the threats and ended up in Rhode Island to start a new life."

A bit of moisture collected in Kayla's eyes. She could now see why Trevor had always attempted to sidestep the conversation whenever the topic had been broached in the past since it brought back painful memories. But Kayla was still confused as to why the family would blacklist Trevor based on what she knew now. He was a hero and should have been celebrated for saving her and Amara's life.

Kayla took a glance over to Amara once again, who continued to wipe her eyes and remain quiet. She walked over and gave her a tight hug, rubbing her back. She then approached Trevor and leaned over, giving him a hug.

"I'm so sorry you went through all of that, but how could everyone abandon you and not consider you a hero after what you did? Me and Mom might not be here if you didn't save us."

Trevor remained silent.

Although she was sympathetic to what had happened, Kayla couldn't help but feel a tinge of annoyance coming through. She felt like this story was purposefully given to her in pieces and there were still some important details needing to be fleshed out.

"If there's something else I need to know, this would be the best time to tell me."

Both Trevor and Amara continued to look at the ground and refused to give Kayla any eye contact while remaining quiet.

"Hello? Is anyone going to speak up?"

Trevor glanced up momentarily in Kayla's direction before quickly putting his head down again.

Kayla's agitation grew as the silence wore on. "I may not be good at reading people's minds, but I can certainly read body language. And there's definitely something missing from this story. And since you both are always on me to be upfront and tell the truth, I'm asking you to do the same for me now."

Trevor continued to look down at the wood flooring of the deck.

"A painful truth beats a lie every time. And your refusal to tell me the rest of this story is still a lie in my book," Kayla said.

Trevor momentarily lifted his head and made eye contact with Amara. She wiped the tears from her eyes and gave him a simple nod.

Trevor's face tightened as he bit his bottom lip. "Before I tell you this, just know I love you more than words can say, and I truly believed keeping silent for so long on what I'm about to tell you was the best thing for your well-being."

Kayla closed her eyes, attempting to conjure up all the strength she could muster to endure what she was about to hear.

"The man threatening you and your mother was no stranger." Trevor stopped and swallowed hard. He looked Kayla straight in the eyes. "He was your biological father."

Kayla froze and had trouble registering what she'd heard. There were moments in people's lives when receiving some shocking news rendered them speechless, confused, and ultimately short-circuited their spatial awareness. Kayla was suddenly dropped in such a moment as she continued to stare at Trevor.

Her peripheral vision quickly faded, along with her sense of any sounds in the area. She could see Trevor's mouth continue to move, but she couldn't register what he was saying. Her trip through suspended animation abruptly ended upon realizing her lungs were not taking in enough air, leading to a touch of dizziness enveloping her head. She squeezed her eyes tight and took in her first meaningful breath in what felt like an eternity.

"I . . . I'm not understanding what you're saying," she said.

"Me and your mother were engaged at the time, and your . . . your father was an ex-boyfriend who would stalk us from time to time. We never thought it would become serious enough that he would threaten you and your mother's life."

Kayla turned her head toward Amara with wide eyes. She didn't say a word and waited for any sign from Amara to confirm this unthinkable turn of events.

Amara looked at Kayla with red, swollen eyes and offered a slight nod, a subtle way of validating the devastating news Trevor had dished out.

"I'm so sorry, Kayla," Amara said, struggling to get the words out.

Trevor wiped a tear trickling down his left cheek. "I know I should have told you a long time ago, but I really didn't know how."

The initial shock wore off as Kayla's emotions finally caught up with the thoughts processing in her brain. A flood of moisture filled her eyes. Her sense of space and time was back to normal, but she struggled to find words that would match how she truly felt hearing this unbelievable confession.

She stood on shaky legs and refused to offer any eye contact to Trevor and Amara. She calmly left the deck and entered the house without turning around to see if she was being followed. She promptly grabbed her duffle bag, left out of the front door, and approached her car. She did hear some commotion behind her but refused to acknowledge what was happening. She started her car and drove off, as she could hear Trevor's and Amara's voices trailing off in the distance.

# **Chapter 37**

Amara held her arms high, attempting to wave Kayla down and prevent her from leaving. "Kayla, please don't go!"

She watched as Kayla drove up the street and out of sight, stopping at the edge of the driveway with Trevor by her side. She immediately turned and, without looking at Trevor, marched back into the house. She didn't bother to hold the door for him and ran straight upstairs and into the bedroom. She grabbed her car keys on the nightstand and exited the room, almost knocking Trevor over.

Trevor put his hand out. "I'd suggest you give me the keys and let me drive."

Amara didn't push back since she knew her eyesight was impaired as a result of her crying. She promptly handed the keys to Trevor, and they both departed the house in search of Kayla.

Amara sat in the passenger seat, rubbing her eyes and attempting to clear her vision as she peered up the street to see if Kayla's car was within sight. She dialed Kayla's cell, but she didn't answer. A combination of fear and anger consumed her.

"I kept trying to tell you we should have told her a long time ago, but you didn't want to listen!"

Trevor let out an exasperated sigh. "Yes, and we've talked about this plenty of times. But as I've told you in the past, I never knew how I would even bring up the subject. It's one thing telling her I'm not her real father, but it's another thing to say I'm also the man responsible for killing your biological father."

"I admit that's a tough conversation to have, but at least if we told her sooner, she would have respected the fact we were upfront with her and didn't attempt to hide anything from her for so long. Do you know how hard it was for me to keep my promise to you and stay quiet about this as I waited and waited for you to finally say something to her?"

"I think telling her when she was younger would have been worse. There's no way a child can handle news like that. It would have been too traumatic."

"So, when were you planning to tell her? If my memory serves me correctly, you kept promising you would say something before she went to high school."

"Yeah, but she was already nervous about going to high school. It wouldn't have been fair for me to drop this bomb on her during that time. It would have ruined her high school years before they even started."

"And what about during high school? You also promised to say something before she started college."

"I know, but she was doing so well in high school with her studies; I didn't want to give her this news and risk messing up her grades."

Amara narrowed her eyes. "It sounds like, to me, you're making excuses as to why you didn't say anything."

Trevor remained quiet for a moment. "Okay, Amara. Do you really want to know why I didn't do it? I couldn't find the nerve to do it because I was afraid. Big bad Trevor Devereaux was scared. Is that explanation good enough for you?"

"Why didn't you flat-out tell me instead of making all kinds of excuses? A man can feel vulnerable or afraid sometimes. That doesn't make you any less of a man." Amara stopped talking and focused her attention back on the road. "We can talk about this some more later. We need to worry about finding Kayla."

Trevor continued to drive out of the community and approached I-95. The car cabin remained quiet as they both rotated their heads from side to side, scanning the area.

"So, where do you think she's heading?" Trevor asked.

"My guess would be Jordyn's house."

*****

Twenty minutes later, they neared Jordyn's house. Amara focused on the driveway, hoping to see Kayla's car. Not only did she not see Kayla's car, but Naomi's Corolla was also nowhere to be found.

Amara dialed Naomi's cell, but it went straight to voicemail. She proceeded to dial Jordyn's cell but also received no answer. She made one final call, attempting to call Kayla, and as she expected, received no answer.

"Of course, no one wants to pick up their phone," she said.

Trevor pulled into the driveway. "Let me knock on the door to see if maybe Jordyn is home."

Amara remained in the car as Trevor ran up the porch, knocking on the door. She saw the door swing open as Jordyn appeared. She quickly exited the car and ran to the porch.

"Sorry, but I haven't heard from Kayla. Is everything okay?" Jordyn asked.

"She left the house in a rush and didn't say where she was going. She's usually pretty good about letting us know where she's going, and we were just a little concerned," Trevor said.

Amara did her best to keep a calm demeanor, even if her thoughts were proving otherwise. She noted the time and said, "Do you mind if we stay here for a little bit to see if she shows up?"

"Sure, no problem. Come on in," Jordyn said.

Amara sat on the sofa in the living room with Trevor by her side. She focused on the goldfish swimming gently in the fish tank against the wall. Except for the sound of the air bubbles popping in the tank, the remainder of the house was silent.

Amara turned to Jordyn. "Can you do me a favor and call Kayla to see if she maybe picks up for you? I've been trying but haven't had any luck getting her."

Jordyn called and received no answer. "She's not picking up."

"Thanks for trying," Trevor said. "We're sorry to barge in like this, but to be perfectly honest, we had a little disagreement with Kayla, and she left the house upset. We're concerned because she wasn't in the best condition to be driving around."

Jordyn nodded as silence momentarily enveloped the room once more.

"Do you expect Naomi to be home anytime soon?" Amara asked.

"She had some errands to run, so I'm not exactly sure. If you want, I can call her if you need to speak with her."

"No, that's okay," Amara said before quickly looking at her phone, which buzzed with a call. Her eyes widened, hoping and praying to see Kayla's name appear on the caller ID, but that wasn't the case. "These telemarketers won't leave me alone."

Amara struggled to keep her anxiety from blossoming as she began tapping the heel of her foot against the hardwood floor. She gazed out the living room window, hoping and praying the familiar Honda Civic would come rolling up the driveway. It also occurred to her that if Kayla did see her car, she would probably turn right back around and leave.

Moisture collected in her eyes once more as she fought to hide her emotions.

*****

Fifteen minutes had passed, and there was still no sign of Kayla.

"I know we've only been here for a short time, but I don't think she's coming," Amara said, looking at Trevor. "We probably need to continue driving around to see if we can spot her."

"Okay, fine with me." Trevor pointed to Jordyn. "Can you please do us a huge favor and let us know if she shows up at your house or reaches out to you?"

"Sure thing, Mr. Devereaux."

# Chapter 38

Mason opened his eyes and stared up at the ceiling. He twisted his head to the right and winced in pain from the stiff neck that had set in overnight. He wasn't surprised his body would endure some form of discomfort since he was relegated to sleeping on the living room couch after his disastrous night out with Leah. He had no one to blame but himself and his absent-minded habit of forgetting special occasions. He actually felt lucky the locks hadn't been changed when he'd arrived home from his solo dining experience, which would have forced him to sleep in his car. However, the bedroom door had been locked, providing him no other choice but to sleep in his clothes.

He continued to stare up at the ceiling, kicking himself for completely guessing wrong as to what Leah had been thinking and admitting to taking money from the joint account. He did have comfort in feeling that was a hell of a lot better than her finding out he'd been cheating on her. He was happily content with pushing that skeleton much farther into the closet.

He relished in the fact he had a couple of more hours to lounge around before heading to the gas station. Saturday morning meant it was Noah's turn to open up the business, and there was no need for Mason to wake at the crack of dawn. Yet, it wouldn't have been all that bad if he left earlier, which would have given Leah less of a chance to see him and continue her onslaught of less-than-complimentary words.

"One . . . two . . . three," he whispered, struggling to sit up on the couch and keep his neck straight in the process. He grabbed the back of his neck and rubbed gently. Then he slowly twisted his head to the right, which didn't result in any pain. He attempted to twist his head in the other direction but stopped once the discomfort kicked in. He figured a hot shower might help loosen up his neck, but that meant gaining access to the bedroom for a change of clothes and having to muster up the energy to deal with Leah once more.

He grunted upon standing and shuffled over to the bedroom door before twisting the knob to find it was still locked.

He tapped lightly. "Are you up, Leah?"

His question was followed by complete silence.

He knocked again, but a little harder. "Leah, I need to get in there to grab a change of clothes. Can you let me in, please?"

He finally heard movement on the other side of the door, but Leah remained quiet.

"Okay, I give up. You proved your point. And just so you know, my sleep on the couch was horrible, and I woke up with a stiff neck. So, if you intended to make me feel uncomfortable sleeping on the couch, it absolutely worked, and I'm paying for it now." Mason paused to listen out for any response but heard nothing.

"Come on, Leah. Enough playing games. Will you open the door?"

After the silence persisted, Mason plodded his way back to the couch in defeat and eased back down to sit. As soon as he made contact with the couch, he heard the lock on the bedroom door click.

"Of course, you wait until I sit back down," he whispered.

He stood once more and approached the bedroom door before slowly opening it. He surveyed the room to see Leah sitting up in bed. She stared at him and didn't offer to say anything. Mason saw this as an opportunity to grab his clothes and run out before Leah could assault him with any more words.

After grabbing his last article of clothing, he took a step to leave before his luck ran out.

"Does the number two ring a bell?" she asked.

He stopped in his tracks and said, "No."

"Not that I'm counting, but that's the number of times you forgot our anniversary in the five years we've been married. And based on my quick calculation, that's forty percent of the time."

He stood still with a solemn look on his face. "All I can say is I'm sorry, and I'll make it up to you."

"That's the same bullshit you gave me before, and I'm still waiting for you to make it up to me—whatever that means." She shook her head in disgust. "What happened to the man who used to give me flowers once a month or surprise me with a night out on the town every once in a while?"

"I'm still the same man, a little older, a little more worn down, and a little more forgetful."

"Are you breaking down because you passed your marriage warranty? Five years or two forgotten anniversaries, whichever comes first? And in your case, they both happened at the same damn time."

"Is this where I'm supposed to laugh?" Mason sighed heavily. "Look . . . I said I was sorry. I didn't forget our anniversary on purpose. I just have a lot on my mind."

"And our fifth anniversary wasn't one of those things on your mind? What else do you have going on in that brain of yours that made you forget our special occasion?"

"I don't know. If I'm being honest, it seems like we've been drifting apart these past couple of years. I know we haven't been able to spend much time together with you traveling, but I understand work is a priority."

"Is this the same excuse you have for the other time you forgot our anniversary? Which, by the way, was before I started traveling with this new job. We were spending more time together back then, so what made you forget then?"

Mason tilted his head to the side. "Do you get some type of joy out of me being your personal piñata?"

"I wouldn't treat you like a piñata if you didn't deserve to be hit."

"I really don't have the energy to argue with you now. I just want to take my shower, eat breakfast, and drag myself to work. Is that okay with you?"

Leah glared at him for a moment. "Since you're being honest, I'll return the favor and let you know I'm struggling to hold back the thought you may be hiding something else from me. You up for playing the guessing game again so we can see what other skeletons come flying out of your mouth?"

"The only secret I had was the one I told you yesterday," he said, staring back at Leah.

Leah continued to look at him without saying a word.

"So, are we good now? Can I go take my shower?"

Leah nodded. "And before you ask, I think another night on the sofa is in your future."

# Chapter 39

Jordyn dialed once more, hoping Kayla would pick up, to no avail. She could only imagine what Kayla might have found out that had caused her to flee the house in such a hurry. Her best guess was she received confirmation she was adopted. Jordyn couldn't fathom how Kayla must have felt hearing that news. She began typing on her phone.

*Your parents came by my house, looking for you. Hope you're okay. Please reach out to me as soon as you can.*

Jordyn also quickly realized how Kayla must have felt when she'd performed her disappearing act and had left her in the dark over that one weekend, even if those circumstances were a little different.

Her mind raced, thinking about all of the ominous possibilities that could be occurring at this moment. She regretted not having a car to help search for Kayla. She wondered if she had decided to make her way back to school, which was the only other destination Jordyn could think of.

She slowly rocked back and forth on the porch swing, gripping her phone tightly, waiting for any sound effect on her phone to go off, indicating Kayla's attempt to communicate.

Jordyn looked up the road and spotted Naomi's Corolla approaching. Naomi pulled up into the driveway, and before she could turn off the engine, Jordyn jogged to the car.

"We have a little situation here. Kayla's parents showed up at the house a short time ago, looking for her."

"Wait, what are you talking about?"

"They had some type of disagreement with Kayla, and she ran out of the house, upset, and they have no clue where she was going."

"I'm assuming you all tried reaching out to her?"

"Yes, but she's not responding."

"Okay. Grab your keys and lock the front door. We can drive around town to see if we can find her."

*****

For the next half hour, they drove around the town of Wakefield, looping through a few of the commercial areas and carefully scanning the streets for any sign of Kayla's Honda Civic.

"Can you think of any places around town you know she likes to go?" Naomi asked.

"I'm thinking she may have gone back to Flagstone."

"I thought about that, too. I guess that's our next stop."

"I figured that would be part of the plan, so I brought my school ID. I'll check the dorm room once we get there. Hopefully, my hunch is right."

*****

An hour later, Naomi and Jordyn arrived on campus. A light rain had begun to fall, limiting the amount of foot traffic on campus. Octagon Park was relatively empty except for a few students briskly walking around with either hoods or umbrellas covering their heads. If Kayla had come back to campus, Jordyn knew there would be little chance she would be out walking around in the rain.

Outside of their dorm room, Jordyn couldn't think of any other destination for Kayla to go on campus. It was all or nothing, and she hoped their search would end at the dorm room.

Naomi parked in the lot behind Dario Hall. Jordyn's eyes focused on the first row of parked cars near the building. Ever since the tire incident, Kayla had been parking her car in that location to remain in view of the outside dorm cameras. Although, Kayla's Civic was nowhere to be found.

"I'll be back," Jordyn said.

She reached for an umbrella sitting on the floor behind her and exited the car. She gave a quick scan of the parking lot to see if she might have missed Kayla's car. With no luck, she shuffled her way inside the dorm. After scanning her ID to enter the lobby, she walked briskly down the hall, envisioning Kayla sitting on her bed when she entered the room.

She arrived at the door, inserted the key, and pushed the door open. She took a few steps in and immediately set her sights on Kayla's bed, which was empty. She focused on the cracked bathroom door, but there was no light emanating from inside, ending any hopes of finding Kayla in the room. She walked farther inside to make sure Kayla's duffle bag wasn't sitting around anywhere, indicating she might have come back at one point.

Jordyn sighed. "Where are you, Kayla?"

She dialed her number once again, which went straight to voicemail. Then Jordyn stood with her hands on her hips, contemplating what to do next. She quickly ran through her contact list and dialed Avery's number.

"And what do I owe the pleasure of speaking to you, Jordyn? You rarely call me. Is everything okay?" Avery asked.

"Depends on how you answer my question. Is Kayla with you?"

"No. I thought she mentioned she was going home this weekend."

"She did, but from what I've been told, she had some big argument with her parents and left her house upset, but didn't say where she was going."

"How did you find that out?"

"Her parents came to my house in a panic, looking for her, and told me what happened."

"Oh, that's not good. Where are you now? Do you need me to search for her on campus?"

"I'm on campus now. I'm calling from our room; she's not here."

"I'm assuming you tried calling or texting her?"

"Yes, but of course she's not picking up."

"Okay. I'm sitting in my dorm now. I can throw on something and run around campus a little bit to see if I can find her."

"Sounds good. Please let me know if you hear from her."

Jordyn exited the room, making her way downstairs and back to the car.

"No luck. She's not in the room."

Naomi closed her eyes and leaned her head against the headrest. "I'd say we call her parents to see if they have any updates."

Jordyn dialed. "Hi, Mrs. Devereaux. I'm checking in to see if you had any luck finding Kayla?"

"Unfortunately, no. We've been checking all around our area, and now we're making our way up to the school."

"We're at the school now, and we can't find her. She's not in our room, which was the only place I can think she would go on campus. I'm sorry, but we should have called you earlier and told you we were heading up here. Do you want to speak with my mom?"

"No, that's okay. I'll let Mr. Devereaux know you're already on campus, and we'll continue looking in town. Please let us know the minute you have any new information."

Jordyn disconnected.

"I'm trying my best to remain calm, but the longer we can't find her, the more worried I get. Have you tried calling her again?" Naomi asked.

"I've called about five times in the past hour and sent about the same amount of text messages." Jordyn grimaced. "Kayla is pretty levelheaded, so I trust she wouldn't do anything that would put herself in any danger."

"I hope you're right," Naomi said as she started the car. "It's been a long afternoon. I say we look around campus a little more, and if we don't find her, we should end our search for the day and try again tomorrow. Unless she shows up between now and then."

*****

Jordyn's stomach grumbled as they exited the campus. It was late in the afternoon, and she hadn't eaten anything since having breakfast.

"There's an Italian restaurant about a mile from campus that has some pretty good pizza. Are you okay if I place a to-go order and we pick it up on our way home to eat for dinner?"

"I'm good with that, darling. I don't think we have many leftovers at home, so it makes sense to pick something up."

Naomi pulled into the parking lot of Rusty's Italian Restaurant. She surveyed the lot for an open spot, which was few and far between. She eventually found parking available, off to the side of the restaurant.

"I guess the food here is good based on the crowded parking lot," Naomi said before shutting off the engine.

"I'm sure the order isn't ready yet since we got here a little early," Jordyn said. She studied her phone, making sure she hadn't missed any text messages or calls from Kayla. "So, how long do we need to wait before we can report someone missing?"

"It's a good chance Mr. and Mrs. Devereaux have already reported her missing. I'd say, once we get home, we call them and get an update on their search unless they call us first."

Jordyn tried calling Kayla again.

"Don't you think you've called enough?"

"Probably, but you never know if, by some chance, she picks up on the tenth time."

Jordyn looked at the time after waiting a while longer. "Okay, I think the pizza should be ready. Be back in a few."

Jordyn exited the car and walked across the parking lot, toward the entrance. Her eyes suddenly widened with alarm upon seeing a familiar car parked. It wasn't the exterior of the car that caught her attention, but the distinct red disco ball hanging from the rearview mirror inside.

She slowed her gait as she peered in through the windshield to see if there were any occupants inside. After confirming the car was empty, she rotated her head, scanning the parking lot to see if anyone was in the area. The grumbling in her stomach was replaced with a nervous knot, not knowing if she was being watched.

She neared the entrance, keeping a watchful eye on any activity with patrons flowing in and out of the restaurant. She watched four young gentlemen leave as she purposely stopped walking, putting her head face-first into the phone, and glanced back to see which direction they were heading. Her attention then shifted away once she noticed they were walking in another direction, away from the car. She then set her sights on two gentlemen sitting on a bench by the restaurant. At a glance, they both looked to be middle-aged with one wearing a dingy white baseball cap and the other displaying a clean-shaven head. Jordyn couldn't immediately tell if they were together since their faces were buried in their phones. Neither one of them bothered to look up as Jordyn passed by to enter the restaurant.

Jordyn opened the door and was immediately greeted by a large number of customers dining in and others in line for takeout. There was a row of booths running alongside the right edge of the wall with nickel-plated pendants hanging from the ceiling, providing the necessary light for patrons to eat. The left side of the restaurant contained a smaller number of booths, due to sharing space with the takeout counter. An assortment of voices could be heard throughout the restaurant, along with the clanging of silverware against plates as people indulged in their food.

Jordyn inhaled deeply to calm her senses after realizing there was no way she could concentrate on every person in the restaurant without her brain suffering from information overload. Instead, she observed each booth and, through the process of elimination, weeded out the groups she felt, in her eyes, were not possible suspects. She also had to consider the customers in line for takeout.

Jordyn felt awkward staring at customers since her normal behavior entering any establishment was to get in and out as fast as she could without paying too much attention to those around her. Her nervousness increased upon noticing some individuals providing eye contact as she looked their way.

She stood in the takeout line and waited, with four customers ahead of her. She continued to glance around, picking up on the varied conversations going on around her.

"Have you been waiting long?"

Jordyn jumped at the unexpected voice. She turned to see the gentleman in the white baseball cap standing behind her. His baseball cap had seen better days, but he appeared to be a well-groomed man otherwise, with a clean-shaven face and sporting a red T-shirt and faded blue jeans.

"No, not yet at least."

"That's good. I just got here to order some takeout. Hopefully, it won't take too long. I should have done the smart thing and ordered ahead."

Jordyn forced a smile. "Yeah, it's pretty busy."

"Have you eaten here before?" the man asked.

"Yes, it's one of my favorite places to eat," Jordyn said, attempting to inject energy into her response.

"This is my first time here, but if the crowd is any indication, I'm thinking the food is probably good."

Jordyn nodded without providing any additional feedback. Her social battery was extremely low, and she preferred not to carry on any further with this unexpected interaction. She also hoped this gentleman felt the same and wasn't a chatterbox by nature.

She focused her attention back in front of her, as she was next in line. Luckily, the conversation had ceased, and Jordyn eventually stepped forward to receive the pizza pie she'd ordered.

Out of common courtesy, she waved at the gentleman before departing and said, "Have a good evening, sir."

He smiled and waved. "*Adios*, young lady."

She made her way toward the exit with the pizza box in hand. She thanked an older woman for holding the door for her as she exited.

After taking a few steps into the parking lot, she heard a voice trailing behind her.

"Excuse me, young lady."

She twisted her head around to see the same gentleman with the white baseball cap. "Sorry to disturb you again, but I thought you looked very familiar when we were talking inside. Do you go to Flagstone?"

Jordyn instinctively shook her head. "Uh . . . no."

The gentleman stared with squinted eyes. "Are you sure?"

"Yes," Jordyn said to reconfirm her lie.

"That's very odd. I could have sworn I saw you leaving Dario Hall a short time ago."

Jordyn swallowed, attempting to combat the dryness in her throat. Her hands grew clammy, but she couldn't tell if it was due to holding the hot pizza box. "Sorry, but that wasn't me. I . . . I need to go now."

"Hold on. Why are you in such a rush?"

Jordyn leered at him, with an edge of impatience mixing in with her fear. "I told you I don't go to Flagstone, and I also told you I need to go. So, please get out of my face!" Without any further hesitation, she started walking briskly away from the gentleman.

"Sorry, we couldn't talk more. Can you do me a huge favor and tell your roommate I said hello," the man shouted in her direction.

Jordyn bit her bottom lip, and her muscles tightened upon hearing his comment. There was no doubt in her mind she'd just come face-to-face with the mystery car driver. She wasn't sure of his intentions with that comment, but if taunting was a criminal offense, he had just committed first-degree murder in her mind.

She jogged back to the car and didn't turn around for fear he might be following her.

She quickly sat in the car, placed the pizza box on the back seat, and said, "Can we please go? Like, right now?"

"What's the matter? You act like you've seen a ghost. Is everything okay?"

Jordyn hesitated to speak, thinking about whether she ever mentioned the story of the car to her mother. "I'll tell you later, but can we please go?"

Naomi shrugged and started the car. Jordyn slouched far down in the seat.

"JoJo! Don't play around with me now. What's going on? Who are you trying to hide from?"

Jordyn remained quiet as Naomi drove out of the parking lot and onto the street. She eventually raised herself back up in the seat. "Um . . . I don't know if I told you, but Kayla's car was vandalized on campus a couple of weeks ago. Someone punctured her front tires with a knife."

"Oh, no. Sorry to hear. So . . . what does that have to do with you ducking in your seat?"

"I'm sure I just met the person who did it."

"And does this person have something against you? Or better yet, does this person have something against Kayla?"

"Yes to your Kayla question, and I don't know about me. I think it's probably guilt by association. He knows I'm her roommate, and he made a comment about it. I didn't feel comfortable talking to him and just wanted to leave and go home. I also think he may have been following us."

"Following you and me, or you and Kayla on campus?"

"You and me. He said he saw me come out of Dario Hall not too long ago. And now we both end up at this restaurant. I don't think that's a coincidence."

Naomi looked in the rearview mirror. "I hope you're wrong, but I'll keep my eye out behind us." Naomi stopped talking momentarily and displayed a wrinkled brow. "And what could sweet ol' Kayla have done to get someone mad at her?"

"It's a long story, Mom. Can we stop talking about it now?"

"Okay. I see you're a little agitated. I'll leave it alone for now."

The rain had stopped, and the sun made a short-lived appearance before it descended beyond the horizon. Naomi sped along the local two-lane route, with no streetlights. A thick cluster of pine trees lined both sides of the road.

She squinted in the rearview mirror as a set of headlights came into view.

"Glad to see we're not the only ones on this lonely road," she said.

Jordyn leaned over, squinting into the sideview mirror. "Is it just me or is that car moving up on us a little fast?"

"If the person is in such a hurry, they can easily go around us. There's no one else coming in the opposite direction."

Moments later, the vehicle came within a few feet of Naomi's bumper and proceeded to tailgate, with no apparent interest in moving around them.

"What the hell is that car doing?" Naomi asked.

Jordyn squinted once again in the sideview mirror, struggling to get a glimpse of the silhouette inside the car. "I can almost guarantee that's the same man I was trying to get away from."

The driver began flicking their high beams and intermittently blowing their horn.

"Go around me, asshole!" Naomi yelled as she pressed on the accelerator to try to create more distance between them.

The mystery vehicle continued with the pursuit and sped up to keep pace.

Jordyn pushed her right hand up against the dashboard, attempting to brace herself from the high rate of speed brought on by this unexpected chase.

"It might be a good idea to slow down a little, Mom. I think I see a curve coming up ahead."

With the speedometer pushing seventy, Naomi didn't have much time to slow before the approaching curve. She glimpsed in the rearview mirror and noticed the psycho driver must have been familiar with the road because they had already decelerated. She pressed on the brake, doing her best to limit her speed before the curve was upon them.

"Hold on!" she shouted as she pulled the steering wheel to the right. The rear tires temporarily lost their grip on the pavement. Naomi could feel the rear of the car sliding into the oncoming lane.

Jordyn put both hands on the dashboard and closed her eyes to brace for possible impact. The rear tires suddenly regained traction, allowing Naomi the chance to safely negotiate the turn.

"Thank God," she said.

She looked back in the rearview mirror and saw the headlights from the mystery driver had cleared the turn and continued to pursue her car.

Jordyn took a glimpse at her phone. "The GPS is showing the highway is only a couple of more miles up ahead."

Naomi kept driving, constantly looking in the rearview mirror to confirm the distance between them and the trailing car.

"Look out, Mom!" Jordyn said, eyes wide.

Naomi observed a deer running across the road in front of them. She slammed on her brakes as the car veered to the right and missed sideswiping the deer by a few feet. She struggled to maintain control as the car skidded to a stop, partially blocking both lanes. The deer continued to bound its way across the road and disappeared into the woods.

Unfortunately, there was no time to experience any sense of relief as the car behind came barreling in their direction. Both Naomi and Jordyn closed their eyes as the car veered sharply to the left in an attempt to avoid them. The car successfully navigated around them but could not maintain control as it ran off the road and catapulted into the woods. An ear-splitting bang could be heard as smoke suddenly billowed from the car's impact with a tree.

Jordyn cupped her hands around her nose and mouth in disbelief.

"Are . . . are you okay?" Naomi asked, rubbing Jordyn's arm.

Jordyn was at a loss for words and could only offer a slow nod.

Naomi took her foot off the brake and slowly drove her car to the side of the road, out of the way of any oncoming traffic.

"What should we do?" Jordyn asked, her body trembling uncontrollably.

"We need to get this person some help. Call 9-1-1!"

# Chapter 40

Trevor sat on the deck as the light emanating from the outdoor wall lantern reflected the silhouette of a man defeated. With slumping shoulders and a beer in hand, he peered out into the darkness of the backyard. He always dreaded the moment when Kayla would find out he wasn't her biological father. He'd thought about how he would tell her and what her initial reaction would be. He'd imagined her reaction wouldn't have been a pleasant one and thought he could handle the moment. But what had transpired during the day was a true wake-up call and presented him with a bitter dose of reality. He hadn't been ready for what happened. He was never going to be ready. Now the aftermath included a missing stepdaughter, a distraught and angry wife, and a mountain of guilt ravaging his insides.

He'd reached out to the local police station a few hours earlier to report Kayla missing and impatiently waited with his phone in hand, hoping for someone to call with good news.

He finished off his bottle of beer and contemplated whether or not to go back inside to see how Amara was doing. She'd been sheltered in their bedroom for the past few hours and hadn't come out. They'd had arguments in the past where she would give him the silent treatment for a while, but those minor disagreements paled in comparison to the gargantuan chasm of disdain he knew she felt toward him at this moment for waiting so long to tell Kayla. It also hadn't helped that he'd made Amara promise not to say anything to Kayla until he'd found the courage to move forward with the tough conversation. He couldn't make sense of how his initial heroic act to save both Amara and Kayla had turned into such a massive cross to bear. And now he was most likely sitting at his lowest point, wondering if he should have ever moved forward with the brutal confession. As Kayla mentioned to him, a painful truth beats a lie every time, but his experience today had proven this statement might not be one hundred percent accurate.

His thoughts were interrupted by the sound of a dish rattling inside the kitchen, signifying Amara had finally made her way out of the bedroom. He contemplated going inside and asking how she was doing, but he knew what the answer would be. That was if she answered him at all. He also knew the only thing she wanted to hear come out of his mouth was someone had found Kayla. And those words would remain elusive as he continued to wait for any updates on Kayla's whereabouts.

He closed his eyes, attempting to drag himself away from his pity party and find the courage to step inside and check in on Amara. He stood with his hands on his hips for a moment before making his way from the deck and into the kitchen. He sat at the kitchen table, watching Amara put away a few plates in the dishwasher. She didn't turn around, but he was almost certain she'd heard him come in.

"Did you hear anything yet from the police?" she asked without turning around as she loaded a few wine glasses into the dishwasher.

Trevor hesitated, caught completely off guard that she'd initiated the conversation. "Unfortunately, no. Nothing at the moment."

She finally turned around to face Trevor. "Just so you know, I'm about to put on my sneakers and drive around town some more to help look for her."

Trevor grimaced. "I can't stop you, but I'm not sure if that's such a good idea. We looked all over the place during the day and couldn't find her. And I'm not sure what kind of luck we would have trying to find her at night now."

Amara peered at Trevor with narrowed eyes. "It doesn't matter to me if it's day or night. The fact is Kayla is missing and we have no idea if she's in danger, hurt, or something worse. And if anything happens to my little girl . . . I don't know what I would do."

Trevor knew he was in no position to argue. He so desperately wanted to believe they could find her at night, but the chances were extremely remote. If he hadn't heard back from anyone during the night, he was planning to wake up early in the morning and continue the search. He was tempted to approach Amara and give her a hug, yet he was unsure of how she would react. He imagined she wouldn't have been interested in experiencing any type of physical touch from him.

He decided to stay seated and remain quiet. He tilted his head down, accepting the fact that silence was most likely the best policy at this time.

He jumped at the sound of glass breaking. The stem from a wine glass Amara had been holding rolled by his foot while shards of glass scattered along the floor around her. He focused his eyes on Amara, who stood unbalanced and swaying back and forth. He jumped up and rushed toward her as she collapsed to the floor. He grabbed her by the arm, attempting to prevent her head from crashing to the floor.

"Amara!"

# Chapter 41

Mason opened the cabinet, putting away his toolbox after what he considered a busy day of servicing cars. He wiped his brow from the sweat that had developed working in the garage. The air had always been stagnant in the garage, and with the weather slowly heating up, he wasn't looking forward to being trapped here, working on cars during the summer months.

Noah had left for the evening, and Mason was tasked with closing up the shop. Most working-class individuals looked forward to leaving their jobs to go home, eat dinner, and relax. Mason, on the other hand, did not share that same sentiment—at least not this evening. With Leah still on the warpath because of his inexcusable mental relapse regarding their anniversary, he seriously contemplated sleeping in his car at the gas station for the evening.

He felt his phone vibrating in his pocket and wiped his hand on a rag sitting on a workbench before answering. Eva's name appeared on the caller ID.

Before he could say anything, he heard her sniffling on the other end. "Eva, are you okay?"

"N . . . no. Caleb was in a car accident."

"What? How bad was it?"

"Bad enough that a police officer came to my door to tell me he was rushed to the hospital."

"Do you know where this happened? And what's his condition?"

"It happened on Route 2, and I don't know anything about his injuries. He's at Rhode Island Hospital, and I'm heading there right now."

"So sorry to hear about this. I'm closing up the gas station now. It may take me a little bit to get there, but I can meet you at the hospital."

Mason hung up the phone and then picked up his pace to ensure the garage was properly locked. He felt numb from receiving the disturbing news. Caleb had been like a brother he never had ever since they were football teammates in high school. They'd come a long way from the carefree young boys back in the day when they'd first met to the grown men they were now with spouses and real-life responsibilities. They both shared best man duties at each other's wedding and traveled together on several vacation destinations. They consoled one another during difficult times and celebrated together during various life milestones. Their bromance became so strong that when Caleb was unable to father a child due to a medical issue, he approached Mason to see if he would be willing to act as a sperm donor so that he and his wife could experience the joys of having a family of their own. Mason initially declined but decided to move forward with the request, which resulted in the birth of Caleb and Eva's son, Owen. They'd all agreed to have Mason remain in Owen's life whenever possible. They'd also agreed to keep this a secret from anyone else within their inner circle, which led Mason to remain tight-lipped about it, even after he'd met and married Leah.

All of those memories flashed before Mason's eyes upon hearing about the accident. He proceeded to lock up the station, then jumped into his car, completely unaware if his best friend would even be alive once he arrived at the hospital.

# Chapter 42

Mason arrived at Rhode Island Hospital and was directed to the emergency room waiting area. He approached Eva, who was sitting in the room, and gave her a tight hug.

"Thanks for coming out here so fast," Eva said, wiping her watery eyes with a tissue.

"Of course."

"I can really use the company right now," she said.

Mason sat beside her. "Any news on Caleb's condition?"

"Nothing yet. He's in surgery now, and I was told a doctor would be out soon to give me an update."

"Do you know where he was coming from?"

"He told me he had to make a quick stop at Flagstone, and then he was planning to grab us something to eat. I tried calling him a few times because he was taking so long to get home, but I didn't think anything of it because this isn't the first time he's been out longer than expected."

Mason looked up as he saw a doctor enter the room, but he proceeded to the other side to consult with another family.

"By the way, where's Owen?"

"I left him with my neighbor. I figured this wasn't the best place for him to be now."

Mason nodded.

"When was the last time you talked to Caleb?" Eva asked.

"Maybe a few days ago. Why?"

"I just felt something was off with him during the past few weeks. Didn't seem like his normal self. Not sure if you picked up on anything."

"Not that I can think of. He seemed to be okay the last time I talked to him."

Eva grimaced. "I also found out recently there was another car involved in the accident. There were two witnesses from this other car that gave statements to the police. They said Caleb was driving recklessly and tailgating them. And when they stopped short to avoid a deer, he ran off the road, trying not to hit them."

"Doesn't sound like Caleb to be driving crazy like that."

Eva shook her head. "I don't know what to think anymore. This is all just a bad dream." She noted the time. "I've been here for over an hour and still haven't heard anything about his condition."

Mason rubbed his hand across Eva's back. "I'm sure we'll hear something soon. And hopefully, it's good news."

"I sure hope so."

Silence followed as they both continued to wait. Mason's lips curled in disgust, now regretting his decision to recruit Caleb in his quest to get even with Jordyn and her roommate. At the time, it had seemed like a great idea, considering Caleb was well aware of Mason's secret relationship with Naomi. Caleb was also aware of his car tires being flattened by Jordyn's roommate and the confrontation Mason had with them at the gas station that led to the stabbing incident. And since Caleb had been working on campus as a groundskeeper, the opportunity had existed for him to fly under the radar and secretly harass Jordyn and her roommate for the trouble they'd caused.

Mason let off a heavy sigh, not only for being impatient as they waited for an update on Caleb's condition but also knowing he'd completely lied to Eva when she'd asked about the last time he'd talked to Caleb. It hadn't been a few days, as he'd stated, but more like a few hours.

Caleb had called Mason from a restaurant parking lot, letting him know he'd spotted Naomi and Jordyn on Flagstone's campus. He'd been following them and was planning to give them a little scare. He never said what he had in mind, and Mason hadn't had a chance to ask him since Caleb ended the call abruptly after seeing Jordyn approaching. Mason could only imagine the tailgating episode was part of the plan, which unfortunately ended in disaster for Caleb. And now he had to deal with the realization his decision to enlist Caleb on his revenge tour might have potentially cost him his life.

# Chapter 43

Jordyn sat at the kitchen table and shoved a few spoons of oatmeal into her mouth before pushing the bowl aside. She'd woken up with a mildly upset stomach, most likely brought on by the stress from the previous day's intense events. Kayla was still missing, and Jordyn had to also contend with the thought of replaying the horrific crash she'd witnessed the previous night in her mind. She was thankful the 9-1-1 call she'd made might have saved the driver's life. They'd hung around the crash site until emergency personnel had arrived. And Jordyn was able to verify the body on the stretcher as the same gentleman she'd briefly talked with at the restaurant. The EMT had confirmed he still had a pulse and loaded him into an ambulance before speeding away. Both Naomi and Jordyn had provided statements to the state police on the scene and eventually departed, arriving home late last night.

"Aren't you going to try to eat a little more? Some hot oatmeal may do your stomach good," Naomi said.

"I don't have too much of an appetite now."

Naomi stood and rubbed Jordyn's back. "Let me at least make you some hot tea with lemon."

Jordyn nodded and closed her eyes, attempting to will the discomfort away.

Naomi walked over to the stove and turned on the flame to heat the kettle. "Hang in there. I know yesterday was a difficult day for both of us, but we'll get through it."

"I barely got any sleep. Kept thinking about Kayla and then the accident. This is all just a little too much for me to handle right now," Jordyn said.

"There's an old saying—hope springs eternal. It simply means we need to have hope no matter the difficult circumstances we may be facing. We just need to have faith that things will turn around today," Naomi said with her hands up in prayer.

"Do you think Kayla is okay?" Jordyn asked.

"In my heart of hearts, I think she is."

"Do you think we should go out looking for her again today?"

"We could, but I imagine with the parents reporting her missing, the police are doing what they can to help with the search."

Jordyn grabbed her phone, wondering if she should even try calling again. "I practically slept with the phone in my hand the entire night, hoping to hear back from her. It's the absolute worst feeling when you're trying to desperately reach someone and they're not calling back."

Jordyn stood and approached Naomi, giving her a tight hug. She peered out of the kitchen window and set her eyes on the tire hanging from the tree in the backyard, gently swaying in the breeze.

"You can stop warming the tea kettle. I think I need some fresh air. I'm going to take a walk outside in the backyard."

"Okay, whatever you think is going to help you."

Jordyn opened the kitchen door, walking down a few wooden steps and onto the grass. It had been a while since she'd taken a leisurely walk in the backyard, and even longer since she'd sat on the tire to collect her thoughts.

She walked toward the tree where the grass around the tire had disappeared long ago under the wear and tear caused by her constant foot traffic during her younger years. The grass had never recovered, resulting in a solid patch of hard dirt, outlining exactly where she would drag her feet on the ground as she swung back and forth.

She approached the tire and grabbed the rope, tugging gently to make sure it was still strong and secure enough to hold her. She then focused on the massive tree branch holding the rope, which had grown in size and thickness since the last time she remembered it. She proceeded to sit on the tire with her phone tightly in hand. She had flashbacks of herself as a youngster, running to the tire on the weekends and spending a few hours just swinging and making up stories of adventure as she flew back and forth in the air. It was amazing to her how an old tire, connected to an old rope, connected to a one-hundred-year-old oak tree, could lead to so much joy as a kid and now wondrous nostalgia as a young adult.

She suddenly jumped, almost losing her phone in the process as it vibrated in her hands. She looked at the screen and felt a tidal wave of elation when she saw Kayla's name appear. Her hand shook uncontrollably upon pressing the button to answer.

"Oh, my God! Is this really you, Kayla?"

"Yes . . . it's me."

Jordyn fought to control her emotions as her eyes began to water. "You don't know how good it is to hear your voice. We've been looking all over for you." Jordyn stopped speaking for a second as her moment of happiness suddenly became sprinkled with a tinge of anger. "How come you didn't respond to any of my calls and text messages?"

"I turned my phone off so I didn't get any messages. I just turned it back on and saw all the messages now, but I didn't read them."

"So, where are you now?"

"I stayed overnight at a hotel in Charlestown, and I'm still here."

Jordyn let out a long sigh. "I'm asking you to please . . . please never do this again. You don't understand how worried everyone was, thinking something bad happened to you."

"I'm sorry, but there was no way I could talk with anyone in the state I was in. Matter of fact, I'm still not good but figured let me at least give you a call."

"So, did you call your parents?"

Silence followed on the other end.

"Kayla? Are you still there?"

"Yes."

"Did you hear what I said? Did you call—"

"No. And I don't have any plans to call them right now."

"What? What are you talking about? They're worried sick about you."

"When I'm ready to tell you what happened, you'll understand why I don't want to speak with them now or anytime soon."

Jordyn didn't want to press any further and couldn't imagine what Kayla must have found out.

"Okay, I understand. But they already called the police and reported you missing. Don't you think you should at least let them know you're okay so they can alert the police?"

"My conscience is telling me yes, but my anger is saying no. And based on how I'm feeling now, my answer is no."

"I don't know if that's a good idea. If your parents call me or my mom, that means I need to pretend like I never talked to you. And I don't know if I can truthfully do that."

"Didn't I keep my promise and not tell anyone on the weekend you famously disappeared?"

"Yes, but that's different. At least I contacted you and told you I was okay before I disappeared."

"And that's exactly what I'm doing now, although I admit it's a little later than when you did it."

"Yeah, but in my case, you were the only one who knew I had disappeared. In your case, a lot more people know you're missing, so I'm not the only one worried about you."

"Look, Jordyn, I trust you, which is why you're the first and only person I'll be calling. So, I'm asking you, as my roommate, as my good friend, to please not say anything to my parents or your mother. Can you do this for me?"

Jordyn let out a massive exhale. "I don't know. You're putting me in a tough situation."

"If I would have known this was going to be your reaction, I wouldn't have called you."

"You're killing me, Kayla!" Jordyn paused and let out a hefty sigh. "Okay, you have my word—I won't say anything."

"Okay, thanks. I owe you big time."

"And how long do I need to play this game of keeping secrets?"

"I don't know. I need more time to think and figure out what I'm doing."

"Are you at least planning to come back to school?"

"Eventually. I'm just not sure when that will be yet. For now, I'll work on my assignments online."

"Please be safe out there and call me whenever you need to talk."

Jordyn hung up the phone and craned her neck up to the sky. Her brain struggled to process the whirlwind of intense emotions revolving around in her head. They were mostly feelings of joy, considering Kayla was alive and well. All of those doomsday thoughts floating in her mind since yesterday had thankfully not come to fruition. However, Kayla's request to keep quiet about the situation initiated a whole new level of stress. She struggled to imagine how she could keep a straight face and lie to her mother about Kayla's whereabouts once she walked inside. She also prayed she wouldn't get a call or text from Trevor or Amara.

*****

After sitting outside for roughly an hour, she held onto the rope and closed her eyes tightly, attempting to get up the nerve to enter the house. She started to walk toward the house, focusing on controlling her facial expression and putting on the most intense poker face she could muster.

She opened the kitchen door to see Naomi sitting at the table, sipping coffee from a mug.

"Did getting some fresh air help you?"

"Yes, it helped clear my head. My stomach feels a little better, also."

"Good. So, what time did you want me to take you back to school?"

"It doesn't matter to me."

Naomi took another sip from her mug. "I was thinking, before I take you back, you can ride with me in town to run a few errands. We can also be on the lookout for Kayla. And once I'm done, I can bring you back to school. How does that sound?"

Jordyn shrugged. "I'm fine with that."

Naomi tilted her head to the side. "Are you okay?"

"Yeah, I'm good."

"Seems like your whole demeanor changed after coming back in from outside."

"No, I'm just thinking about Kayla."

Naomi studied her face further. "Okay. Come over here and give me a hug."

Jordyn approached and leaned over to give Naomi a warm embrace.

Naomi continued to hold on tight. "Don't worry, darling. I have a good feeling Kayla will be found somewhere safe and sound. You can call it a mother's intuition."

# Chapter 44

Kayla sat on the motel bed, staring at the wall. The curtains were drawn so no one could see inside the first-floor room. A dull yellow glow emanated from a lamp sitting on the nightstand next to the bed. Except for being away at college, this was the only other time she could remember sleeping in a bed outside of home. And if the thin mattress with box springs pushing against her back all night was any indication of how comfortable motel beds normally were, she contemplated whether or not she could spend another night in the room. She imagined that even if she'd slept on a higher quality mattress, her sleep would have been severely disrupted by her thoughts, moving back and forth at warp speed, attempting to process the events that had occurred the previous day.

She rubbed her temples to help soothe the headache that had been with her most of the night. She also longed for a cold bottle of water to help rehydrate her body and quench her thirst.

Given what she knows now, she would have never decided to confront her parents about her family history. As the famous proverb says, curiosity killed the cat, but in Kayla's case, it had truly killed her soul. She couldn't have imagined a more devastating confession from the man she had known as her father. Finding out she was adopted would have been easier to handle. The fact that her stepfather, who she thought was her real father, had actually killed her biological father was nowhere near a selection on her menu of potential scenarios.

But she did understand Trevor deserved a great deal of grace for saving her and Amara. They might not be around to experience this moment if he hadn't intervened. Her main gripe revolved around the lies and deception that had carried on much longer than she felt they should have. Although, she did struggle to figure out at what point would have been the most opportune time during her childhood to present this confession.

Her thoughts turned to her real father as she wondered why he'd even threatened them with a knife. What had he looked like? Did she get her height from him? How had he and Amara met? Did she have any half-brothers or sisters somewhere out in this world? These questions, and many more, floated around in her head.

She knew Amara would have the answer to many of these questions, but she couldn't even think about her now without getting sick to her stomach. In Kayla's eyes, Amara remained on the hook for being complicit in her silence, and in some ways, might have committed the greatest crime. She couldn't fathom her decision to keep things quiet all of these years and not even think about telling her or pressuring Trevor into moving forward with the confession sooner.

Kayla sat quietly as another tear trickled down her cheek. Her heart remained in a chokehold, and she truly didn't know if forgiveness would ever be possible at this point.

She wiped her eyes to clear her blurred vision and flipped through the text messages she'd received yesterday. She purposely skimmed over the messages and didn't read them in detail, except for one of Trevor's messages that did catch her eye and raise cause for alarm.

> *If you get this message, please call me back ASAP. Your mother was admitted to South County Hospital.*

# Chapter 45

Late Sunday afternoon, Naomi sat on the couch, rubbing her right knee, which ached after dropping Jordyn off at school and driving back home. Unfortunately, there had been no signs of Kayla on the trip to town earlier in the day, and Jordyn had confirmed she wasn't in the dorm room when they'd arrived on campus. Naomi kept up hope that Kayla would be found sooner rather than later, but the longer she remained missing, the tougher it became to keep up her optimism.

She clicked on the TV remote and searched through the guide for something interesting to watch. Her focus on the TV was interrupted by a knock on the door.

"Who the heck is that on a Sunday afternoon? This better not be who I think it is," she whispered.

She stood and peeked out of the living room window to see an unfamiliar car parked in the driveway. On occasion, there had been folks coming by the house, attempting to interest her in changing her phone or internet service, but they normally didn't come by on a Sunday.

She cautiously opened the door to see a middle-aged woman standing there with a smile. She wore form-fitting black jeans and a white, tunic top, showing off a svelte body frame. She had jet-black, wavy hair dropping down to her shoulders. The scent of passion fruit wafted from her body and caught Naomi's attention.

"Hello, ma'am. How can I help you?"

"I'm so sorry to bother you on a Sunday afternoon, but I wanted to start out by saying I'm not a salesperson, just in case you were wondering."

"I had a hunch that was the case. They normally don't come around on Sundays. So, if you're not selling anything, what can I do for you?"

"I'm hoping I have the right house, but do you know someone named Mason?"

Naomi gave the woman a questioning stare. "Yes . . . I know of someone named Mason."

"Okay, good. Is he a friend of yours?"

"I'm sorry, but what's this all about?"

The woman continued to display a pleasant smile. "Since I don't want to waste your time or mine, let me be upfront with you. I've been made aware Mason has visited this house a few times and, being the curious wife I am, I wanted to know who he was visiting."

Naomi did her best to take cover from the atomic bomb that had just been dropped directly on top of her. Her thought process was completely shattered as she attempted to regain her composure and keep her body language steady. "Oh . . . I see. Well . . . I was a client of his car repair shop, and he did some work on my car a time or two."

The woman nodded. "Okay. Very interesting. Forgive me if this comes off a little rude, but what does that have to do with him coming to your house?"

"He was actually doing me a favor and took me back home after I dropped my car off instead of me waiting for the car to be fixed. And once it was done, he came back to pick me up once my car was ready," Naomi said, completely stunned at her ability to think so quickly on her feet and communicate this blatant lie with confidence.

The woman glared at Naomi for a few seconds before responding. "That's mighty nice of him. You must be a special client." She looked down for a moment before setting her eyes back on Naomi. "So . . . that would explain two occasions of him coming to your house. And if my sources are right, there were at least a few other occasions I'm aware of. Any chance you can explain those other visits?"

Naomi stood with her hands on her hips, looking away from the woman momentarily. "I'm sorry, but I can't remember another occasion when he might have come here."

"Unless my sources are wrong, I swear he was here again, a time or two."

Naomi shrugged. "Sorry, I can't offer you more information."

She pursed her lips and studied Naomi intently with narrowing eyes. "Maybe I'll just talk to Mason to see if he could help me out."

"I think that's a good idea."

"I apologize if this is all coming off a little accusatory, but I hope you can understand why I might be concerned."

"I completely understand."

The woman raised her hand. "I'm sorry, I don't know where my manners are. My name is Leah."

Naomi raised her hand and offered a fist bump instead. "I'm Natalie. Nice to meet you."

Leah folded her fingers to oblige with an aggressive fist-bump. "Oh, okay. I guess this is how we greet each other in your neighborhood."

Naomi shrugged. "Forgive me, but I'm kind of a germaphobe."

Leah gave Naomi a cursory glance up and down. "Nice chatting with you. Enjoy the rest of your day," she said before departing.

Naomi closed the door and bit her bottom lip. "That son of a bitch had a wife!" she muttered under her breath. "How the hell did I miss that?"

She shook her head in disbelief. *I should have just admitted to the entire affair, but that would have resulted in some hair-pulling, and I'm in no condition now to be fighting. And who the heck are her sources? I hope no one was spying on us.*

She watched as the car pulled out of the driveway and accelerated down the road. She could only imagine what was about to transpire once Leah arrived home to confront Mason. She would give anything to be a fly on the wall to witness that bloodbath of a conversation.

# Chapter 46

Leah studied the reflection in the rearview mirror, watching the house disappear in the distance. She tightened her grip on the steering wheel as an image of Angela Bassett came to mind—the iconic scene where she threw her cheating husband's clothes in his car and lit them all on fire as she watched them burn.

"That woman is definitely lying," she said out loud. "I should have pushed her more, but I'm almost certain she didn't know Mason was married by the look on her face when I introduced myself as his wife."

She stopped at a light and pulled up her Find My app to confirm if Mason was still out. She'd always suspected something was going on during the past year, which had prompted her to place the AirTag in his car recently. She kicked herself for not acting sooner once she'd started tracking him coming to the same address multiple times. She'd initially given him the benefit of the doubt since she couldn't find any other clues he might have been cheating, but that had been a mistake. She was a firm believer in going with her gut, and as was the case most of the time, her gut hadn't steered her wrong.

Now, she did admit the timing of her visit to the woman's house could have been better. With Mason still concerned about the well-being of his friend, Caleb, she was hoping this visit would have been a false alarm, with no reason to cause any ruckus when she arrived back home. Although the woman never admitted to an affair, Leah had to decide whether to move forward and confront Mason with her suspicions or let it slide for now, at least until Caleb's status was no longer in doubt.

# Chapter 47

Kayla pulled into the visitor parking lot and shut off the engine. She was coming to the hospital completely blind as to what had happened or what condition Amara was in. She refused to reach back out to Trevor and decided she would get all of the details she needed once she arrived. She was also completely aware there was a good possibility she might see Trevor at the hospital, but she couldn't let that deter her from seeing Amara, especially if this visit involved a life-threatening situation.

She walked through the revolving doors and toward the guest service center. She approached the gentleman sitting behind the desk.

"Hi, sir. I'm here to see Amara Devereaux," she said, unsure if this was the correct pavilion she resided in.

The gentleman typed a few keystrokes on the computer in front of him. "She's in ward B on the third floor, room 345. And please, be aware you have about two hours left before visiting hours are over."

Kayla signed in and affixed the visitor label to her shirt before proceeding to the elevator. She had no clue what to expect upon entering the room. Would Amara be awake? What kind of machines would she be hooked up to? Would she be in any pain? And would there be any awkward moments of seeing Trevor sitting in the room?

She entered the elevator and pressed the third-floor button. A sudden sense of guilt overwhelmed her, knowing her last interaction with Amara wasn't a pleasant memory. She was still highly upset at the situation but didn't want this grudge to interfere with her duty as a daughter to love and support her mother as she attempted to recover from whatever was ailing her.

She exited the elevator and was immediately hit with the sterile scent of alcohol in the air. She followed the signs to room 345 and stopped before entering the room. She motioned the sign of the cross and took a step inside.

Her eyes immediately shifted to the left, where the bed was positioned. Amara's eyes were closed, with her head and back propped up at a slight angle. Kayla's fear of seeing her mother hooked up to a breathing machine was unfounded as the hospital equipment surrounding the bed was kept to a minimum. Outside of an IV stand and a machine keeping track of her heart rate, there was no other equipment to be found.

A small hint of a smile tugged at the corner of Kayla's lips. Sound from a TV affixed to the corner wall could be heard, along with the various beeping sounds coming from the heart rate monitor.

She approached the bed and stared at Amara. She found it hard to believe a little more than twenty-four hours ago, she had stormed out of the house and hadn't wanted anything to do with her. She placed her hand on the side of Amara's forehead and gently stroked it.

She flinched upon seeing Amara's eyes open.

Amara squinted for a moment then displayed a massive smile. "I . . . is that really you, Kayla?"

Kayla struggled to keep a straight face and prevent a smile from forming. "Yes, it's me in the flesh."

Amara slowly reached her arms up, looking for a hug. Kayla bent down and obliged. She tried pulling away, but Amara kept holding on. Kayla was surprised and elated to see Amara's strength remained, regardless of her medical situation. Amara finally let go.

"What happened?" Kayla asked.

"I . . . I don't know. I was in the kitchen and started to feel dizzy. The next thing I knew, I was waking up in the emergency room."

"Did you talk with the doctors yet?"

"I vaguely remember some doctors coming in, but I honestly don't remember what they were talking about."

"Do you feel any pain?"

Amara lifted her arms and bent each leg. "I'm feeling a little pain in my right hip, but other than that, I think I feel fine."

"That's good. I'll go to the nursing station shortly to see what information they can give on your diagnosis."

Amara's smile quickly dissipated. "Where did you go? We were worried sick about you."

Kayla fought hard to control the negative emotions still festering on the surface of her mind. "I ended up staying at a motel overnight."

"I understand you were upset about the situation, but you could have at least told us you were okay."

"I admit I probably should have texted you and let you know I was all right. But after the news I received, I hope you understand why I may have not been thinking straight."

"Yes, that makes sense."

Kayla struggled to stay focused on the task at hand and just concentrate on Amara's recovery. There were so many questions she needed answers to, but she felt odd asking Amara while she lay in a hospital bed.

Amara looked at the IV sticking in her arm then turned her attention back to Kayla. "I'm so sorry for not telling you sooner."

Kayla closed her eyes to focus on an appropriate response. In any other situation, she would have lashed out at this moment, following through with the anger still lurking within her. However, based on the current circumstances, she figured it would be wise to proceed with a measured response, especially not knowing Amara's health status.

"If I'm being honest, I can't say I'm truly ready yet to accept your apology."

"Okay, I can respect that."

Silence followed as Kayla was unsure of how to carry on without any anger seeping into her tone.

"I'm sure you have questions about your biological father. I can answer any questions you have if you want to talk about it?"

There were plenty of questions Kayla had surrounding her real father. But with the resentment she felt still coursing through her veins, she was unsure if she had the mental capacity to handle this talk. She didn't acknowledge Amara's offer and decided to remain quiet.

"His name was Dylan," Amara said.

Kayla continued to look down at her hands without saying anything.

"We started out as friends in college, and since we were both from the Richmond area, we continued to see each other after we graduated. And a few months after graduating, we took the relationship to another level and started dating."

Kayla shifted in her chair. A part of her wasn't ready to hear the story now, but she couldn't deny her curiosity, which was in full bloom, so she continued to listen.

"And if you're wondering where you got your height from, it was definitely from him. He played basketball at the school and stood about six-foot-five."

Kayla nodded, finally reacting to that interesting fact.

"As with many relationships, things started off fine, but it didn't last for long. We were still dating when I got pregnant with you, and that's when his attitude seemed to change. He started drinking and became verbally abusive. I kept trying to get him to go to counseling, but he refused. He eventually lost his job as a marketing consultant and things kept getting worse. I knew that wasn't the right situation for me and decided to break up with him."

Kayla finally looked up. "And how did he respond to the breakup?"

"Not good. We weren't living together, but he began to stalk me at my apartment. I filed a restraining order against him, which worked for a while. Fast forward to a few months later, and I was almost nine months pregnant with you when I met your fa—" She immediately stopped. "I mean, I met Trevor at a diner, where he worked as a short-order cook. I started to go there every weekend for breakfast, and we became friends."

Kayla closed her eyes tight, doing all she could to remain calm upon hearing the mention of the man formerly known as her father.

Amara paused. "I can stop if you don't want to hear the rest of the story."

Kayla sighed. "That's okay. You can go ahead."

Amara nodded then continued. "I went into the diner like I always had one weekend and suddenly went into labor. Trevor was a huge help in calling for an ambulance and keeping me calm before they arrived. Thankfully, I made it to the hospital just in time before you were born. And I'll never forget, but the next day, Trevor came to visit me in the hospital to see how I was doing and get his first look at you. I remember he was afraid to hold you because you were so small." Amara stopped to clear her throat. "During those first few months I was back home, he would come by a couple of times a week after work to check in on me, and the relationship eventually evolved into dating. I thought something was wrong with him because there were very few men I knew who would be willing to get involved with a single mother who just had a baby and had an ex-boyfriend who continued to stalk her. Once I realized he was genuine about the situation and there were no strings attached, that told me all I needed to know about Trevor's character as a man. We got engaged after a year of dating, and I should probably stop there."

As tough as it was for Kayla to hear these stories, she felt a strange sense of peace. This was the missing link in her quest to find out who she truly was, where she'd come from, and validation of her existence. Yet, she still struggled with the traumatic way in which all of these events had unfolded and reflected back to the first positive affirmation she remembered reading on Jordyn's desk.

*I am more than my circumstances dictate.*

That gave her some hope that she could somehow push through and make the most of this difficult hand of cards she'd been dealt.

She swiped with the back of her hand, wiping away a tear falling from her eyes as she continued to look down. Her attention was quickly diverted to a doctor walking into the room.

"I'm sorry. Is this a bad time? Do you want me to come back?" she asked.

"No, it's okay. I wanted to speak with someone, anyway, regarding my mom's condition."

The doctor continued to walk over toward the bed. "After running a few tests, we did discover some abnormalities with your EKG readings, which we'll need to investigate further. In addition, your blood pressure was very low. Have you had any issues with your blood pressure in the past?"

"It's always been borderline low but never to the point where it caused me any issues," Amara said.

"We can prescribe you medication to help keep your pressure up to normal levels." The doctor focused her eyes on Kayla. "Were you the one who called 9-1-1 when your mother passed out?"

"No, wasn't me."

Amara interrupted. "It was my husband."

"In that case, I would suggest you give your husband a huge hug the next time you see him. Based on the records I see here, your husband had to perform CPR on you because your pulse rate was very low once you passed out. This helped keep you stable enough until the EMTs arrived to transport you to the hospital. It could have been an entirely different story if he hadn't stepped in to help you."

"Oh, I didn't know. He was here earlier in the day but didn't mention anything to me."

"That makes him a humble hero. Now that you know, you can personally thank him." The doctor inspected Amara's chart. "There are a few more tests we would like to perform, which will result in us keeping you for at least another night. So, I would relax, enjoy the visit from your daughter, and we'll try to get you out of here and back on your feet as soon as we can."

# Chapter 48

Mason closed his eyes, overjoyed with relief after talking with Eva and hearing Caleb had regained consciousness a day after his surgery. He had a long way to go after suffering a broken right leg, a dislocated shoulder, a concussion, and severe facial bruises from the impact with the airbag. Although extremely battered and bruised, his seat belt had ultimately saved his life.

Mason had arrived home from the hospital and, with Sunday being the only day he had off during the week, he'd planned to kick his feet up and rest for the remainder of the evening. Leah had been out running errands for most of the afternoon, allowing him a moment of peace. The eventful day quickly caught up with him and he eventually dozed off watching TV.

A short time later, Mason was roused from his sleep after hearing someone stirring in the apartment. After his eyes adjusted, he noticed Leah putting away groceries in the kitchen. He didn't immediately acknowledge her presence and continued to close his eyes every so often. He felt a nudge on his leg, realizing he must have fallen back asleep.

He rubbed his eyes to clear his focus and could see Leah sitting on the edge of the couch by his feet. He cleared his throat. "What time did you get back?" he asked, still attempting to regain complete consciousness.

"Maybe an hour ago. How's Caleb doing?"

Mason mustered a small grin. "Much better. He's awake now but has a long way to go to heal up from his injuries."

Leah offered a guarded smile. "Happy to hear."

Mason stretched and sat up on the sofa. "Were you gone the whole time while I was at the hospital?"

"Yes. I ran around to a few other places besides the market."

"Good for you. It's a good time to be out with this nice weather."

Leah didn't respond and proceeded to rub her forehead.

"What's the matter? Not feeling well?"

"I guess you can say that."

Mason shrugged. "Well . . . either you are or you aren't."

"I'm fine physically."

"Okay. So, what's going on inside that head of yours?"

"I'm not sure where to begin," she said, looking down at her hands.

"I can't help you since I have no clue what you want to discuss."

Leah leaned over and grabbed the remote, turning off the TV.

Mason rubbed his fingers against the stubble on his cheeks. "I guess this is something serious."

Leah finally turned her head, looking at Mason with furrowed eyebrows. "My mother once told me intuition is a muscle, and the more you trust it, the stronger it gets," she said.

Mason sat, completely perplexed as to why Leah had started her conversation with this odd reference.

"And I must say, my intuition has grown by leaps and bounds this past year. And because of this, I learned to trust my gut more."

It wasn't until she finished her second statement that Mason's brain activity began firing on all cylinders as an ominous thought bubbled to the surface of his mind. He refused to immediately submit to any of these worst-case scenarios floating around in his head and figured he'd let this play out some more to see where Leah was going with this banter.

"After leaving the market, I made a quick trip away from town and to this quiet rural community not too far from us."

"Okay," Mason said with a touch of uneasiness reflecting in his voice.

"I came across a nice mid-century, rustic-styled home with a gorgeous front porch. It had somewhat of an old southern charm to it."

The house description sounded all too familiar for Mason. As much as he wanted to deny this frightening development, an image suddenly became all too clear in his mind with his worst-case scenario knocking on the doorstep. He could see Leah reaching into his closet, grabbing the skeleton by the neck, and dragging it out into the open, ready to stomp it into oblivion. He immediately realized the jig was up and his cover was blown wide open.

"I had a nice chat with a pretty little lady who told me she was a friend of yours. I believe she said her name was Natalie."

Mason at least gave Naomi credit for lying about her name, but it didn't matter at this point. He was trapped in a corner and now had to try to fight his way out. However, he was content to keep quiet and see how much more information Leah would provide before he offered his rebuttal.

"I did find out some unfortunate news while speaking with Natalie. She initially denied it, but after spending a little more time with her, she told me you two were actually more than just friends. I thought that was odd, with you being married and all, but then she told me she didn't know you were married."

Mason struggled to remain calm and not react to his worst fears coming true.

"Any of this sounding familiar?" Leah asked.

Mason only offered a simple shrug.

"I'm sure you can imagine things got a little tense during our discussion, and before you knew it, everything ended with a little fist contact. And once I was done with her, I figured the next logical step in the process was to come home and confront you," Leah said, clenching her jaw. "So, unless you can miraculously pull a rabbit out of your ass to explain all of this to me, this conversation is not going to end well for you."

Mason tried with all his might to determine if Leah was telling the truth. He thought he knew Naomi well enough that even upon her finding out he was married, she would never admit to Leah they were both in a relationship. But above all else, Leah's fist reference created a serious pause for concern.

Leah looked pretty good and didn't show any battle scars from a physical confrontation, which could only mean Naomi might have received the worst of it. Even though he was upset with the way Naomi had broken up with him, he never wished any physical harm toward her.

Mason let out a long sigh. "So . . . I guess me dealing with Caleb's situation doesn't mean anything to you, and you have no problems approaching me with this accusation while I'm still stressing over his recovery."

"You should at least give me some credit. I was courteous enough to ask you how he was doing first. And once you told me he was doing better, I felt I had the green light to push forward with the conversation since it was weighing so heavily on my mind."

"This is crazy. I would have still expected you to at least give me some grace after I spent the afternoon at the hospital and let me rest for the remainder of the day instead of you dragging me into whatever suspicions you have going on in your head."

Leah's eyes narrowed. "Stop it, Mason! Just stop it. I see what you're doing, and it's not working. You're just trying to stall and invite me to your pity party. Well . . . I'm declining the invitation, and I need you to stop playing around right now and give me a damn good explanation as to your relationship with this woman."

Mason shook his head. "I'm guessing this is where you imagine I would start making up all kinds of excuses and deny what she said was true."

"You're damn right! And knowing you, I don't think you would have the balls to admit it now, anyway."

Mason suddenly found himself at a dangerous fork in the road. Going to the right meant dropping off an immediate cliff with no parachute if he admitted to the affair. Going to the left meant walking across a field with land mines buried at every turn if he tried lying his way out of this predicament. And he only had a millisecond to make his decision on which way to go.

Mason put his hands up in the air. "I honestly don't have much to say other than you got me. I'm guilty of stepping out on our marriage. Is that what you want to hear?"

Leah immediately tilted her head down and closed her eyes. "No, this is something I never wanted to hear. So, how long has this been going on?"

"I don't know. Long enough."

Leah pounded her fist on the coffee table. "I knew I should have listened to my gut sooner. I should have had you exposed months ago. This makes no sense. I feel like I'm in The Twilight Zone. So, give me a reason, Mason. Why did you do this? And don't give me any bullshit about me traveling too much because, without this job, we probably wouldn't have been able to keep a roof over our heads."

"I'd be lying if I said it didn't have something to do with it. You were traveling so much at one point, and we barely saw each other. I felt like we started to drift apart."

"And your solution was to cheat on me? That was supposed to bring us closer together? What kind of wacky logic is that?"

"It's not like I planned to do this."

"So, basically, what you're telling me is you took advantage of the opportunity. When the cat's away, the mice will play. Was that your thought process?"

Mason shrugged again. "If that's what you want to call it."

Mason was a bit surprised Leah's reaction wasn't as bad as he'd imagined it would be. She was rather subdued after hearing his cheating confession. He figured dodging a flying chair or some wild swings from her fists would have been part of his fate once he'd admitted to cheating on her. She was unexpectedly tame, considering the circumstances.

"May I ask how you found out where she lived?"

"You can ask, but I'm not going to tell. Let's just say I have my sources."

Leah suddenly stood up from the sofa as Mason kept a watchful eye on any sudden movement from her, indicating some form of retaliation might be coming his way. Instead, she calmly grabbed her bag and car keys. She approached the apartment door and reached for the knob before turning back to Mason.

"You know, it's funny. I guess we were meant for each other in some ways. Let me ask you a question. Have you been trusting your intuition lately?"

Mason shrugged. "Why are you asking?"

"Because you were so wrapped up with your lady on the side that you probably never thought to yourself some of my trips for work may have involved more than just business. You weren't the only mouse playing in the field."

Leah smiled, stepped outside, and slammed the door shut.

# Chapter 49

The following evening, Naomi eased her foot on the brake upon nearing her house. The sun was roughly an hour from setting, as a decent amount of light still filtered through the sky.

"You gotta be kidding me."

She was mentally exhausted from a ten-hour shift she'd completed, and the last thing she needed was some unexpected company. And this wasn't any ordinary company, as the Dodge Charger parked in her driveway indicated another surprise visit from Mason.

She pulled to the side and came to a complete stop, roughly a hundred feet from her driveway. Her car was halfway hidden behind a large oak tree standing along the edge of the road. She assumed it wasn't a coincidence Mason had shown up the day after his wife had unexpectedly knocked at her door and dropped the bombshell news. She could only imagine what might have happened during their confrontation. *Did she kick him out of the house? If so, he damn sure isn't welcome at my house, looking for shelter.*

There were many possibilities as to his reasons for showing up, but there was one thing she did know—she was completely pissed now, knowing he was married while they were dating. She directed a part of this anger toward herself for not catching on to any clues he might have had a ring on his finger. But all of her thoughts didn't matter. What mattered was the conniving man, whom she'd recently had a relationship with, was now trespassing on her property, and she had the golden opportunity to tell him how she truly felt.

Naomi opened the glove compartment and sifted through some paper before she grabbed a can of pepper spray in the corner. She'd recently purchased the can for protection and wondered if there would ever be a chance for her to use it. Depending on the outcome of this interaction, her first opportunity to unleash the burning mix of ingredients might be sooner than she'd thought.

Although tired, she felt grateful the joint pain in her knees had been kept to a minimum during the day. Unlike the last time Mason had unexpectedly showed up at her house, she felt better equipped to handle any physical demands that might come out of this interaction.

She stepped on the pedal and slowly drove toward the house, but instead of turning into the driveway, she parked on the street to avoid blocking Mason's car from leaving.

"Okay, you bastard, let's see what brings you to my doorstep this time," she whispered.

She exited the car and placed the pepper spray in the back of her jeans pocket. She purposely left her bag in the car and only grabbed her house keys, allowing more freedom for both of her hands. She walked on the grass instead of behind the car in the driveway to get a better angle of vision to confirm if Mason was present in the car. She noticed him calmly sitting in the driver's seat with the engine not running. He remained facing forward with his window down and did not initially look her way as she approached. She stopped roughly ten yards from the passenger door before he finally acknowledged her presence by looking in her direction. Naomi stood firm with her arms folded.

"I'm sure you're probably tired of me showing up at your house unannounced," he said.

Naomi continued to stare without saying a word.

Mason looked her up and down. "I'm happy to see you appear to be okay."

"And why wouldn't I be?"

"I was just a little concerned about your situation based on the events I was told took place yesterday."

"Are you talking about the unexpected visit I received from your wife?"

Mason nodded. "I was under the impression there might have been a physical confrontation, and I figured it was only right for me to check in on you and make sure you were all right."

Naomi laughed. "This is actually unbelievable. You're talking like me finding out you were married is no big deal."

"Sorry about—"

"Don't even say it, and let me finish talking to make sure I have this right. You, being the upstanding gentleman you are, decided to check in on your ex-mistress who you thought might have been physically harmed by your rightfully jealous wife who somehow found out we had something going on and also found out where I lived."

"Yeah, I guess that's about right."

"This sounds like a real live soap opera and doesn't even seem real to me. Also, don't you think your decision to visit me at this particular moment makes the situation exponentially worse? Do you even have a clue how your wife found out? And does she know you're here right now, checking in on me? How do you think she'd feel about that?"

"I have no idea how she found out, and I don't think she cares right now if I'm here, because it turns out karma came back to bite me pretty quickly."

"Let me guess. Did you find out she was cheating on you?"

"You got it."

Naomi let out a hearty laugh. "Wow, you can't make this stuff up. So you both deserved each other. It's just very unfortunate I was an unsuspecting casualty in this cheating scandal. I will say this does make me feel a smidge better, but if I'm being honest, I still have the urge to grab you by the neck with my bare hands and squeeze as tight as I can."

Mason pointed to himself. "I don't get any credit for showing concern and wanting to check in on you?"

"Now you're being completely stupid about the situation. Did you even think how I might react if I ever saw you again after knowing what I know now? Words can't describe how I'm feeling right now. I let you into my home. I let you into my life. I let you into Jordyn's life. I let you into my whole world, and you were nothing but a deceitful bitch all this time." Naomi's face hardened. "And truth be told, I'm more upset at myself for not catching on to your cheating ass. Shame on me, but I can tell you this will never happen again."

"I totally get why you're upset, and you deserve to be. But I think things could have turned out much better for the both of us if you could have handled the conversation a little better."

"And what's that supposed to mean?"

"You could have maybe not admitted to my wife we had something going on."

Naomi raised an eyebrow in confusion. "I never did admit we were together."

"That's not what I was told."

"You were told wrong. I simply told her you did some work on my car a few times, and that was about it." Naomi aggressively shook her head. "Wait, why the hell am I even arguing with you on this? None of this is my fault. It's all your fault, so don't try to turn things around on me and make me look like I'm the bad person." Naomi suddenly pointed to the street. "I'm done with you, I'm done with this discussion, and I need you to get off my property now before things get ugly."

"And what's that supposed to mean? I'm here, talking to you calmly and looking to have a civilized conversation."

Naomi focused her eyes on the ground to her right and spotted a softball-sized rock. She reached down to pick it up and held it in her hand. "I'm not going to tell you again."

A vertical crevice developed between Mason's eyes "Oh, now you want to threaten me? And what are you planning to do with that rock if I don't move in time?"

Naomi had reached her boiling point. Her rational thought process had been short-circuited by a sudden jolt of rage. On pure instinct, she cocked her arm back and tossed the rock at the rear passenger window of Mason's car, shattering the glass into a thousand fragments. Mason reached up to cover his head with his arm as some projectile shards of glass came hurtling his way.

Naomi stood frozen for a second as she snapped back to reality, surprised she'd thrown the rock.

"Have you lost your damn mind?" Mason yelled.

Her adrenaline spiked after seeing Mason open his car door. She immediately reached into her back pocket, grabbed the pepper spray, and aimed at Mason's face before pressing the trigger. A stream of liquid connected with his face as he instinctively twisted his head and shielded his eyes with the crook of his elbow. He dropped to one knee with his hands cupping his face.

Naomi started to sprint toward the house while reaching into her pocket for her keys. She scurried up the porch steps and reached the door, frantically sifting through a few keys, attempting to locate the correct one to open the door. She peeked over her shoulder, using her peripheral vision to determine Mason's location. He was no longer kneeling and had stumbled his way toward the porch steps.

"Don't let me get my hands on you," he said, ascending the steps.

She pushed the key into the door lock, twisted the knob, and made her way inside before quickly slamming the door shut. Seconds after she locked the door, Mason hit the door with a thud, violently shaking the knob.

"Open this damn door, or I'll break it down!"

Naomi backed away from the door as Mason continued to pound against it. Several massive blows followed, shaking the doorframe as it continued to stand firm from his vicious attempt to gain access to the house.

Naomi ran to the living room windows to ensure they were all locked. She then backpedaled toward the stairs while Mason's assault on the door continued. She started to make her way upstairs when the banging ceased. She jogged up the stairs and into her room, grabbing the aluminum bat from under her bed. She felt a strong sense of déjà vu as a similar scenario had played out a few weeks ago when Mason had unexpectedly arrived at her door, attempting to profess his apologies. But this time, his motivation to get into the house was fueled by pure rage.

She edged toward the bedroom door and closed it before twisting the knob to lock it. She remained quiet, listening for any movement beyond the door to track his location. She pulled out her phone and contemplated calling 9-1-1; however, based on past experience, she knew it would take too long for any police officers to show up in her rural neighborhood. She changed gears and focused her attention on Trevor, who from her recollection, did not work too far from the house.

She dialed, and after a few rings, her call went to voicemail, which she didn't bother to leave a message. She pulled the phone away from her ear and listened out further for any sounds indicating Mason's presence. She ran over to the bedroom window and parted the curtains ever so slightly to take a peek at the driveway, confirming Mason's car was still parked.

She tapped her phone again and called Jordyn, who picked up after a couple of rings.

"I got myself into some trouble with Mason and need help ASAP," Naomi said, skipping all of the greeting pleasantries.

"W . . . what's going on? Where are you now? And what kind of trouble?"

"I'm home, and Mason is trying to break into the house. I'll explain later, but I need help now."

"Did you call the police?"

"No, because I know it's going to take them forever to get here. I tried calling Mr. Devereaux instead since I figured he didn't work too far from here but didn't get him."

"I can call the police for you. Are you sure all of the doors and windows are locked in the house?"

"Yes."

"Where in the house are you now?"

"Upstairs in my bedroom. He was trying to break the front door down, but he stopped. I have no clue where he—"

Naomi heard the shattering of glass downstairs. Her body locked up with fear, now completely aware Mason had no doubt forced his way into the house.

"Mom? Are you still there?"

"He's in the house. I heard a window break downstairs," she whispered.

"Oh, God. J . . . just stay in your bedroom with the door locked. I'm calling the police now. I promise we'll get you out of there safely. I love you, Mom."

# Chapter 50

Jordyn hung up from the 9-1-1 operator and prayed the police would be dispatched as quickly as possible. She immediately dialed Kayla's number.

"Where are you?"

"In my car now. I'm about to grab a slice of pizza, and then was planning to head back to school. Why? Is everything okay?"

"No. I don't know what happened, but Mason is after my mom and he broke into our house. I called the police, and I know it's going to take them forever to get there. So, I was hoping your father could get out to the house to help my mom. Can you please give him a call and tell him my mom needs help ASAP?"

There was a pause.

"Kayla? Are you still there?"

"Yes. But I haven't spoken to him since . . ."

"Listen to me, Kayla. I don't know what happened at your house that caused you to run out, and I apologize for not sounding sincere about your situation, but if my mom doesn't get help now, I don't even want to think about what could happen. So, I'm begging you to please set aside whatever grudge you have with your father and call him to ask for help."

After a few more seconds of silence, Kayla finally responded. "Okay . . . okay. I'll give him a call."

# Chapter 51

Kayla remained in the parking lot of the local pizzeria in town, staring at her phone. Her hunger was replaced with a mountain of anxiety with the news Jordyn had dropped on her. The onset of this sudden stress was further compounded by the thought of trying to push her animosity aside and call Trevor to ask for help. Under normal circumstances, she would have rehearsed what to say; however, there was no time to practice any lines. Ms. Fisher needed help, and she needed it now.

Kayla dialed.

After a few rings, Trevor picked up. "Kayla! You have no idea how happy I was to see your name pop up on my screen. I was praying so hard to hear back from you. Are you okay?"

"As good as I can be."

"Mom told me you stopped by the hospital last night to see her. Thanks for reaching out to—"

"Sorry . . . Trevor, but I'm not calling now to reconnect with you and patch things up. We have a long way to go before I can even think about getting to that point, if I ever get there."

"Wow. Okay, that was a lot to take in. If I'm being honest, I'm a little thrown off by you calling me by my name, but I understand. We can save that all for another day. So, what's the reason for the call?"

"I just got off the phone with Jordyn, and Ms. Fisher's boyfriend broke into their house and is after her. I guess they were fighting, and we can use your help to run out to the house to make sure she's okay."

"I knew I shouldn't have trusted that man. My shift is scheduled to end in an hour, but I should be able to run out early. Give me a few minutes, and I'll make my way there."

"Thanks, I'll let Jordyn know."

She disconnected and texted Jordyn, informing her that Trevor would be on his way shortly. She punched in Jordyn's address on her phone to see how far the drive would be. She hated to think Ms. Fisher was trapped in her home with Mason lurking, potentially to do her some physical harm. She wasn't sure how long it would take Trevor to arrive at the house, but she imagined having two people to help was better than one. She also would never forgive herself if she chose to continue with her trip back to school without even attempting to see if Ms. Fisher was going to be okay.

She reached into her duffle bag, confirming the knife was still confined in one of the inside pockets. Not that she was eager for another conflict with Mason, but at least, this time, she would have Trevor as backup.

She shifted the car in gear, noting thirty minutes were all that separated her from a potential round three confrontation with Mason.

# Chapter 52

Naomi stood still by the bedroom door. She heard a few creaks from the floorboards downstairs and the crackle of glass shards being smashed by what she assumed were Mason's footsteps. She followed his footsteps and heard water running, most likely coming from the bathroom sink.

She looked over to the bedroom window and contemplated tying her bed sheets together, around the bedpost, opening the window, and lowering herself as far as she could down to the ground. She'd seen that play out in a few movies and wondered if it was even possible in real life. She shook her head, wiping this scenario from her mind, not wanting to risk falling twenty feet to the ground based on an unproven movie stunt. The only alternative option was to hope Jordyn had successfully contacted the police and they miraculously showed up early. If not, she thought if Mason did get past the locked bedroom door, she had a clear shot at knocking his block off with one good swing.

She momentarily placed the bat between her legs and wiped her sweaty palms on her jeans. She needed to have a good grip on the bat if she had any chance of successfully incapacitating him with a few forceful swings.

She placed her body up against the wall, several feet from the door, and waited. She had home-field advantage on her side by knowing exactly where the loudest floorboards were located in the house. There was one exceptionally loud squeaky floorboard by the foot of the stairs on the lower level, which was the same one she'd just heard Mason step on. She heard footsteps soon follow as he ascended the stairs, with each step becoming louder as he neared. She could tell when he arrived at the top of the stairs because the footsteps temporarily stopped. She imagined he was surveying the upstairs hallway before proceeding further.

She hadn't thought about closing the other bedroom doors to at least make it more of a guessing game for Mason to figure out where she might be. Besides the linen closet, her bedroom was the only other door closed, making this game of hide and seek much more easy for him to figure out.

Naomi motioned the sign of the cross and closed her eyes. She was relieved to know the bedroom doors were all original to the house and made of solid heavy oak. That at least offered some additional resistance for Mason to contend with.

She heard the footsteps resume in the hallway as they slowly traversed across the wood flooring until they stopped right outside her bedroom door. She could hear her heartbeat pounding in her ears while she also fought hard to control her breathing. She looked to see the doorknob gently twist clockwise. This was followed by several knocks against the door.

"I know you're in there, Naomi. I'm not looking to hurt you. I just want to talk and see if we can figure this whole thing out."

Naomi remained still without saying a word.

"I was completely wrong for not telling you I was married, and I hope you accept my deepest apologies. I also forgive you for smashing my car window and spraying me with pepper spray. I'm not going to lie, it burned like hell, but it feels better now. I promise, if you open the door, I'll be a complete gentleman and we can talk this over like civilized adults."

Naomi continued to refrain from answering. She found it hard to believe he would think she was that gullible to go for his sorry-ass attempt at coaxing her to open the door. *I was born at night, but not last night.*

There was a moment of silence before the doorknob rattled rather aggressively. A few seconds later, she heard his footsteps walking away from the door and eventually descending the stairs. She couldn't imagine he was giving up that easily.

She continued to stand firm with her fingers experiencing a tingling sensation as she held a firm grip on the bat. She walked a few steps toward the door, placing her ear against the wood surface. She heard a few items being shifted around in the kitchen. She feared he would find her toolbox sitting in the kitchen pantry, containing an assortment of items he could use to his advantage.

She noted the time, attempting to gauge how long it had been since she'd talked with Jordyn. She imagined it wasn't too long ago, but time had a funny way of slowing down during moments of heightened anticipation. Time was not the only factor working against her, as her left knee started to ache, no doubt agitated by her frantic scramble to get away from Mason. She'd done a good job of ignoring it until now. She had no choice but to grin and bear it, hoping she could escape this moment without any further injuries.

She heard the creaking of a door, followed by a few light thumps of items being moved around, before it became silent once more. She swallowed hard, attempting to soothe her dry throat, and tugged on her blouse to peel it away from the skin on her chest, which had generated a great deal of moisture. She wanted to so desperately sit on the bed, take pressure off of her knee, and gulp down a cold bottle of water to help reenergize her body.

The loud creaking noise at the foot of the stairs garnered her attention once more, indicating Mason was about to ascend the steps for another visit.

Naomi repositioned her body against the wall as the sound of his footsteps eventually approached the bedroom door. She fought to regulate her breathing and waited in silence. She looked at the knob, which twisted ever so slightly, and, without warning, an ear-piercing bang rang out. She didn't think it was a gunshot, yet she didn't want to take any chances and jumped away from the door, moving to the corner of her room to distance herself from the sound.

Seconds later, the same banging sound repeated a few more times as she assumed he must have been hitting the doorknob with something heavy. Her assumptions were correct after she heard what sounded like the doorknob hitting the floor in the hallway. He then started banging on the door, but it continued to stand firm and didn't open.

The banging subsided for a moment and was followed by the sound of wood cracking. She could see the gap between the door and the frame widening ever so slightly and she didn't know how much longer it would hold.

She neared the door and held the bat up high, making sure she was in striking distance. With the sound of one last crack, the door flung open, and Mason stepped inside, holding a hammer. His eyes were tinted red from the irritation caused by the pepper spray.

Without hesitation, Naomi swung the bat at his hand, dislodging the hammer from his grip and connecting with a few of his fingers in the process. He let out a painful yell, and before she had a chance to take a second swing, he put his head down and charged at her as they both went tumbling to the ground.

Naomi lost her grip on the bat, which rolled into the bedroom corner and out of reach. Mason had her pinned to the ground, using his full body weight to restrict her movement. He clenched his jaw, holding the few fingers on his right hand, which had taken the brunt of the hit.

"Are you happy now? I think you might have broken two of my fingers," he said while continuing to grip his fingers in pain. "Just for that, I'm gonna keep my full weight on you so you can share some of my pain."

Naomi lay on her back against the hardwood floor. Her hands were free, but she struggled to muster enough energy to fight him off. Much of his weight was centered around her stomach as he straddled her, disrupting her normal flow of breathing and limiting the amount of air she could take in.

Mason noted her facial expression, which showed signs of distress. "I see you're not liking this one bit. You deserve it after what you did to me and my car."

Naomi made one last-ditch attempt to thrust her hips upward and turn her body sideways to break free. Her efforts were in vain, as she could barely lift her hips off the ground with the excess weight pinning her to the floor. She closed her eyes, attempting to concentrate on getting enough air so she wouldn't pass out. Her energy had completely run out, and she was at the full mercy of whatever Mason chose to do.

Moments later, she heard a car door slam in the driveway.

Mason tilted his head up toward the window but couldn't see out into the front yard based on his positioning on the floor, straddling Naomi.

"Who's that? Did you call someone for help?"

Naomi only had the energy to shake her head, denying she had tipped anyone off.

"Don't you lie to me. Did you call the police?"

She shook her head once again.

Mason glared at her. "I don't trust you enough to get up off of you and look out the window, so I'm going to ask you nicely not to make a peep if someone calls out to you. You understand me?"

Naomi nodded her head. She felt lightheaded and hoped whoever it was could quicken their pace to help her.

Mason continued to sit on her but did shift his weight just enough to allow for some deep breathing.

A knock at the door soon followed.

"Naomi? It's Trevor. Are you okay?" he yelled.

Naomi closed her eyes, surprised to hear Trevor's voice and extremely thankful help had finally arrived.

Mason looked at Naomi, totally confused. "Who's Trevor?" he whispered. "And before you answer, I need you to talk very softly."

Naomi cleared her throat and tilted her head off the floor, closer to Mason to make sure he could hear. "He's a friend of mine who's going to come in here and kick your ass," she said in a soft-spoken tone.

Mason suddenly shifted his full weight back on Naomi as she groaned in pain. "As much as I want to continue sitting on you, I'm going to stand up in a few seconds, and I need you to be completely quiet. I swear if you talk, scream, or make any other attempt to tip him off to where we are, it's lights out for you. Is that clear?"

Naomi nodded.

Mason eased his body off of Naomi and stood. He flexed his fingers and grimaced in pain before looking around for the bat. He walked into the corner of the room and picked up the bat with his uninjured hand. Then he looked back at Naomi, making sure she kept her word and remained quiet. Mason edged toward the bedroom entrance and stopped, listening for any additional sounds below.

Trevor knocked a few more times before stopping. Naomi remained on the floor, taking in deep breaths to fill her lungs with some much-needed oxygen. She surveyed the room, searching for the hammer Mason had dropped. She spotted it by the doorway, but there was no chance of her scrambling to get it without Mason stopping her. She then looked to her right as her body lay parallel to her wood-grained dresser. At the far edge of the dresser, a white-laced runner ran over the edge and dangled to the side. Although she couldn't see on the dresser surface, she was well aware of the items resting on top of the runner—a jewelry box, a brushed nickel lamp, and a few picture frames. As she looked up more carefully, she could see one of the picture frames hanging on the edge of the dresser, most likely shifting as a result of her wrestling match with Mason.

Naomi's thoughts were interrupted by the crunch of glass as she imagined Trevor had found his way in through the broken window.

Mason stood against the wall, holding the bat with one hand.

"Naomi?" Trevor called out.

Mason glared at Naomi once more, shaking his head to reinforce his demand for her to remain quiet, before turning his attention back out into the hallway.

Naomi found the strength to prop herself up on the floor and immediately reached for her knee, which had stiffened up quite a bit since she'd taken a tumble to the ground. She then looked back up toward the dresser, focusing on the picture frame, and realized opening her mouth to make a sound wasn't the only way to alert Trevor of her location. She figured the frame could be coaxed into falling from the edge with a gentle tug on the laced runner. She was certain the sound would be loud enough for Trevor to hear, but she also knew that would be a huge gamble. This plan would all be predicated on Trevor reacting fast enough to rush upstairs and engage with Mason before he had a chance to take his anger out on her. She imagined she could also play dumb and deny she did anything to cause the frame to fall if he didn't catch her in the act.

With a slight nod of her head, Naomi decided it was now or never. There was no way she would allow Trevor to walk upstairs, completely unaware of Mason's location, and risk him being ambushed by a surprised sneak attack with the bat.

She carefully eyed Mason, waiting for the right opportunity to reach up and tug on the runner. With his eyes focused on the hallway, Naomi grabbed the edge of the runner, gently pulling it in her direction at about the same time Mason spun his head around, catching her hand in the cookie jar. He started to charge in Naomi's direction, but it was too late as the tug on the runner resulted in the frame shifting far enough to teeter over the edge and come crashing to the floor.

Mason continued his rush toward Naomi with his fist cocked. Before she could raise her hand to protect herself, she felt a blow to her head, and all of her senses suddenly fell silent.

# Chapter 53

Trevor stopped dead in his tracks after hearing the commotion upstairs. He had now received confirmation he wasn't alone, and it was up to him to find out the source of the sound. He regretted heeding Amara's advice and putting the gun back in the safe at home over a week ago. This would have been the most opportune time for him to have it holstered to his belt.

He quickly made his way out of the living room and into the kitchen. He focused his eyes on a knife block sitting on the counter and proceeded to pull out a large chef knife from one of the slots. He wasn't too fond of this weapon based on his past traumatizing experience, yet he didn't have much else to choose from.

He gripped the knife in his right hand and walked toward the staircase. He tried his best to stealthily tiptoe his way across the wood flooring, but his attempt to be quiet was foiled by an extremely loud squeaky floor joist at the foot of the stairs. He paused, wincing slightly, and remained still, listening out for any further sounds upstairs. He grabbed onto the railing and slowly started his ascent.

His sight was limited by the narrow staircase and further challenged by the second-floor landing, positioned to the left, which wouldn't have been visible until he cleared more than half of the steps. If someone were crouched on the second-level floor by the staircase, he wouldn't know it until his head cleared the landing.

With heightened senses, he crept up the stairs, holding the knife by his side, ready to strike if someone attempted to ambush him.

He stopped midway up, attempting to limit the creaky sounds generated by his footsteps. This noise also interfered with his ability to listen out for any sounds up above that might indicate someone's presence. He continued up the stairs and shifted his footing to the right edge of each step, to avoid putting weight on the middle floorboards, which he surmised had taken a beating from years of foot traffic. His strategy paid off as the creaking sounds did subside, allowing him a better chance of covering up his exact positioning.

He took one last step, providing him the opportunity to peek over to the left and onto the second-level floor. All was clear as he temporarily relaxed his grip on the knife. He reached the top of the landing and now had to contend with figuring out which room the noise had originated from. He carefully looked over the top floor layout and counted a total of five doors from within his field of vision. He stood closest to a door, much narrower than the rest. He thought this was perhaps some type of linen closet. It was also the only door closed on the second level.

He took a step toward the door, grabbed the knob, and gently pulled. As suspected, several shelves lined the inside of the closet with nicely folded towel sets stacked on top of one another.

His next focus was on a door to his right, which, from his angle, contained small, beige-colored tiles stretched along the floor, indicating this was a bathroom. He took a few steps, nearing the entryway. The narrow bathroom contained a toilet, pushed up against the wall at the entrance on the right, a white porcelain sink, mounted along the wall, and a clawfoot bathtub on the opposite side. There didn't appear to be many hiding places in the bathroom.

He quickly stuck his head in the room to look over the edge of the tub to ensure no one was hiding in it. Then he suddenly stopped and twisted his head toward the hallway, thinking he'd heard a sound.

The breeze outside had been picking up throughout the day, so the noise could have been the wind hitting against the windows. He most certainly couldn't assume that was the case and kept a firm grip on the knife.

He exited the bathroom and imagined the three remaining doors were all entrances to various bedrooms. But before he took another step, his eyes zeroed in on one of the bedroom entryways, displaying some damage to the doorframe. He also observed a doorknob resting on the floor, along with a hammer. He tightened his grip on the knife and edged toward the room.

As he closed in on the door, he spotted several large cracks on the wood finish by the lock, indicating someone must have forced their way into the room. He shifted his eyes into the room and, to his horror, Naomi's body was sprawled out in the corner of the room.

Trevor's attempt at being quiet had suddenly ended as he rushed to Naomi and kneeled by her side. He immediately saw swelling on her left cheekbone, indicating some type of blunt force trauma had occurred.

He kept the knife in his right hand and grabbed her wrist with his left, feeling for a pulse. A sense of relief flowed through him as he felt a strong pulse, signifying her heart was still beating, as it should, and circulating blood throughout her body. He proceeded to pinch Naomi on the arm to see if she reacted but received no response.

Not wanting to completely let his guard down, he looked over his shoulder, by the bedroom entrance, to make sure he had no unexpected company.

He focused his attention back on Naomi and observed the rise and fall of her chest, making sure she appeared to be breathing normally. As an added safety measure, he positioned his arm under her back and gently rolled her on her side to prevent her tongue from potentially blocking her airway. He then grabbed his phone with every intention of calling 9-1-1 but suddenly stopped after hearing a car door outside. He jumped up and looked out of the window to see Kayla exiting her car on the street. Trevor hadn't expected her to show up at the house and now he had somebody else to worry about.

As she walked up the driveway, she stopped by the Dodge Charger, momentarily looking at the shattered back passenger window. Trevor waved his hand, attempting to get her attention and signal for her not to come inside. She didn't look up and continued her march toward the house. He raised his hand again, intending to knock on the window, and that was when he heard a creaking noise behind him, indicating the presence of someone else.

Trevor twisted his head and turned his body, immediately bending his knees slightly, setting his balance, ready to engage with the knife displayed prominently in his right hand. He immediately ducked in an attempt to avoid a bat that came barreling toward his head.

After successfully avoiding the bat, he followed with a swipe of the knife to the person's mid-section, cutting a hole in their shirt. The person stumbled back a few steps, creating distance between them and allowing Trevor to confirm this was indeed Mason.

Trevor wasn't sure if the knife penetrated any of his skin, as he didn't see any blood forming on his cream-colored T-shirt.

Trevor darted his eyes down and realized they were only a couple of feet away from Naomi's unconscious body on the floor. She was completely vulnerable, and he didn't want to risk her being injured any further from this confrontation.

Before Mason could gather himself and raise the bat to swing again, Trevor charged, pushing Mason toward the doorway and away from Naomi. Mason lost his grip on the bat, and it rolled onto the floor, stopping by the foot of the bed. Since Mason did have a slight size advantage, he successfully pushed back, temporarily stopping Trevor's momentum.

Mason immediately reached to grab Trevor's wrist to wrestle the knife away from him. Trevor observed Mason favoring his left hand more while they both fought for control of the knife. He figured Mason might be suffering from an injury to his right arm or hand. This provided Trevor an advantage, allowing him to maintain possession of the knife and stun Mason with an elbow to the jaw.

Mason stumbled into the hallway and inadvertently stepped on the doorknob lying on the floor, making him fall backward, crashing to the floor. Without hesitation, Trevor jumped on top of Mason and placed the knife against the side of his neck.

"Don't make me do this!" Trevor shouted.

Mason stopped resisting, most likely still stunned from the elbow as well as the hard fall to the ground.

Trevor's attention was immediately diverted toward the staircase as he heard footsteps and saw Kayla appear. He continued to position the knife against the side of Mason's neck with his thoughts suddenly drifting to the one other time he had participated in a confrontation involving a knife.

He looked at Mason then back up at Kayla, who didn't say a word, but the horror written all over her face told him all he needed to know. What cruel swing of fate would put him in a position to potentially end a second person's life with a knife and have Kayla as a witness this time around?

Trevor's breathing slowed, and the spike of adrenaline that fueled his aggressive actions began to subside. He glanced at the blade touching Mason's neck and softened his grip on the knife. He proceeded to slowly pull the knife away, watching a drop of blood form on Mason's neck from a small puncture wound.

Without warning, Mason took a swing, and his fist connected with the side of Trevor's temple. Trevor leaned to the right and eventually slouched to the floor with his equilibrium thrown off.

"Stop!" Kayla screamed.

# Chapter 54

Mason lifted himself off the ground and snatched the knife away from Trevor, taking advantage of his dazed state. With Trevor lying on his back, Mason kneeled next to him and returned the favor by putting the knife up against his neck. He then glanced up and noticed the young lady take a few steps closer while displaying a pocket knife.

"Get off of him!" she shouted.

Mason shook his head. "Not this time. I've had enough of you threatening and stabbing me with your knife. I'm the one with the advantage this go-around, so I'd suggest you put your little knife down and kick it over to me or your father is going to have some serious problems."

The young woman looked at Mason, then down at Trevor before dropping the knife and kicking it, as instructed. "Okay, I did what you said. Can you please let him go?"

"I can't make it that easy for you." Mason pointed to his right forearm. "You caused me a lot of problems when you stuck me with that knife. I've been trying to think of a fitting punishment for a while now, and it looks like things are finally working in my favor. I'm getting some pleasure seeing the worry on your face and you wondering what I'm planning to do in this situation." Mason stopped and focused his attention beyond the young woman and over toward the steps. "Where's your buddy? Jordyn? Is she going to come running up the stairs to save the day?"

The young lady remained quiet and wiped a tear from her cheek.

"Don't get all soft on me now. I guess you're not so tough without that knife in your hand." Mason squinted his eyes as a thought came to mind. "By the way, I just realized this is the third time we've come face-to-face with one another, and I never found out your name. Do you mind telling me your name so I can address you properly going forward?"

Mason suddenly looked perplexed, watching a smirk develop on the young woman's face.

"Her name is Kayla, you son of a bitch!"

Mason twisted his body in the direction of the unexpected voice shouting from behind him. He turned just in time to catch a glimpse of a bat approaching his head before everything faded to black.

# Chapter 55

Kayla ran to Naomi, giving her a massive hug, before kneeling and stroking Trevor's head. "Are you okay?"

Trevor nodded. "I'll be fine. Just need to rest here a little more to clear my head."

Trevor focused in on Naomi and put his hands up in prayer. "Thank you." He rubbed the side of his face. "By the way, that was one hell of a swing coming from someone passed out a few minutes ago."

Naomi grimaced. "You don't know, but it took every ounce of energy in me to swing that bat on a balky knee and deal with this headache I'm feeling now." She looked down at Mason who had fallen face-first onto the floor. "I don't know if I killed the bastard or not, but it was either him or us, and I take us all day every day."

Kayla smiled as she could now see where Jordyn had come up with that expression.

Trevor slowly sat up, with his hands extended behind him, providing support to remain upright. He blinked a few times in quick succession, attempting to help clear his head. Then he reached over to Mason, who lay out only a few feet from him with a sizable knot protruding from the side of his head. He grabbed his wrist to feel for a pulse. "His heart's still beating. Looks like he's just taking a nice nap."

Moments later, a siren could be heard in the distance.

Kayla ran into the bedroom and peeked out of the window to see a police vehicle pull up behind Mason's car. "The police are here."

Naomi shook her head. "I guess better late than never."

# Chapter 56

Kayla watched the influx of student activity in Octagon Park. She sat on top of a blanket with her legs crossed, absorbing the bright sun shining in the sky. It had been a few weeks since the harrowing incident at Jordyn's house, and she fought hard during this time to adjust back to a normal way of college life.

She completely understood the events taking place at the house could have ended much differently. No lives were lost, and outside of some bumps and bruises, everyone had made it out without any major injuries. She was the only one who'd walked away unscathed physically, but she was paying for it from a mental standpoint.

She'd experienced many sleepless nights since the incident, blaming herself for distracting Trevor and allowing Mason to get the upper hand during their wrestling match. If it wasn't for Naomi's heroics, Kayla couldn't have imagined anything good coming out of the confrontation for Trevor.

She was also amazed at how quickly her emotional pendulum had swung from one side to the other when it came to her feelings toward Trevor and Amara. She'd never thought she would feel so much anger and resentment toward them at any point in her life after finding out about the secret they'd been holding on to for so long. And, within a forty-eight-hour period, after she'd found out the news, both Amara and Trevor had experienced life-threatening events that had slapped Kayla in the face with a reality check. Any grudge she'd held against them would not have been worth its weight in gold if they were no longer around to receive the hateful energy she was throwing their way.

This by no means meant she'd completely forgiven them for holding on to the secret for so long, but it shortened the time span for how long she believed total forgiveness could possibly be achieved. She understood this journey of forgiveness would be a marathon and not a sprint. She had to take it one day at a time, and her more frequent conversations with both Amara and Trevor indicated there had at least been some progress made on the communication front.

Kayla couldn't remember how long it had been since she could walk on campus, feeling carefree and without fear of being watched. She was grateful the encounters with seeing the red disco ball car, as she now referred to it, had come to an end. Based on Jordyn's scary tailgating experience and her description of the accident, the car was completely totaled, and had no shot of seeing the road ever again. But, the mystery remained as to who the driver was and whether they'd even survived the accident. Kayla didn't wish death on anyone and hoped the driver made it out alive. But, for now, she successfully pushed aside any fears that this person might ever come back, although she would always keep that open as a possibility.

Her thoughts were interrupted after seeing Jordyn walking her way.

"I figured I would find you here, at your favorite spot on the lawn."

"After being imprisoned in our dorm room for weeks, I'm trying to make up for lost time and enjoy campus life,"

Kayla said, moving over to give Jordyn room to sit on the blanket.

"I can't believe we only have a few more weeks until finals and then summer break," Jordyn said.

"I know. This semester went way too fast, but I'll be happy for it to end. I don't want to go through another semester like this ever again."

"So, what are your plans for the summer?" Jordyn asked.

Kayla shrugged. "I don't know. Probably look for a job so I can start saving up some money for my traveling aspirations."

"Nice. Any thoughts on where you want to go?"

Kayla smiled. "Hawaii would be nice, or maybe Madrid. But that's more of a long-term travel goal. For now, I'd be happy to go anywhere outside of Rhode Island. And what about you?" she asked before tilting her head to the side. "And don't tell me you have plans for more clinical trial testing. I don't want you coming back next semester glowing in the dark." Kayla laughed.

"No, I think those days are done. I'll probably go back to working at the convenience store to pick up some pocket change."

Kayla and Jordyn both stopped talking as a shadow in front of them suddenly appeared. They both looked up to see Avery standing there with a wide smile, showing off her pearly white teeth.

"Have you both lost your mind? Whose idea was it to have a party without me?" Avery asked.

Both Kayla and Jordyn pointed to one another.

"If you have room for me to sit, I guess I can forgive and forget," Avery said while squeezing onto the last bit of space on the blanket. "So, does this mean both of your prison sentences in your dorm room are over?"

"Thankfully, yes," Kayla responded.

"Now that's what I'm talking about," Avery said before pausing with a look of concern on her face. "You know what this means?"

Both Kayla and Jordyn shook their heads.

"It means hunting season is officially open for you both. It's time to go on the prowl and stalk your next boyfriend trophies, your honey-boo, your better half, or maybe your worst half—whatever you want to call him." Avery stopped and looked at Jordyn. "Honestly, I can't speak for you because I don't know your relationship status, but if you need a man, just let me know, especially if you like the tall ones. I know just where to go to find a good candidate for you."

"Do you think about anything else other than boys?" Kayla asked.

"Of course. It's not like I think about them all twenty-four hours of the day. I do need to find time to sleep, you know."

Both Kayla and Jordyn laughed.

Avery took out her phone. "Okay, I think it's time for a selfie to celebrate this beautiful day."

Avery handed her phone to Kayla to take advantage of her longer reach, and they all squeezed into the picture frame and smiled.

It had been quite some time since Kayla could laugh and truly enjoy her college experience. She reflected back on reading the positive affirmation from Jordyn's calendar earlier in the day.

*"I'm a capable, vibrant being that radiates success. I deserve every drop of happiness, love, and joy that comes my way."*

*So true*, Kayla thought.

# Epilogue

Amara was released from the hospital after three days and diagnosed with a heart arrhythmia. She was given medication to control it and to stabilize her blood pressure. Although her relationship with Kayla had taken a major blow after the family secret was revealed, she felt a huge sense of relief not having to worry about when and how Kayla would find out. She remained optimistic she could eventually patch things up with Kayla and develop a healthy relationship. She also understood this would all depend on if and when Kayla was ready to move forward and open to healing the relationship.

Amara's relationship with Trevor temporarily took a few steps back after dealing with the aftermath of the confession. She held a deep resentment toward Trevor for making her promise not to say anything to Kayla, and then holding on to the confession for so long. Amara also realized Trevor technically saved her life twice, and there was no way she could completely sweep that under the rug and continue to hold a grudge against him. It didn't happen overnight, but she eventually overcame any negative feelings she had toward Trevor and stayed true to her marriage vow, *for better or worse.*

Trevor had no lasting physical injuries from his confrontation with Mason. He continued to thank and praise Naomi for coming to the rescue. Although, that was where the good vibrations stopped for him. He continued to struggle and second-guess his decision not to pull the trigger sooner and let Kayla know he wasn't her biological father. And now he had to deal with the consequences of a stepdaughter who might or might not ever forgive him for his voluntary silence.

He also felt uncomfortable and insecure regarding his relationship with Amara after the confession. She did come around after a while, and things appeared to be mostly back to normal. But in his mind, he always had the burden of knowing this stain on the relationship, caused by his procrastination to confess, would be etched in stone and never go away.

Naomi recovered from the ordeal at the house, but she did suffer from PTSD as a result of the altercation. She did have to move forward with court proceedings due to the incident and was liable for property damage for throwing the rock through Mason's car window. But that was where her liability ended, as the court found her innocent of any other charges after determining all of her actions afterward were considered acts of self-defense.

Her financial situation improved immensely after a surprising development centered around her caregiving duties. Naomi was devastated by the passing of a long-time client who she had considered a true mother figure. Her passing was even more difficult to process since this client did not have much family around to support her. But unbeknownst to Naomi, her client turned out to be a millionaire on the down low, and before she'd passed away, she'd adjusted her will, leaving Naomi with a large sum of money. With this money, Naomi was able to pay for her much-needed home repairs, put money aside for Jordyn's college fund, and purchase a new vehicle. This financial blessing proved that hope truly did spring eternal.

Jordyn owed a great deal of gratitude toward Trevor and Kayla for coming to Naomi's rescue. She was grateful no one sustained major injuries and the tumultuous Mason era had ended.

Her heart broke for Kayla after she found out about her devastating family secret and admired how she was able to push through the trauma of hearing this news and finish out the rest of the semester.

Through Kayla's recommendation, Jordyn started counseling sessions with Ms. Crawford to help get her through the various life challenges she'd been experiencing. She also learned her lesson and made it a point to not hold back on keeping secrets from Kayla whenever necessary to help prevent any future misunderstandings from turning into disaster.

Leah filed for divorce from Mason as the relationship collapsed under the weight of trust issues, irreconcilable differences, and mostly due to the infidelity that ravaged their marriage. She accepted a relocation offer from her job and settled into a new apartment in Charlotte, North Carolina. This offer came with a pay raise and allowed her an opportunity to spend more time with her new man, who owned a luxury condo in the downtown area. And by the way, she kept the AirTag in Mason's car to continue to track him whenever she felt like it.

Mason suffered from long-term concussion symptoms after the altercation at Naomi's house. Headaches, light sensitivity, and dizzy spells were some of the symptoms he experienced at alternating times. His recovery took longer than he would have hoped, and he could never look at an aluminum bat the same way.

Mason's decision to break into Naomi's house and cause her physical harm cost him a moment of his freedom. He was charged with assault and battery resulting in a ninety-day jail sentence and a hefty fine.

After completing his time in jail, he moved forward with selling the Last Chance gas station to a developer who planned to build a larger and much more commercialized rest stop on the land. The proceeds from the sale of his business allowed him to move out of town and figure out his next chapter of life in Savannah, Georgia, where his father grew up.

He remained in contact with Eva and Caleb, who had fully recovered from his accident. This move out of town prevented him from spending quality time with Owen, but he had plans to one day travel up north to visit him.

His divorce proceedings with Leah couldn't have come at a better time. He was never one hundred percent sure he was ever ready for marriage and his challenging five years with Leah had proven his point. But he did learn one valuable lesson during his years of marriage—karma could really be a bitch.

And by the way, he finally discovered the AirTag underneath the seat of his car and received the answer to Leah's secret source.

Kayla successfully finished her spring semester with passing grades, allowing her to maintain her academic scholarships. Although her mental health session with Ms. Crawford had been short, she took her advice to heart and did what she could to practice the art of recognizing whenever negative energy had a grip on her mental state. This by no means prevented tough times from happening every so often, but it made her better equipped to handle challenging times whenever they did occur. Her ability to deal with difficult circumstances and continue to live life to the fullest proved without a shadow of a doubt that what didn't kill you made you stronger.

# Acknowledgements

"Reading gives us someplace to go when we have to stay where we are"
Mason Cooley

I would like to thank everyone who decided to take a chance on reading my book and I hope this fictional world I created allowed for a moment of respite from your daily lives.

I would greatly appreciate it if you could leave a review to provide me insight into your opinions of the book. This would ultimately help me improve my craft as an author and continue my pursuit of offering the best reading experience possible for any future projects I might embark on.

This book would not have been possible without the help of a few notable individuals.

First and foremost, I would like to thank God for giving me the imagination, creativity, patience, and determination needed to write the 83,500 words that make up this manuscript.

Second, I would like to express my gratitude to my wife and daughter for their patience and support while I dedicated countless hours to brainstorming and typing on the computer to create this story. I'm also thankful for their valuable feedback as beta readers and for their input into the book cover design.

# Acknowledgements

Additionally, I want to extend my thanks to Kristin for her dedicated editing work on the book and, NoahKEaton, for designing the book cover.

Lastly, I encourage everyone to keep reading and letting their imaginations run wild with books that transport them into fascinating fictional worlds. Until next time!